Enjoy, Gene

MARK'S PASSION

The Story of a Spiritual Calling

GENE VANDERZANDEN

CreateSpace
Seattle

MARK'S PASSION, The Story of a Spiritual Calling

Copyright © 2015 by Gene Vanderzanden. All rights reserved.
Printed in the United States of America. No part of this book may be used or reproduced in any manner whatsoever without written permission, except for brief quotations embodied in articles and reviews. For information contact the publisher through the website http://www.markspassion.com.

Biblical quotations are taken from the New Revised Standard Version of the Bible, copyright © 1989 by the National Council of the Churches of Christ in the USA. Used by permission.

This novel is a work of fiction. Except for the historical figures and events, all names, characters, and incidents are either the product of the author's imagination or are used fictitiously. Any resemblance to actual events, locales, organizations, or persons, living or dead, is entirely coincidental and beyond the intent of either the author or the publisher.

ISBN-10: 1523308850
ISBN-13: 978-1523308859

PRAISE FOR MARK'S PASSION

"In Mark's Passion, the man behind the gospel becomes fully human as he faces his own frailties and strengths, and his need to know love. Insights into the life he lived, his surroundings, the social structure and political struggles of the time are wonderfully presented as an intriguing story."

—Stella Cameron, *New York Times* bestselling author

"The New Testament comes alive in Mark's Passion while you follow one man's journey as he attempts to put the life of Jesus into the written word. A well written story that relates much of what happened to the early Christians after the death of Christ." —DeeAnn Fuchs, author of the Drasana series

"At last, a historical novel based on the latest New Testament scholarship."
—Deacon Lloyd Snider, Archdiocese of Seattle

The historical events depicted in this book are factual. You will learn a great deal about the origins of the gospels and the realities of life faced by the early Christians. The names of actual people and places are shown in their English spelling, and I avoided archaic language to help you enjoy the story.

To see illustrations, links and maps that relate to the 1st Century events and to learn more about what New Testament scholars are saying today, go to www.markspassion.com.

WHO WAS MARK?

Other than some legends and claims, very little is known about the author of the Gospel according to Mark. According to the best-attested tradition, Mark began the gospel in Rome where he served as an aid and interpreter for Peter. Many have confused the evangelist with the John Mark mentioned in the Book of Acts or Mark the cousin of Barnabas mentioned in Paul's letters, but Hippolytus of Rome stated that these other Marks were different persons from the author of the gospel. Similarly, two ancient churches in Alexandria claim to have been founded by Mark the evangelist in 49 AD, but this would have been nearly two decades before the gospel was even written. The name *Marcos* was very common, and beyond his association with Peter, history left us nothing of certainty about what the inspired writer was like.

Based upon references in the texts, the consensus of New Testament scholars today is that Mark's gospel was written first—about 66-69 AD—during the Jewish rebellion against Rome. They believe that Matthew, Luke and John followed later, which differs from the traditional understanding. Mark's gospel had been thought to be an abbreviated version of Matthew's, not its predecessor.

Clearly, Mark was a human being, inspired by God to accomplish a vitally important task. He used his natural abilities with the help of God's grace and succeeded in a remarkable way. Can we picture what this endeavor looked like? I don't attempt to settle the questions about the identity of the forward-looking evangelist or resolve which of the various legends, claims and relics are authentic—if any. I simply explore what life could have been like for the person called to put what was known about Jesus in writing.

*With many such parables Jesus spoke the word to the crowds
as they were able to understand it.
Without parables he did not speak to them.
But to his own disciples he explained everything to them in private.*

Mark 4: 34

1

A shrill voice broke through the mid-morning silence. "Peter is dead!"
"What?"

"Peter is dead!" Niko screamed at Mark, whose head had dropped in sleep to his writing table a few minutes earlier. "Wake up! I'm telling you, Peter is dead. They crucified him!"

"They what?" Mark lifted his head a few inches and tried to shake off the haze.

"They took Peter—the soldiers took him. They crucified him!"

Mark was quickly waking, but the words were not yet making sense. "Crucified? Peter?"

"Yes! They crucified our leader." She began shaking him with her hands. "Everyone is talking about it in the market. They took Peter and some others."

"Oh, God." Mark was awake now and beginning to comprehend. He had been working at his table since dawn and dozed after the others went out. Raising his head he asked, "When? How?"

"This morning. It wasn't in the Coliseum, but in the circus at Vatican Hill. Soldiers took a group of the brothers over there and some women too. They crucified them all. They say most of them are still hanging there gasping, but Peter is already dead!"

Confronted by the harsh reality, Mark let his head drop into his hands. It had only been a few days since the guards had arrested Peter and put him in the Mamertine Prison. "That's terrible," he moaned, trying to deal with the awful news. He couldn't imagine his mentor being dead and was too shocked to absorb the agony.

Niko began asking questions, "How could he die so fast? It usually takes a day or more." She also couldn't make sense of what she heard.

"He's getting older," Mark answered as his shock began turning to grief. "Over 60—maybe almost 70. And if he lost much blood, well . . ."

Niko sobbed. "That horrible Nero. Ever since the Fire he's been attacking us."

Mark quickly traced back over the events of the last two months. The Great Fire of Rome started during the night of July eighteenth and raged for six days, devastating half of the city. Some said Nero initiated the fire, sending out men pretending to be drunk, so he could reclaim the land for a new palace. They said he watched from the Tower of Maecenas on the Esquiline Hill while singing and playing the lyre.

The blaze began in shops below the Caelian and Palatine Hills. The night was windy, and the flames spread rapidly, expanding through an area of narrow streets and flammable housing. In this area of Rome there were no large stone buildings or open areas to impede the inferno as it spread along the slopes.

The population fled first to areas untouched by the fire and then to the open fields and rural roads outside the city. Looters and arsonists were reported to have spread the flames by throwing torches. Some angry groups even tried to hinder measures being taken to halt the progress of the blaze.

Nero sent in food supplies and opened gardens and public buildings for refugees. Six days of organized clearing brought the conflagration to a halt before it reached the Esquiline Hill. Of Rome's districts, three were completely devastated and only four escaped damage, including the Trastevere—across the Tiber River, where most of the Christians lived.

The Emperor tried to fasten the guilt on the Christians and ordered executions to appease the population. Some were killed by ravenous dogs, some nailed to crosses, and some set aflame; when night came, fires consuming the corpses lit the sky.

Mark stood up and clenched his fists. "Those pigs! They are taking our leaders from us. First they beheaded Paul, now Peter. Damn them!" He was red with anger. Mark seldom cursed, but the brutality of the Romans had reached the point where his feelings could not be expressed any other way.

"I hate them." Niko was too fearful and angry to even consider Jesus' teaching on forgiveness.

Mark was devastated. They had executed the one person he most respected and loved in Rome, his guiding light and trusted friend. The reality that was beginning to sink in left him speechless. The shock was too sudden and too great.

"Will they come for us, Mark?" Niko was referring to her husband, Antonius, and their little Stephanos. The couple had arrived in Rome three years earlier, from Actium on the west coast of the Greek mainland. Antonius was an expert stone mason, and in Rome his skills were in high demand. Mark was paying them a small sum for meals, a couch, and space for his writing table in their little hovel in the marshy area at the base of the Capitoline Hill. Niko was pregnant with their second child.

"I don't know." He tried to disguise his thoughts. The persecutions had been continuous, and there was no end in sight.

"Oh, Mark!" Niko fell into his arms, shaking.

Instinctively, Mark embraced his sobbing friend, trying to give her comfort, but her fears were too intense. Niko let her weight rest in his supporting arms, and he caressed her neck and shoulders. Having a woman's body close to his was an infrequent experience for him. He was thirty years old and not yet married. Women trusted him. He liked them and showed them respect, but Peter kept him busy every day. He had little time and even less money—no means of supporting a family.

Mark felt Niko's breath on his shoulder. On many nights he heard the sounds she made as she lay with Antonius, the giggles, murmurs, moans, and sighs. He frequently longed for the intimacy other men enjoyed, which his devotion to his work prevented him from having. He was growing tired of being alone. He wanted to love and be loved. There was a void in his life that only mutual devotion could fill.

Then his mind snapped back to the tragedies of the day. Peter had been killed, and the Emperor was on a tirade. This wasn't the time to think about his personal needs.

He helped Niko slide down to the floor and rest her back against the wall. "We all have to be strong now," he told her.

"Yes, strong now," she agreed.

Then through the door came the elderly neighbor who cared for Stephanos while Niko was out. The woman carefully lowered the child down to the floor.

Niko smiled. "Come to mama." The boy toddled over to his mother as if nothing that happened that day could be more important than getting back to her. She grabbed the smiling child in her outstretched arms and smothered him with wet tears and warm kisses.

2

Mark wanted to run to Vatican Hill, but his good sense kept him sealed in the house.

As Niko prepared the evening meal and they waited for Antonius, he picked up the document on his writing table. Fingering it carefully, he glanced at some lines near the beginning.

As he passed by the Sea of Galilee, he saw Simon and his brother Andrew casting their nets into the sea; they were fisherman. Jesus said to them, 'Come after me, and I will make you fishers of men.' Then they left their nets and followed him. He walked along a little farther and saw James, the son of Zebedee, and his brother John. They too were in a boat mending their nets. Then he called to them. So they left their father Zebedee in the boat along with the hired men and followed him.

Mark had heard Peter tell the story often. Of course Peter spoke in the first person, using the words 'he' and 'me' of eyewitness testimony. Mark had penned the story as a narrative. Usually Peter pushed vigorously through his talks, often leaving out details that Mark wished to know, like the location and date of what he was describing.

Mark's thoughts circled around his relationship with the Christian leader. His parents came into the faith when Peter was the *episkopos*, or overseer, of the church community in Antioch of Syria. Mark had only vague memories of those days. He was just a boy when the head of the apostles left their city for Rome in the second year of the reign of Claudius.

Peter traveled often while he resided in Rome. He sailed to Jerusalem, Caesarea, Damascus, and all over the Empire. Wherever he was needed, he went.

As Mark neared adulthood, his father, acutely aware of the lad's intellectual abilities, placed him as an apprentice to learn the crafts of language and writing. About the time that Mark had developed these skills, Peter paid a visit to Antioch. That's where the two met—his father introduced them. Peter said, "You are from a fine family, and I need a man with your abilities. Will you come with me?" And without stopping to think about what this might entail, the young Christian agreed.

"I said yes to Peter as quickly as Peter said yes to Jesus," Mark muttered quietly. For eight years he had stayed at the apostle's side, translating the fisherman's rustic Aramaic into polished Greek. Mark compiled pages of notes and sometimes addressed groups in Peter's place. They were constantly on the go, meeting with visitors from all over the Empire. Mark couldn't imagine why he was picked for the job—others were just as competent, or more. He only recently realized what may have been his mystery qualification: he said yes. It was that simple; he had said yes, and the rest was history.

Mark wanted to write a complete narrative about Jesus. Peter said that sounded fine, but showed more interest in meeting personally with potential converts to the faith. Mark hoped to document that Jesus was the divine Son of God. Christ said he would return, but the years were wearing on, and the original eyewitnesses were getting old. Mark wanted to clearly make the case in writing that Jesus is who he said he was.

Mark also wanted to show what authentic discipleship is like. According to Peter, the original twelve often failed to live up to Jesus' expectations—including Peter, himself. When Peter told those stories, listeners tended to lower their eyes and examine deeply their own faults. It led them to want to do better. Mark believed that if people could hear stories of the downfalls of these early saints and take the lessons into their lives, the whole world would be changed.

But now Peter was dead. Mark wouldn't have him to follow around anymore. There might no longer be a role for him. He had no idea what the church leadership would do. He felt like a ship that had set out on a clear course, but an unexpected gale had blown the entire journey adrift. He had no idea where new guidance would come from, but he was clear on one thing—whatever it took, he would complete the writing of the gospel.

3

As Mark continued to wait for Antonius, his thoughts drifted back to his home in Antioch. He pictured one special person he left behind there—Lydia, a beautiful girl with sparkling eyes and cascading brown hair, who was blossoming into the fullness of womanhood. Her shy smile was captivating, and her deep dark eyes displayed the essence of her tender heart. Lydia and her family were members of the Christian community and had been friends for many years. She was four years younger than Mark, and both families assumed they would marry.

The two first noticed each other at Lydia's oldest sister's wedding feast. When they filled their plates and looked for a place to sit in the crowded house, it put them together in a corner. They didn't say much; neither was the talkative type. Mark was fifteen years old and getting interested in girls. Lydia's cheeks looked incredibly soft, and even though he usually didn't act without thinking, he reached out and touched them with his fingertips. Her skin was even softer than he had imagined. Suddenly, he realized how foolish this must seem, but Lydia didn't seem to mind. She just looked at him with big warm eyes and smiled. From that day on, almost every time he glanced her way she was looking at him, and her magnetic smile drew him into a bond that was both unfamiliar and unexpected.

A few months later, when Mark's brother Habib got married, they sat together watching the bride and groom dance. When the music stopped the couple in the middle kissed, and everyone applauded them. Mark found himself being kissed, as well. Lydia had grabbed his head with both hands and pressed her lips to his. Mark didn't know what to think, but he liked it. When he put his hand to his lips, Lydia blushed, but when he broke out in a big boyish grin, she smiled and kissed him again. After that, neither thought of themselves as a child anymore.

During his apprenticeship they didn't see each other very often, but they felt close, whether they were together at a big gathering or miles apart. Mark couldn't support a family until he concluded his apprenticeship, and Lydia seemed content to wait. But when he finished, instead of becoming betrothed, he left Antioch. He still felt attached to Lydia, but now it was with loss and longing, and he wondered how she felt about him.

It was getting late, and Antonius had not yet come home for dinner. Niko was showing signs of nervousness and complained that the food was getting dry. Stephanos was fussing. His mother tried to keep him occupied, but her mind was elsewhere.

Mark was concerned too, but trying to hide it. He thought about how different from him Antonius was—a short, powerful man, with the heavy frame of one who worked with tools and stone. His black beard was full and curly—an entirely different kind of man from Mark, who was at his best with books and preferred to shave every day. Mark liked to stay clean and wanted to look well-groomed. But, despite their differences, they had become good friends.

Dusk was settling in over the neighborhood. Some families were closing their doors, when in walked Antonius, obviously weary, with sweat across his brow.

Niko rushed into her husband's arms. "You've heard?" she asked.

"Yes. What a horrible purge this is."

"Did they crucify them? That's what they were saying in the market."

"They crucified them all. The soldiers did it. There weren't a lot of people watching."

"And Peter?" Mark wanted every bit of information about his patron.

"Peter too. Yes . . . He pleaded with them, though. He said he was not worthy to die like Jesus. If they wanted to crucify him, would they do it upside down?"

"Upside down!" two voices exclaimed.

"Upside down. I don't know how exactly. The soldiers made a sport out of it. They used ropes and nails and got him up there." The stone mason was waving his arms as he described the unwieldy torture.

Mark leaned in towards Antonius. "We heard he was the first to die."

"That's right. Those who saw it said his face got red, like a vulgarus beet. His eyes were bulging. No one knew how long he could live, hanging that way. He seemed to handle it for a couple of hours, then suddenly he started convulsing and grimacing. It must have been terribly painful at the end. Those bastards . . ."

"At least it was over quickly for him."

"Yes. Thank God."

Niko brought up another concern. "Do you think they will burn him?"

"No! It was amazing! Like Christ was watching over him. When he stopped moving, Cato took Albus and just walked up to the soldiers and asked for the body. The centurion stuck his spear in Peter's side and said, 'Take him.'"

"So they just carried him away?" she asked.

"Yes!"

"Where did they put him?" Mark wanted more detail.

"Well, there was a little garden not far away. I got there just as they were carrying him to it."

"You went there!" Niko was horrified.

"Yes. Cato said we should hide him as best as we could to keep the Romans from getting his remains. They dug a hole and put him in it."

"You shouldn't have gone."

"Well, it was good that I was there. I had my chisels and I saw a stone. I inscribed the letters Cato told me to cut—Πέτρος ΕΝΙ—Peter is here."

Mark broke in, "So we will know where his bones are, but nobody else?"

"Yes. Cato is very smart."

Antonius abruptly changed the conversation. "Mark, you are not safe here. They may come for you next. The brothers were talking. They said you must get out of Rome."

"But how?"

"They elected Linus to succeed Peter as bishop, and he has arranged passage for you to Philippi. You can meet the bishop there—Alexios. He will take you in."

"But when?"

"Tomorrow morning. A ship is leaving from Ostia harbor. You must pack your things tonight."

"But soldiers will see me carrying a bag."

"They thought of that. You must pack now. Albus will sneak your bag to the pier where the river turns west, away from the via Ostia. Do you know the place?"

Mark nodded.

"Then tomorrow morning you can walk there like you are just going to work. A small boat will take you down to the harbor."

"Will I be able to pass by the guards?" Mark was not a bit sure.

"No one knows. But you've got to try."

It all was so sudden. A few hours earlier Mark was not even thinking of leaving Rome. Now his patron was dead, and he was being told to pack his belongings. There were so many people he wanted to say goodbye to. "You have been such good friends. I owe you so much. You and the others have been generous to me. I can't just *leave*."

"You must. They want you to finish the gospel. You can't do that here."

"But . . ." Mark hesitated, yet he knew they were right.

"Linus also said they are grateful to you. You have been a great help to Peter and the whole community. But that's changed. Now they are thinking of the future, and you need to be where you can finish putting the gospel in writing."

"I guess that's right," Mark agreed.

"Now. Pack quickly. Then we eat. I am very hungry."

4

Mark set about packing his belongings. There wasn't much to put in the bag—a blanket to sleep in, one extra tunic (which fortunately was clean), a pair of sandals that were showing wear, a comb, and an iron *novacila* razor for shaving. He found a bronze medallion of the Holy Spirit descending like a dove, a gift from Peter that held memories of their times together. He also picked up a small silver cross, a present from his mother when he left Antioch. When she first pressed it into his hand, he was shocked. No one then thought of the cross as anything but an image of Roman cruelty, but over the years he had grown to see it as a sign of Christ's love. His eyes became moist. I have to hurry, he thought, forcing himself to concentrate on the packing.

He grabbed two togas, one with a bit of red border. It wasn't a *praetexta*—the toga with purple borders that officials wore in imperial ceremonies. *Madder* red was one of the cheapest dyes available, but the elders thought the garments added a level of dignity in important meetings. Mark never felt it was his. The toga was just placed with him for his use. He folded it carefully. It's no use leaving it here, he told himself as he put both in the bag.

Then he picked up his writing materials—a few sheets of loose parchment and eight reed pens made from the hollow stems of marsh grass. They were perfect for writing on parchment. One end formed a nib or point. A writing fluid filled the stem, and the writer squeezed the reed, forcing the fluid into the nib. Mark had heard about inks from India and China, but he never had the means to acquire them.

The writing table was too big to carry, and the couch belonged to his hosts.

All that remained to pack were the *codices*—booklets made of folded sheets of parchment or papyrus. As an apprentice, Mark learned how to fold the papers so that each sheet formed two leaves or four pages of writing surface. Multiples of the folded sheets could be attached to one another with binding threads. They were quite common; merchants used them for recording purchases and payments.

Mark preferred the codex to the scroll, which was made by attaching sheets end to end to make a continuous writing surface. He had used both, but found the codex easier to work with. Books also suffered less damage when carried around.

With a codex you read the text by turning the pages, while a scroll was read column by column, holding the rolled ends in both hands. Jews continued to use scrolls for their writings, but Christians almost universally adopted the codex. No one in authority made a decision about this—it just became a convention among the church communities. For the most part, availability and practicalities determined what the believers did. It was not the paper that was sacred, but the message on it.

Two of the books were new, with not a letter on them. There also was a narrative of Jesus' last days. The brothers used it for instructing *catechumens* in the faith. When Peter spoke about the passion of the Lord, he offered more details than the document contained. Mark wanted to add these points; they showed how much Jesus suffered and how much he loved.

Another codex contained some sayings of Christ. Peter didn't know who compiled them, but he said they were accurate. "That is what Jesus said—those were his words," Mark could hear Peter's coarse voice attest.

There were copious notes from Peter's many speeches, not in any order, just jottings Mark made while listening to the leader share his testimony.

Finally, he gazed at a booklet that looked almost new. He had begun writing in it after the Fire, and only a few pages were filled in. Opening it, he read,

The beginning of the gospel of Jesus Christ, the Son of God.
As it is written in Isaiah the prophet:
Behold, I am sending my messenger ahead of you;
he will prepare your way.
A voice of one crying out in the desert,
'Prepare the way of the Lord, make straight his paths.'

"I absolutely must complete this," Mark whispered.

As he stood there fingering the booklet, Niko came up behind him and handed him a bundle of food. He smiled and put it in the bag.

"Good," Antonius said as he picked up the bag in his strong hands. "Albus will be here soon."

At that moment the man appeared at the door. "Here," Antonius told him as he handed him the bag. "Mark will meet you at the pier at first light." Albus nodded and disappeared as quickly as he arrived.

The house was still while the family ate. Except for a few playful sounds from Stephanos, very little was said.

Mark helped Niko clean up the table; she always appreciated that. He wanted to say something, but couldn't find the words. Neither could Niko.

Then they settled in for the night. Mark lay on his couch and tried to sleep. That didn't seem likely, though. He was thinking about John, and what Peter had told him about the burly relative of Jesus.

John the Baptist appeared in the desert proclaiming a baptism of repentance for the forgiveness of sins. People of the whole Judean countryside and all the inhabitants of Jerusalem were going out to him and were being baptized by him in the Jordan River as they acknowledged their sins. John was clothed in camel's hair, with a leather belt around his waist. He fed on locusts and wild honey. And this is what he proclaimed: 'One mightier than I is coming after me. I am not worthy to stoop and loosen the thongs of his sandals. I have baptized you with water; he will baptize you with the Holy Spirit.'

I am so unworthy for this task, Mark thought. I am a lowly sinner—just like those who went out to John. So often I have let my enormous pride influence my choices. How can I accomplish anything for Christ?

He prayed silently, Jesus—my Lord—I am sorry for all my transgressions. I hate how selfish I have been throughout my life. My sins are as countless as the stars. Peter said that you always forgive, but I still don't see why you do. I am made of clay. Surely you must be made of pure love, or you would have struck me down years ago.

Then he thought about the days ahead. I must be as steadfast as John the Baptist. No one told him what to do. He just saw the need and followed the passion in his heart. In my small way, he silently vowed, I have to summon that kind of courage and do what I can to pass along the gospel. If it is the will of Christ, it will bear fruit. If it is not, it won't matter.

5

The next morning when only a slight purple hue had crept into the dark sky, the household got up. Everyone was quiet, supposedly to avoid waking Stephanos. Mark drank some water, ate a hunk of dark emmer bread, and was ready.

"God be with you my friend," whispered Antonius as he gave his guest a firm hug.

"And with you," Mark replied.

Niko approached him. Their eyes met, and she embraced him affectionately. Mark's last words were simple. "I must go." Then he slipped out the door.

As Mark left the house the cold air slapped him in the face. There was a thick fog from the river, and he thought, that's good; it will be darker.

He walked only a few paces, when his ears picked up the sound of footsteps. Then he saw a light. Instinctively he ducked behind the wall that enclosed a nearby pagan temple.

Tromp, tromp, tromp, tromp, the sound drew closer. It was a group of Roman soldiers. Mark's heart raced.

They approached the house he came from, and one of the soldiers said in a hushed voice, "The door is open. Go in, but take them alive." Mark peeked over the wall.

With no further word from the squad leader, the guards rushed into the building. Niko screamed.

"Get out! I'll kill you!" the stone mason shouted, meaning every word.

The leader yelled, "You come with us or we will kill the woman. I'll cut her throat, but first I'll put my dagger through the new child." Niko put her hand to the round of her belly and held her breath. The Romans didn't invent terrorism, but they perfected it. Roman soldiers take a vow to kill anything—be it animal, barbarian, or Roman—when commanded to do so, and they understand how brutality is the most expedient way to gain cooperation.

One of the soldiers grabbed Stephanos and held a knife to his neck. "You try anything and I'll cut his throat."

"Now follow me." The one in charge motioned to the door.

The captors and victims trudged to the street. From the shadows, Mark heard two of the guards smash and cut up the family's belongings, then run to rejoin the group. They would have set the dwelling ablaze, but since the Great Fire they had been ordered not to use that method of oppression. The neighbors were familiar with these quick, brutal attacks; it would be up to them to clean up the debris.

An anguishing scream came up from the depths of Mark's soul, but it did not escape his lips. Those dirty bastards! They will take my friends to the Coliseum. Images of their fate flashed through his mind. He had not witnessed any of the executions, but had heard of believers getting mauled by beasts or being burned alive as prominent citizens watched with delight.

Then before he had time to release his anguish he was struck with another blow. They were coming for me! His purple anger turned to deep red guilt. I was Peter's assistant. This is the day they would come for me. His mind, though clouded, simply could not deny the facts. Yesterday they executed Peter and today they were rounding up those who worked with him. I was supposed to die today—not these good people. He broke down and wept bitterly, overwhelmed with remorse for how his presence in their home had been the cause of their cruel fate.

Remembering the urgency, his brain partially regained its function. "I've got to get to the pier," he muttered. This was not just to save his own skin, which would enter the mind of any human being; it also was for the sake of the gospel.

6

When Mark reached the point where the Tiber River turned west, he immediately saw Albus. The half hour walk had been without incident, but he was not yet in the clear. He approached the man and without looking at him, listened.

"Everything is ready, over there." Albus pointed toward a small boat with one mast. It could seat two, plus the oarsman. "Your bag is in the boat."

Mark nodded. Should he tell Albus about the raid? There didn't seem to be time.

"Get in." The instructions were clear. Mark followed them, trying to express his gratitude through his eyes. Albus nodded to the oarsman, and the boat moved away from the pier.

Rome had been located about 20 miles in from the sea, the farthest upstream ocean-going vessels could reach and the lowest point bridges could be built, across from the Trastevere neighborhood near a small island. The Isola Tiberina was dedicated to the god of medicine. People who were ill sometimes spent the night there and left little figurines representing the parts of their body that needed healing.

Since those early times, ships had become larger and silt had reduced the water depth. Now the principal harbor was at the mouth of the river. Small boats like the one Mark boarded could float down to the harbor in a few hours, depending upon the direction of the wind and the endurance of the oarsman. Mark leaned back. Amidst the creaking of the oars and the lapping of the waves, he had time to assess his situation.

On one hand everything that was happening made sense. He was moving away from an area of danger toward a region outside of the zone of persecution. It was as though invisible hands were guiding him to a place of safety where he could pursue his work. Mark took a deep breath of the fresh morning air; he felt very grateful.

On the other hand everything he had hoped for was crumbling. The man he had followed since his apprenticeship was dead, cruelly executed. His friends were suffering martyrdom. The Emperor was celebrating his tenth anniversary, and the church was losing its leadership. The signs were contradictory. Could this mean the end is coming?

He remembered what Peter had said about the end of the age.

As Jesus was making his way out of the temple area one of his disciples said to him, 'Look, teacher, what stones and what buildings!' Jesus said to him, 'Do you see these great buildings? There will not be one stone left upon a stone that will not be torn down.' As he was sitting on the Mount of Olives opposite the temple area, Peter, James, John, and Andrew asked him privately, 'Tell us, when will this happen, and what sign will there be when all these things are about to come to an end?' Jesus began to say to them, 'See that no one deceives you. Many will come in my name saying, 'I am he,' and they will deceive many. When you hear of wars and reports of wars do not be alarmed. Such things must happen, but it will not yet be the end. Nation will rise against nation and kingdom against kingdom. There will be earthquakes from place to place and there will be famines. These are the beginnings of the labor pains.'

Mark could not think of a more apt image for describing the days since the Great Fire. Every detail fit. It all seemed to be happening right before his eyes.

Jesus said, 'Watch out for yourselves. They will hand you over to the courts. You will be beaten in synagogues. You will be arraigned before governors and kings because of me, as a witness before them. But the gospel must be preached to all nations. When they lead you away and hand you over, do not worry beforehand about what you are to say. But say whatever will be given to you at that hour. For it will not be you who are speaking, but the Holy Spirit.'

There was more in what Peter had related, but Mark needed to keep his thoughts in the present. His friends' martyrdom must not be in vain. Their witness could convert many hearts, if only people paid attention. And the gospel still needed to be preached to all nations. When the written narrative is complete, it will help with that mission. I have to do it, he vowed. I simply must.

Mark began to pray; Lord Jesus—help me—guide me—keep me from losing hope . . . The words failed to develop in his weary mind, but he sensed that Christ understood.

Reaching into his bag, he found the medallion that Peter had given him. Fingering it carefully, he gazed at the image of the Holy Spirit, then he closed his eyes and lifted his mind to the heavens. You are my leader now.

As the small boat continued down the river, Mark thought about his relationship with the leader of the apostles. From the beginning Mark liked working with him. Peter's gift was how quickly he could move into action, while Mark liked to take in details and think them through. They made a good team, and over the years Peter had become less impulsive, while Mark had grown in courage.

Shortly after Mark settled in Rome a situation came up where a presbyter was failing in his spiritual role. Peter began dictating a scathing letter, and in the middle Mark put down his pen and asked, "Might it not be wiser to talk personally with the man and maybe offer him a different job, one in which he would be better suited?"

Peter stared at Mark for what seemed like an eternity. Then he sprouted a broad grin and said, "You are a smart young man. I can put him in charge of our buildings and coordinating renovations. He will be excellent at that!" From that day forward, their relationship became more of a partnership, even though Peter was undeniably the boss.

In March of the current year, Peter was fretting about the lack of money. "It is so frustrating. We never have enough to pay to get what is needed done." The apostle was at his best when inspiring people with his total dedication to the Lord, but administrative details often escaped his grasp.

Mark replied, "We should have enough. There is plenty coming in."

Peter frowned. "I know, but they take it."

"What? Who takes it?"

"Various people. I can't watch them every minute."

"Who, for instance?" Mark asked.

"Well, Judas always had his hand in the bag. It started there. Money is a great temptation, you know. Through the years I've had my suspicions, but I never know what to do. Now, I think it is Lucius."

Hearing the name of the deacon in charge of the church treasury surprised Mark. "Lucius? No."

"Yes. I think so."

Mark thought for a moment, picturing the man slipping coins he was supposed to be protecting into his garment. "What if . . . What if one person records the amounts that come in and go out, and another keeps hold of the balance? They would keep each other honest. That's what men do who run businesses."

Peter's eyes lit up. "Of course! That might do it. We can't change human nature, but we can put some ropes around temptation." The former fisherman grabbed his young assistant by the shoulders and gave him a hearty embrace.

With happy memories floating through his mind and the medallion clutched firmly in his hand, Mark drifted into much-needed sleep.

7

Ancient Rome colonized Ostia, where the river meets the sea, for one reason—salt. Romans like their meat, and plenty of the tasty preservative could be raked up in the nearby flats. A naval fort there also provided defense against enemy ships wishing to sail up the Tiber.

Claudius was on the throne when city officials proposed relocating their harbor away from the silt that had begun to block large ships from reaching their docks. He approved construction of a new artificial basin in the second year of his reign, but the mammoth project took over twenty years to complete. Nero celebrated the official opening just a few months before the Fire, but ships had been using the new port for two years.

As the little boat approached the docks, Mark noted the familiar outlines of the place. Peter and he had passed by a number of times, but this was his first occasion to board a ship there. The vessel he would sail in looked sea-worthy, with a sturdy mast for supporting a large square sail and an angled foremast for attaching a sprit. He noted the oarlocks and hoped that plentiful winds would make rowing unnecessary.

The captain was Cretan, from a long line of sea going families. Outside of Crete they called him Minos because no one could pronounce his given name. It meant king, and Mark observed that the crew responded exactly as Captain Minos ordered—instantly.

His greying hair and well-tanned face gave confidence to his clients, whether they were sailing with him or shipping freight. "Climb aboard," he said with a big smile. "Stow your bag there in the bow. We sail on the next tide."

Mark was wondering what the plans were for the voyage when the captain approached him. "You want to know how we go?" Greek obviously was not his first language. "We go along mainland to Sicily and take on cargo at Syracuse. Then we head east to Athens. And our last, we go north to Philippi. It take three weeks or so. The wind, He decide how fast we go."

"I imagine you have made this trip many times."

"Oh yes. I been all over the sea. I sail all my life; my father teach me, and his father teach him." Minos apparently liked to brag about his career. "I go to Egypt. I go into Black Sea. I go to Spain too, never beyond."

Mark felt safe in the experienced mariner's hands; the broken speech even added to his credentials.

Later that day Mark explored the ship, looking for a place where he might do some work. He spied a ledge along the side. It was below the main deck, out of the wind, but with just enough light for writing. "Ah ha. That will be perfect," he whispered. The cargo area was only half full. Captains such as Minos liked to take on passengers when sailing away from Rome. When heading toward Rome they carried as much freight as possible to satisfy the desires of the citizens.

From his bag Mark removed two codices: the beginning of the gospel and his notes of Peter's talks. The talks were short accounts of things Jesus had done, anecdotes actually, not in any particular order. Mark wanted to present the stories in a way that gave people an appreciation for what Jesus was like. Both his father's conversion and his own faith had stemmed from hearing accounts like these and pondering the implications. He decided to begin with things Jesus did, more so than what he said. Filling a reed pen, he began copying.

> *On leaving the synagogue he entered the house of Simon and Andrew with James and John. Simon's mother-in-law lay sick with a fever. They immediately told him about her. He approached, grasped her hand, and helped her up. Then the fever left her and she waited on them.*
>
> *When it was evening, after sunset, they brought to him all who were ill or possessed by demons. The whole town was gathered at the door. He cured many who were sick with various diseases, and he drove out many demons, not permitting them to speak because they knew him.*

"Hello. What are you doing?" The voice belonged to one of the crewmen. He was short and lean, with recently-trimmed brown hair and a short beard. Strong muscles in his arms and legs evidenced a rugged life at sea.

"I'm writing a story, and I'm copying some notes I made earlier." Mark told him.

"Oh. Who is the story about?"

Mark hesitated for a moment. The seaman's eyes looked sincere, and his broad smile set Mark at ease. "It is about Jesus of Nazareth, the one we call the Christ."

"Oh. I've heard about him. They say he was the son of a god, but I don't know. He was a Jew. Right?"

"Yes, but no ordinary Jew. He was the Son of the Most High."

"He got crucified. Right?"

"Yes. His own people turned him over to the Romans. The governor gave the order," Mark replied sadly.

"What crime was he guilty of?"

"He was a man of peace. He never hurt anyone. But some of them turned against him."

"Why did they do that?" the seaman asked curiously.

"He preached about a new kingdom—the kingdom of God. In this kingdom people treat one another fairly. No one ever takes from another. No one ever uses power over another."

The man shook his head and grunted, "It sounds like a myth. The world is not like that."

"But that's the point. Jesus taught that if we all treat one another the way we want them to treat us, the world will be a better place."

"Yes. Sure. *If* everybody does it."

"Well those of us who follow him want to live that way. Jesus is our model. We try to be like him."

"Read me some of the story." The man was skeptical, but obviously interested.

Mark read the part he had just copied, where Jesus healed Simon's mother-in-law.

"That's amazing! He cured people that easily?" Timon asked.

"Yes. He was divine—the Son of God."

"And so many?"

"He never turned anyone away. He had great love in his heart for all people," Mark attested.

"My mother, she died last year. Nothing could save her."

"Oh. I'm sorry. Did she suffer long?"

"Not too long. She coughed and coughed. Nobody knew what to do. Then she just gave up."

Mark reached out and put his hand on the man's shoulder. "You loved her very much."

A tear slid down the seaman's cheek. "She was a very good mother."

For a moment, silence seemed to offer the most comfort. The man was in touch with his grief.

"My name is Timon. What is yours?"

"Mark."

"It is good to meet you, Mark. I have to get back to work now."

"Good to meet you."

As the man walked away, Mark savored a feeling of satisfaction. People appreciated hearing about Jesus, whether they were ready to turn to him, or not. And when one of his followers reached out to someone in an authentic way, it left an image in the person's mind that the kingdom Jesus preached about just might prevail.

Mark felt good about the conversation; he had many like it while he worked with Peter. The head of the church was vastly more experienced, of course, and possessed the credibility of an eyewitness. When Peter spoke, people listened intently. They were captivated by his stories of Jesus. At first Mark was timid about speaking with people about Christ, but the longer he was at the great apostle's side, the more confident he became.

The next day Mark noticed that Timon was not working with the crew. He asked Minos about him, who replied, "He sick. Bad sweat."

"Oh. Have you given him any medicine?"

"We got no that on the ship. He got to rest—sleep it off."

"Where is he?"

"Back there. You go, if you want."

With little hesitation Mark proceeded to the crew area. Timon was awake, but sweating profusely. Eyeing a jug of water, Mark wet a rag and wiped the man's oily brow and cheeks. They were well-tanned from the sun, but had become unnaturally red and felt hot to the touch. Timon smiled despite his obvious discomfort.

For a long time Mark just sat with him, occasionally wiping his forehead. Timon looked weak and fragile, totally unlike the sinewy seaman he had met the previous day.

The seaman appeared to be thinking. Finally he spoke. "Can Jesus heal me?"

"Yes."

"He was alive when he healed those people. Now he is dead."

"He's no longer visible, but he always is with us," Mark assured him.

"Can you ask him to heal me?"

"I can try."

"Tell him I have my wife and children in Thessalonica. They need me to support them."

"I will do that."

Mark gathered his thoughts. "The way we talk to him is prayer. We think the words in our minds or voice them out loud. Either way he hears us. Do you want me to pray for you?"

"Yes . . . please."

"Lord Jesus," Mark began. "You see how Timon needs you. He does not know you, but you know him. He is a good man. He loves with his whole heart. He loves his mother. He loves his wife. He loves his children. He loves everyone."

"Not so much the Romans!" Timon interrupted.

Mark smiled. "Not so much the Romans. . . But his heart is filled with the desire to do good. Help him. Keep him safe until this illness passes. He needs your care. Please do what you can for him."

The seaman's eyes closed. Mark sat with him and continued praying silently, occasionally wiping Timon's fevered brow.

When he left Timon, Mark went up on the deck and stared at the waves. The sky was cloudless. Two white birds were following the ship, inspecting the activities of the crew. Mark felt hope in his heart.

After a few moments of grateful reflection he went back to where his books were and continued writing.

Rising very early before dawn, he left and prayed. Simon and those with him pursued him and on finding him said, 'Everyone is looking for you.' He told them, 'Let us go on to the nearby villages that I may preach there also. For this purpose have I come.' So he went into their synagogues, preaching and driving out demons throughout the whole of Galilee.

Mark mused, I guess I'm trying to do just like Jesus. I'm traveling around, talking to people about the kingdom, and now I just prayed to heal someone. The original disciples did that too. They felt the passion in their hearts and acted on it. The written gospel can do the same, in its own way. The church has missionaries that go out and teach and bishops and others who stay and support their people. Both will find the written narrative valuable. And as time goes on and the Church continues to grow, we will need a standard to keep the memories of Jesus secure.

He copied another of Peter's stories.

Jesus said, 'This is how it is with the kingdom of God. It is as if a man were to scatter seed on the land and would sleep and rise night and day and the seed would sprout and grow, he knows not how. Of its own accord the land yields fruit, first the blade, then the ear, then the full grain in the ear. And when the grain is ripe, he wields the sickle at once, for the harvest has come.'

Jesus spoke in images and parables—the language of the common people. Peter had told him, "We had to keep it simple." Christ did not pursue the rich and powerful. He just tried to touch the hearts of those he called the 'lost sheep.' He gave them a reason to hope. Mark continued writing.

Jesus said, 'To what shall we compare the kingdom of God, or what parable can we use for it? It is like a mustard seed that, when it is sown in the ground, is the smallest of all the seeds on the earth. But once it is sown, it springs up and becomes the largest of plants and puts forth large branches, so that the birds of the sky can dwell in its shade.' With many such parables he spoke the word to them as they were able to understand it. Without parables he did not speak to them, but to his own disciples he explained everything in private.

The parables were quite simple. The crowds in the villages always got the point. The Jews had been expecting God to establish a new kingdom for them, and by teaching in parables Jesus built upon their hopes. Even while Mark was a boy he understood the parables. The images Jesus used became pictures in his mind. He remembered how his heart burned as he saw the mustard seed grow into a large tree with all the birds flying into it. He wanted the kingdom to grow like that, and the teaching kindled his hopes, even though it seemed far away.

Then he paused and read the last line of text three times. *Without parables he did not speak to them, but to his own disciples he explained everything in private.*

I never noticed that, he said to himself. While the crowds only understood the simple images in the parables, his disciples wanted more, and he explained everything to them in private. That's it! Those who wanted more, got more. Those who wanted to understand Jesus, understood more deeply. Those who grew to love him, entered more fully into the kingdom of God! The insight left him tingling. He had dwelt on these teachings just like the first followers. And after spending eight years with Peter focusing daily on Christ, he had become a totally new person. People will be able to go as deep as they want into the mysteries of God, if they simply spend time with the stories of Jesus. And I will preserve the accounts for them.

The next morning Mark made it a point to see Timon. The sick man told him,

"I am getting better. Tomorrow I will go back to work. Thank you very much for all you did."

"Oh, don't thank me. Thank Jesus."

"I thank you both. If Jesus healed me, it was you who talked to him. You pray very well."

"I have had practice."

"Yes. You are a good man."

8

The next day, as the ship passed between Messana and Rhegium, Mark went up near the rudder control. Captain Minos smiled at him. They were leaving the mainland and would be following the east coast of Sicily. "Tomorrow—Syracuse."

"We made good time," Mark noted.

"Yes. The wind—He good to us."

"How long will we be in port?"

"One day. We get food and water; some cargo for Athens."

"I was wondering why we are going that far south before turning east."

"The crates come from North Africa. No much to load. They want it in Athens."

"I see." Mark was satisfied with the travel arrangements. Ships went where needed, and an extra day did not matter to him.

As the sight of land faded behind them, his thoughts went back to his home in Antioch. He remembered how he felt the day he left for Rome, knowing it would be a long time before he saw his family again.

His aging father was crying as he kissed his son. "You will do good work with Peter, but I will miss you."

"I will miss you, too, Father."

His brothers and sisters embraced him affectionately. Habib, the oldest, said he hoped Mark would return one day to help with the family business.

Lydia and her family also were there to say goodbye. Lydia was sincere and loving—everything a man could hope for—and Mark would gladly have accepted her as his wife. But he was leaving. He didn't know what to say to her, and she held her feelings inside as best as she could. He didn't even embrace her when he left, even though it would have been acceptable for them to do so.

His mother pushed a basket of food into his arms. She had hoped that her youngest son would stay close to home, like his brothers. But being the brightest and best-trained, there was no guarantee. Then she told him, "Take this too," pressing the silver cross into his hand. "Go with God."

Then Mark picked up his bag, turned and walked out the gate. That was it.

As he walked toward the harbor to join Peter he realized that they all must be staring at his back, while he was looking ahead to new adventures. He didn't look back, though; he just stepped forward with a quickened pace.

I was so immature back then, he recalled. Lydia and I could have become betrothed before I left, and I could have returned for the wedding. I was too naive, though. If I had used my head, I'd be a married man today.

With the cool breeze of the sea glancing across his face, he sunk down on the deck. Wonderful memories floated through his mind, but so did many regrets. Warm tears dripped onto his tunic.

Mark went down to his ledge to try to work. While he was thinking about what to do next, he heard a familiar voice.

"Are you are still writing?"

"Yes. Hello Timon. How are you feeling?"

"Pretty good. . . Much better." Mark waited to see what the seaman had on his mind.

"I've been wondering about something. Can I ask you a question?"

Mark nodded.

"How do you know that Jesus was the son of god?"

"The Son of God. . . When he prayed to God or spoke about him, he called him Father."

"But gods are far away. They are not concerned about us here."

"That is true of the gods you learned about in Thessalonica. But the One God loves us."

"How do you know that?" Timon asked.

"Well, the two questions are related. Jesus showed in many ways that he loves us. And when he prayed to his Father he called him *abba*, which means daddy. They have a relationship of love."

"I understand about daddy and son; I am a father too."

"Yes. It's like our human love, only theirs is divine—love beyond anything we can imagine."

"You talk like Jesus is alive. Didn't they crucify him?"

"They did. And his friends laid him in a tomb. But on the third day he was raised."

"How do you know that?"

"They went back to the tomb to anoint his body, and he was not there. They saw only the burial cloths lying where his body had been."

"Someone could have taken the body," the seaman asserted.

"Several of Jesus' disciples witnessed the whole thing. My mentor, Peter, verified the report. Here, listen to this." While Mark opened his notes, Timon sat down on the deck.

When the Sabbath was over, Mary Magdalene, Mary the mother of James, and Salome bought spices so that they might go and anoint him. Very early when the sun had risen, on the first day of the week, they came to the tomb. They were saying to one another, 'Who will roll back the stone for us from the entrance to the tomb?' When they looked up, they saw that the stone had been rolled back; it was very large. On entering the tomb they saw a young man sitting on the right side, clothed in a white robe, and they were utterly amazed! He said to them, 'Do not be amazed! You seek Jesus of Nazareth, the crucified. He has been raised; he is not here. Behold the place where they laid him. But go and tell his disciples and Peter, 'He is going before you to Galilee; there you will see him, as he told you.'

Both men sat in silence. Timon obviously was thinking seriously about what he heard, and Mark was giving him time to do so.

"So he was raised after being in the tomb for three days! He certainly was dead. That is amazing!"

"Yes."

"So now he is alive?"

"Yes."

And no one saw him?"

"Oh. Many of his followers saw him. He appeared to them over a period of weeks."

"What happened then?

"Then he ascended into heaven, but not until after he commanded his disciples to go forth to all nations and tell others about him."

"Just like you did to me?"

"That's right. Just like that."

"How can I learn more about Jesus?"

"Well . . . We will talk more on the voyage. And when you get home to Thessalonica, you can inquire at the *ekklesia*, the Christian community there."

"You have people in my city?"

"Yes. There has been a group there for almost fifteen years."

"Really? Where are you traveling?"

"I am going to Philippi."

"That's close."

"Yes. Very close. Maybe we can stay in contact."

"That would be wonderful!" Timon said excitedly. "What will you do in Philippi?"

"I'm going there to complete my writing. The *episkopos*, the bishop, will give me lodging and meals until I am finished."

"Episkopos—he oversees your group?"

"Yes. His name is Alexios."

"Is there a bishop in Thessalonica?"

"Yes. Every large city has a bishop, if there are enough Christians. I don't know your bishop's name, though. If you ask around, someone will lead you to him."

"They will accept an ordinary seaman?" Timon asked doubtfully.

"Yes, they'll welcome you. We don't distinguish between rich and poor in our communities."

"You are joking!" Timon scoffed.

"No. Jesus ate with the common people. He didn't discriminate between social classes; so neither do we."

"That's amazing; so different."

"Christians are different. We try to live our lives like Jesus did. We are not as perfect as him, but we try our best."

"And if I find the Christians in my town this winter, they will tell me more?"

"Yes. If you sincerely want to learn more about Jesus, they will instruct you."

"I might like that. I will think about it. Thanks Mark." Timon jumped up to go back to work.

Mark rose and gave him a warm hug. "May God be with you, my friend."

At one time Syracuse was the largest city on the island of Sicily. It became a bustling port town with strategic importance at the intersection of shipping routes. The city was founded by Greeks, and the great mathematician Archimedes was born there.

A day in port sounded good to Mark. He wanted to get his feet on solid ground again, and it would be hectic on the ship with the loading of supplies and cargo. He told Minos he wanted to go into town to find a *tonsor* to give him a shave. His iron razor didn't work very well on the tossing ship.

Shaving became popular under Alexander the Great. He thought shaving made it more difficult for enemy warriors to grab his men by the face in combat. Julius Caesar had his facial hairs plucked out individually with tweezers each day. Many cultures detested shaving, but those that embraced it called them barbarians, which meant un-barbered. Mark just wanted a good shave.

Finding a shop, he entered the door.

"Come in. What can I do for you?" the barber asked, while busily cutting a man's hair.

"Primarily a shave," Mark told him.

"I can do that right after I finish this man. It won't be long. Make yourself comfortable."

Mark saw a cushion on the floor, so he sat down and leaned his back against the wall.

"You passing through?"

"Yes. We leave later today."

"Where are you from?"

"I came from Rome."

"Ah—Roma. The great City. . . You look like someone who works with his mind, not his muscles."

"Yes. I am a—scribe."

"Oh. That's a good occupation. Who is your patron?"

Oh, God, Mark thought. This may not be a good place to reveal my identity. What should I say?

"Who do you work for? A great man maybe?" the barber asked again.

"Yes, a very great man." Mark felt every hair on his body quivering.

"What is his name? I may have heard of him."

"It was Peter."

"A rock! Ha ha. I don't think I know any Peter from Rome."

"Did you say Peter?" The seated man who had been silent seemed startled. "Are you talking about the leader of the Christians? Those heathens should all be strung up!"

Mark held his breath and didn't answer.

"Are you one of them?"

The man's face got deep red. He didn't hold back his hatred one bit. Mark kept silent.

"You *are* one of them—and a fugitive too, I bet."

Mark glanced toward the door. If he got up and ran, it would look obvious.

Seeing the movement in Mark's eyes, the man rose up from where he was seated and stared down at him. "Are you running away from the Emperor?" When Mark didn't answer, the man picked up a heavy stone jar from the tonsor's table and smashed it down on his head, stunning him momentarily. "I will call the guards. You won't get away."

The man raised the jar a second time and hit him again, smashing it against his skull. Mark felt a searing pain in his right temple; then everything went dark.

9

When he awoke Mark's head was throbbing. Nothing made sense. Where was he? The walls around him were bare stone. Light appeared from one side.

"Oh, my head," he moaned. He lay there motionless for several minutes, wanting to look around, but his head hurt too much to move it.

Finally, he got up the strength to turn toward the light. It looked like a doorway. *Oh yes. I was in the tonsor's when that man attacked me. But this is not the place—no furniture—no barber tools here.* The bare floor pressed against his body. *How long have I been here?* Each part of his flesh in contact with the floor was sore. *A long time I guess.*

Then he saw that the doorway had an iron gate across it. *What!* He looked again, studying the pattern of the bars. *Is this a prison?* With great difficulty he rolled his aching body towards the gate. Lifting his left hand, he felt the cold iron bars and muttered, "Oh, no! Oh, God. I'm in a jail."

Slumping back to the stone floor, he lay there assessing the situation. *The barber was making conversation. Then the silent man, who apparently hated Christians, hit me with a stone jar. He must have turned me over to the guards. What do I do now,* he wondered, and realized he couldn't do anything, lying there unable to lift his head.

He reached up to rub his throbbing head with his free left hand and noticed flakes of dark dry blood on his fingers. *Was he cut too? How bad?* Struggling, he managed to crawl over to a wall. He sat up and leaned his back against the stone, studying the iron bars.

"Oh God— the ship!" he shouted. The gravity of his predicament finally sunk in. *Minos said the ship would sail in the afternoon. What day is this?*

Glancing out the doorway, he looked for clues. The shadows seemed long, but not knowing which way he faced, he couldn't tell if it was morning or evening. Then a cool breeze wafted against his face. It's morning! Have I been here all night? Where is the ship?

Realizing that Minos may have left the harbor with all of his belongings on board, Mark slumped back down to the floor and sobbed. His head ached, and he hadn't yet used his right arm.

He lay on the floor for a long time in a daze. Then pulling his body again up against the wall, he stared out the door and realized it must be midday. Eyeing some bloodstains on his tunic, he allowed his voice to speak the truth. "I am in prison. The man who hit me said he would turn me in, and here I am. The ship is gone by now." Also realizing that he was thirsty and hungry, Mark just sat there, holding his aching head.

"Are you finally awake?" The voice asking the question came from the doorway. "Do you want some water and bread?" Looking up, Mark saw a young soldier, confirming his fears as to his predicament. "I will put it here through the bars. When you finish, put the pitcher outside."

"Thank you," Mark said sincerely. "Why am I here?"

"You started a fight with a citizen. That was not very smart. He called for us saying you are a fugitive. You will stay here until the Promagistrate decides what to do with you." With that, the man turned his back and left.

The water and bread were welcome, even though nothing else in Syracuse seemed to be. He took a long drink from the side of the pitcher, and chewed a chunk of bread. Then, using as little water as possible, he washed the dried blood from his face.

When the shadows out the door grew longer, the young soldier appeared again at the door. "I told my officer that you were awake. He told me to bring you food and water twice a day while we wait."

"Wait for what?"

"We wait for word to come back from Rome as to what to do with you."

"What?" Mark questioned.

"You are a fugitive. Right?"

"No. I left Rome freely. No one was chasing me." Mark assured him.

"The citizen you fought with said you are part of a sect of heathens that Nero is plucking out."

"I didn't fight with the man. He hit me with a stone jar. I didn't even raise my arm."

"He said you bow to your *Christos* and not to our gods."

"I follow the Prince of Peace."

"Even if the one you follow is the son of a king, he cannot overpower Caesar."

The conversation was straying into the wrong territory. Mark needed to seek information, not give it. "I had a little money. Where is it?"

"We will keep it to pay for your food and water. You will be here a while."

"For how long?"

"The Promagistrate sent a letter to Rome asking if we should execute you here or ship you back to Nero. We should hear within two or three weeks."

"But I can't stay here!" His words were of no avail; the soldier turned and walked out of sight.

As the daylight faded, Mark replayed over and over the events of the day. Everything had gone wrong for him. Part of the time he was trying to figure a way out of his situation, even though it seemed hopeless. The rest of his energy went toward his mission. *How will I complete the gospel? I've lost all my notes. I can't finish it just from my memory, even if I do get out of here.*

His head was throbbing a little less now. He swung his right arm in a broad arc. Opening and clenching his hand a few times he told himself, *nothing is broken; just bruised.* But there was little reason for optimism. *I will die a martyr, and no one will even know.*

He had never thought about dying a martyr's death. Peter spoke of the possibility, but Mark didn't give it much attention. Peter's prediction about his own death had proven true. Would he follow his mentor in this as well?

So many have gone by that route, he thought as he traced through names like Paul, James, Stephen, and John the Baptist. John's work was finished when he prepared the way for Jesus. But King Herod had him arrested, and John sat in a prison cell while his fate was determined. John had rebuked the king for marrying Herodias, the wife of his brother. He recalled the story.

Herodias had a grudge against him and wanted to kill him. But she could not, for Herod feared John, knowing that he was a righteous and holy man, and he protected him. When he heard him he was greatly perplexed; and yet he liked to listen to him. But an opportunity came when Herod on his birthday gave a banquet for his courtiers and officers, and for the leaders of Galilee. When the daughter of Herodias came in and danced, she pleased Herod and his guests; and the king said to the girl, 'Ask me for whatever you wish, and I will give it.' And he solemnly swore to her, 'Whatever you ask of me, I will give you, even to half of my kingdom.' She went out and said to her mother, 'What shall I ask for?' She replied, 'The head of John the Baptizer.'

The king was deeply distressed, but he had made an oath in front of his guests. So he gave the order for the decapitation. They brought back the head on a platter.

"Why am I thinking such gruesome thoughts?" he asked himself out loud. The reason was obvious. Mark's situation had many parallels. But the Baptist had fulfilled his calling. Mark was only getting started.

In the darkness, he dropped to his knees. It was some time before words formed in his mind. Then, in the silence of the cell, he poured out his soul in earnest. "Jesus, my Lord. I am failing you. Everything is going wrong. I have no one to turn to but you. It's not for my sake that I pray, but for the sake of the gospel. I am willing to die for you. But I am not willing to die before finishing an account of your life that can inspire people to believe in you. I will not give in to despair, yet I have little reason to hope. If you want me to complete the gospel, you need to open the way."

10

A few days later, some soldiers brought another prisoner to the cell. They pushed the man inside, closed the gate, and locked it. "You will not disrespect a Roman officer!" one of the soldiers bellowed. Then without hesitating, they marched away.

"Rotten bastards!" The man was short and lean, with sinuous muscles divulging a vigorous life. His oily black hair looked seldom combed, and his beard, trimmed to a point, made him look sinister. He clenched his fists often, which appeared to be a habit. The man glanced at Mark and then grabbed the gate, shaking it mightily, but to no avail. Even though it didn't budge, he shook it three more times, showing it how he hated to be overpowered.

Mark disliked the man at first sight. Many of his good friends were strong, like Antonius the stone mason, but this man was a fighter. Mark kept them at a distance.

The man turned toward him and glared. "A little spit—that's all it was."

"What did you do?" Mark asked cautiously.

"I saw a group of soldiers coming down the street. The Duplicarius in charge looked so proud, like he owned the city. I got up a pretty big wad, and when he got right in front of me I let it fly."

"That was risky."

"Ahh—I thought I could get away with it. Most of it landed on the stones. Maybe one little drop hit his toe."

"He saw you?"

"I didn't think so. I ducked behind a column. Then he ordered his men to halt and turn around, and shouted, 'Seize him!'"

Mark couldn't believe that anyone would be so reckless.

"I could have got away, but there was one too many of them."

"So they brought you here?"

"They brought me here. One of them said, 'You're lucky the Promagistrate ordered all executions to go through him. Otherwise our Duplicarius would have stuck his sword through you there on the street.'"

"What will they do to you?"

"I am a lucky man. He told me the Promagistrate is away for three more days. I just might get out of here."

The man was talkative, but turned away from Mark, trying to think of a way out. Mark decided to let him be.

A few minutes later the man looked back at Mark. "What are you in here for?"

"Oh, a citizen hit me and turned me in. They might send me back to Rome."

"Hmm." The man asking the question didn't listen to the answer.

"My name is Mark," he told him, extending his hand.

"Hmm. Arsenos," the man replied, keeping his hand at his side.

"Well, Arsenos—it looks like we will be here together for a few days."

"Hmm." The man turned back to the gate and shook the bars angrily two more times.

When evening came the young soldier appeared as usual at the doorway with a pitcher and a loaf. Motioning to Arsenos he said, "I can't give you anything. You didn't have any money on you, and no one has brought you any food."

"Ahh!" Arsenos grumbled.

As the soldier walked out of sight, the prisoner blurted, "My Korinna; she will bring me some."

"Here." Mark broke the loaf in half and extended it toward the man, along with the water. The man grabbed the pitcher and took several gulps. Then he sat down in a corner, gnawing on the bread, not saying a word.

Mark chose to leave him to his thoughts.

The next morning the soldier brought two portions. Arsenos grabbed a wrapped parcel and looked inside. "Ah ha! My Korinna. She is so good to me." He held up a fig and bit into it.

They sat against the stone walls across from one another eating their food. Neither said a word.

An hour later the two men heard noise from the street. Looking out the doorway, they smelled smoke. People were shouting, "Fire! Fire!"

"What's going on?" Arsenos spoke his question aloud.

"Something is burning."

"I can't see where . . . In the next building, maybe."

Suddenly the young soldier appeared at the door. Unlocking the gate, he shouted, "Outside! Now!" The two prisoners followed as ordered.

Once outside they could see the structure adjoining the jail ablaze. People were attempting to get the fire under control, but to little avail. Mark stood next to the soldier staring at the flames, now shooting up from the roof. Then he heard a voice from behind him say, "This is perfect! I'm out of here."

Mark followed the voice. Arsenos ducked into a narrow passageway, and Mark rushed behind him. The two men crept along quietly so as to avoid suspicion, but didn't waste time. Mark had no idea where they were going, but Arsenos did. He knew the city streets like the lines on his calloused hands.

Running out of breath, Mark realized that they were heading to the harbor. Arsenos made a bee line toward a ship just being untied. "Kastor, can I get on?" he shouted to the captain.

Recognized his friend, the captain waved him on. "Come aboard."

"Can I come too?" pleaded Mark.

The captain peered down at the slender figure standing there in a dirty, blood-stained tunic. He didn't look like much of a prospect. "Can you work?"

"Yes."

"Then get on."

As the boat left the harbor Mark looked for some sign of Minos' ship. It was gone.

"Coil up those ropes."

"Yes sir." He jumped to the task of coiling the lines.

"Now help those men pull up the canvas."

Only nodding, Mark raced to where three men were hoisting the main sail.

He didn't know anything about sailing, but he figured he could pull on a rope. Grabbing it in both hands he copied the motions of the others, but his hands slipped. Feeling a burning sensation ripping through his palms, he grimaced. Then wrapping the rope around his wrists, he pulled with all his might.

When the sail was in place and the ship had gone a little way out of the harbor, Captain Kastor had a talk with his new recruits. "I know you can handle yourself on a ship, Arsenos, but what can your friend do?" he asked.

"He is no friend of mine. I never saw him before yesterday."

"Then why was he with you?"

"We were in . . . the same place. A fire broke out, and we ran to the dock together."

"So you were in jail again, huh? Are you ever going to learn to stay out of trouble?"

Turning to Mark, he asked him bluntly. "Have you ever worked on a ship?" Mark shook his head. "What do you do for a living?"

"I'm a scribe. And I translate. I speak good Greek."

"That won't do us much good out here. I don't suppose you have any money." Mark shook his head again. "Are you running from the Promagistrate?" This time Mark nodded.

"All right. The sensible thing would be to throw you over the side right now." Kastor thought for a moment about his options. "You want to go to Corinth?"

"Yes. Very much."

"Then you will help prepare meals and clean up. You will clean the head. You will do whatever else I think you can handle. And you will get no wine on the voyage. Is that acceptable?"

"Yes. Very acceptable." Mark had no choice—it was the best arrangement he could hope for. The trip would only take a few days. He could handle it.

"Oh, and if the wind dies, you will take an oar."

"Yes. I will do that."

As he headed for the little galley, Mark felt fear streaming through his body. He was not one of the crew, and he definitely was not a paying passenger. Arsenos showed no concern for him, and Captain Kastor could at any moment choose to throw him out. Any of the men on board could turn against him.

At nightfall, he allowed the other men to pick their place to sleep first. Then he tried to make himself as comfortable as possible on the hard decking. But even though he was exhausted, he couldn't sleep.

He had no idea what might lie ahead, no money, and no clothing except for the blood-stained tunic he was wearing. I wonder if this is how the disciples felt as they went out to the villages, he asked himself. Maybe they felt as helpless as I do. He recalled a story that Peter told.

He called the twelve and began to send them out two by two, and gave them authority over the unclean spirits. He ordered them to take nothing for their journey except a staff; no bread, no bag, no money in their belts; but to wear sandals and not to put on two tunics. He said to them, 'Wherever you enter a house, stay there until you leave the place. If any place will not welcome you and they refuse to hear you, as you leave, shake off the dust that is on your feet as a testimony against them.' So they went out and proclaimed that all should repent. They cast out many demons, and anointed with oil many who were sick and cured them.

Mark pondered the parallel. Jesus must have wanted his disciples to feel what it is like to have no source of security, except him. Here I am—totally destitute. I don't know what to expect, if I get to the next town. And the 'house' I am in is only partially welcoming me. He prayed, Oh Jesus, I have nowhere to turn but to you. Take me to where you want me to be. I am your helpless servant, more than I ever imagined.

The next day the wind died, and the ship came to a halt in the middle of the sea. Captain Kastor cursed. "This time of the year there should be plenty of wind. Too much wind or too little—that is the lot of those who sail." The men sat on the deck and waited.

Kastor, perched on the highest point, scanned the horizon for any sign of breeze. The sea was flat and shining in the noonday sun. "Damn wind. Show your face." Spotting a dark area of water to the north, he barked an order to the men. "To the oars!" Every man jumped.

Mark watched the others pull the oars from where they were stacked and followed their actions. The long oars were heavier than he had imagined. Going to the right side, he took a place behind two others and in front of Arsenos. He had rowed a little as a boy in small boats near Antioch, but never in a full sized ship.

"Now pull!" Kastor turned the rudder as the men leaned their bodies and strained on the oars. As the heavy vessel edged ahead, the captain pointed it toward the dark ripples. "Pull... Pull... Pull... Pull." The steady rhythm of his voice kept the men united in their task.

Mark was fully aware that he was the least experienced of the eight rowers and the one in the poorest physical condition, but he was determined to do his share of the effort. "Idiot—watch the man in front of you," came the voice of

Arsenos behind him. "Match his rhythm." Mark did his best, and heaved with the others, dipping and lifting properly during most of the strokes.

"Pull... Pull... Pull... Pull." He wondered how long they would be at this.

As they continued to strain at the oars, Mark found himself drifting back to memories of his home—his mother quietly preparing the meals, his brothers so happy on their wedding days, his father toasting his handsome grown sons, and Lydia watching the festivities and occasionally tossing him a coy smile. He thought, what if I had stayed in Antioch? My life would be so different. By now I would have children around me and a home of my own. And Lydia would cuddle in my arms every night.

He longed for the moment they could be joined in a full and complete union of body and soul. He pictured her soft body next to his. He kissed her ear and listened to her happy giggle. It seemed like heaven, where a man didn't think, but just entered into the motion of life, allowing the feeling to build toward a peak of pleasure.

"Pull... Pull... Pull... Pull."

Mark snapped back into the present reality. He was not in Antioch, but on the open sea, straining on an oar. "Pull... Pull... Pull... Pull." He was getting tired. His body ached, and his hands felt on fire. Still, he continued at his task. The air was stagnant in the close lower deck; he noticed balls of sweat falling off the back of the man in front of him and smelled the pungent odor with each heavy breath. He didn't know how long he could keep it up. "Pull... Pull... Pull... Pull."

Jesus—how long must I do this? The involuntary question had no answer. He had no option but to stay with the labor for however long it took. He began thinking about how long Christ hung in agony on the cross—three hours, and that was after receiving a brutal scourge and carrying the heavy cross beam out of the fortress, through the city streets, and up the hill of Calvary. I have suffered nothing compared to his. I must endure this. If I hope to ever become worthy of his mercy, I need to stay with whatever pain befalls me.

Peter had shared how he reacted when Jesus first predicted his passion. "I rebuked him for saying such things, and he told me,

> *'Get behind me, Satan! For you are setting your mind not on divine things but on human things.' He called the crowd with his disciples and said to them, 'If any want to become my followers, let them deny themselves and take up their cross and follow me. For those who want to save their life will lose it, and those who lose their life for my sake, and for the sake of the gospel, will save it.'"*

With renewed energy, Mark heaved on the oars. His hands were burning and his mind became dazed. Pulling with all his might, he strained to the sound, "Pull... Pull... Pull... Pull."

11

Corinth once was a city-state on the narrow stretch of land joining the Peloponnesus peninsula to the mainland—part way between Athens and Sparta. An important trade city since ancient times, it often got caught in disputes between the other powers.

One and a half centuries before Christ was born, Rome declared war on the Achaean League, and the Romans under Lucius Mummius besieged and captured Corinth. Mummius put all the men to the sword, sold the women and children into slavery, and burnt the city. Corinth remained largely deserted until Julius Caesar re-founded it as *Colonia Laus Iulia Corinthiensis*, the Colony of Corinth in honor of Julius, shortly before his assassination. The Romans rebuilt the city and made it a provincial capital, and the population grew to more than 100,000 Romans, Greeks and Jews.

Mark had never been to Corinth. Peter visited there before Mark joined him and thought of it as one of Paul's cities. The two leaders held each other in mutual regard, and Peter tended to let Paul retain influence over the communities he had founded or nurtured.

Paul lived in Corinth off and on for several months during his missionary journeys. He wrote letters to the Christians there, which subsequently gained wide circulation. Mark had read two of them—one written from Ephesus and one from Macedonia. Paul arrived in Rome in custody, as a citizen waiting to have his case heard by the Emperor. He was held only under house arrest, however, and could have visitors. Mark wished he had spent more time with Paul, but Peter kept him busy.

As soon as the ship was tied to the pier, Arsenos jumped onto it and walked away.

Mark sought out Kastor. "Thank you," he said to the captain. "If I can ever repay you, I will."

"Ahh. Get out of here," the captain growled, although he showed satisfaction for having helped.

It was past mid-day, and Mark felt a gnawing in his stomach. As he walked through the harbor district, he wondered where he should go. He knew no one in Corinth. He had no money, no bag, and no clothing except for the stained tunic he was wearing. The blisters on his hands were burning, and the stubble on his face marked him as a vagrant and someone likely on the run.

Up, he thought. I need to go uphill, away from the harbor. I need to stay away from any Roman soldiers, and I'd better not go into any classy districts; I look too awful. Actually, he looked out of place in any district, but he kept walking, studying the surroundings and looking for options.

People were busy, rushing in and out of shops and houses. An old woman wearing a head scarf glared at him as he passed by her vegetable stand, making sure he didn't grab a turnip. A butcher gave him a long once over, possibly wondering if he should signal the guards. His presence was breaking through the boundaries of their comfort.

He passed several small temples, meeting places for devotees of the gods. The temples just served their own; none of the pagan organizations did anything for outsiders. He saw a synagogue, but had no idea how Jews felt about Christians in this city. I've got to find some Christians, he thought. But how? I can't just walk up to someone and ask.

He continued walking for about an hour, but knew he shouldn't spend too much time out in the open. Then over on the east side of the city, something caught his eye. Near the door of one shop he saw an outline of a fish. His heart raced. It could be an *ikthys*, a pair of intersecting arcs in the profile of a fish, sometimes used by Christians as a secret symbol. Do I dare go in there? he wondered.

After pondering the pros and cons for several minutes, he went up to the door. Inside was a dark-haired woman about his age, arranging a table of sandals. He picked one up, examining the lacing, then smiled and said, "Hello."

The woman smiled in return.

"Do you know where I might find people of the Way?" he asked. The woman did not respond. "I saw the fish," he continued. "You see, I had some trouble and I am destitute." If he was going to seek help, he may as well be honest.

"I will get Longinus." The woman turned and darted into the quarters behind the shop, reappearing with a stocky, light-skinned man with muscular arms, wearing a leather apron.

"I am the sandal maker. Can I help you?" the man asked.

"The kind of help I need does not involve shoes." Mark again chose to stick to the truth. "I am a Christian fleeing from the persecution in Rome. My money was taken away from me along with my clothing."

"Would you like something to eat?"

"Yes, but I cannot pay."

"Come with me."

The man led Mark through a doorway, past his work bench, and into a small living area. "Sit down. I'll get some bread." Reaching into the cupboard, he brought a pottery platter of bread with some olive oil. "Let's see how you feel after you eat something."

"Thank you. I am very grateful." Mark broke off a piece of bread and dipped it into the oil. How much should he explain before the man revealed his feelings? "My name is Mark. I heard your name is Longinus."

"Yes, and Klea is my wife. Did you say you are from Rome?"

Mark nodded. "It is getting very bad. Since the Fire many have been killed. Last week they crucified Peter."

Longinus looked shocked. "We heard about the purge, but you say they got Peter?"

"Yes. It was terrible." Mark related how Peter was executed and answered the man's many questions.

"And you are running away?"

"Not exactly. You see I worked with Peter. I am writing a narrative about Christ. The elders thought it best that I complete it away from Rome, so they sent me to Philippi."

"So you came by way of Philippi?"

"No. In Syracuse, on the way to Philippi, a citizen attacked me for being a follower, and I ended up in prison. I escaped, and now I am here."

"With nothing?"

"With nothing."

"You can stay here with us while we determine what to do. I can only offer you the couch at night."

"That's fine. I am accustomed to couches, and it's better than the hard deck on the ship."

"Good then."

"Oh, there is one more thing." Mark felt that he should lay out the whole truth. "At the last house I stayed, the soldiers came and took the whole family to the Coliseum."

"Hmm."

Mark held his breath.

"Well you get some rest, while I finish my work."

Mark slept while Klea prepared the evening meal.

Later he awoke to the comforting voice of Longinus, "Are you feeling better?"

"Yes. It was tiring on the ship."

"You worked with the crew?"

Mark explained how he and Arsenos got on board and described the work he did with the crew.

"It doesn't look like you are accustomed to hard work." Mark's blistered hands were the giveaway.

"I need a job, if I can find one."

Longinus poured two cups of wine. "What can you do?"

"I write well. If someone here can use a scribe, I can do that. I speak Greek, Syriac, and Old Aramaic. I know quite a bit of Latin, and I have an excellent memory."

"No manual skills?"

"Not actually."

"Well. We'll see what we can find. Now we eat."

The porridge was tasty, and with fresh olives and goat cheese it seemed like a treat. The two men continued to talk throughout the meal. Longinus was hungry for news from Rome. Klea didn't say much, but when Mark smiled her way she looked pleased.

"Would you like to come with us to Eucharist tomorrow?" The sandal maker was speaking of the weekly gathering to celebrate the Lord's Supper.

"Is it Sunday?" Mark had lost track of the days.

Longinus nodded. "We will have an Agape meal after." The sparkle in Klea's eyes indicated that she also enjoyed the gatherings.

"But I have no suitable clothing."

"We will have to do something about that as well. You can wear one of my tunics; we are not too different in height. And I will find you a blade so you can shave that stubble."

The next morning Mark shaved and put on the clean tunic. It was a little large through the shoulders, but that provided a needed extra bit of length over his longer legs.

"We gather in the home of Sosthenes, our *presbyter*," explained Longinus.

Christians typically met in a member's home. They had no other large buildings, and it kept them out of sight. "We like our little community here on the east side. The main body meets in the central district with our bishop, Onesiphorus. He doesn't come over here much. Silas visited us more often." Mark recognized the name of Paul's traveling companion. He knew that Paul had left him in charge of the Corinthians. "We liked Silas better. Our new bishop came from Calophon in Asia Minor. He is a good man, but he doesn't yet know our ways."

Entering the house, Mark noticed how friendly the people were. Every person greeted everyone with good words and a hug—men, women, and children all joined in the celebration.

Mark loved the liturgy: After singing some songs, one of the men read from the Hebrew Scriptures, they chanted a psalm together, and the presbyter spoke about how the words in the historic text related to their present lives. Then the leader said a long prayer, which recalled how Jesus—before he died—established the sacred ritual, when they all ate from one loaf and drank from a common cup. Sosthenes liked to center the prayer around part of Paul's early letter to the community, where the apostle said,

The Lord Jesus on the night when he was betrayed took a loaf of bread, and when he had given thanks, he broke it and said, 'This is my body that is for you. Do this in remembrance of me.' In the same way he took the cup also, after supper, saying, 'This cup is the new covenant in my blood. Do this, as often as you drink it, in remembrance of me.' For as often as you eat this bread and drink the cup, you proclaim the Lord's death until he comes.

Without thinking, Mark blurted out something Peter sometimes added, *And Jesus said to his disciples, 'Truly I tell you, I will never again drink of the fruit of the vine until that day when I drink it new in the kingdom of God.'*

All eyes turned and looked at him.

12

The Agape meal began immediately after the prayer. Sometimes they waited until later, but on this Sunday eating the meal in common was part of their communion in Christ.

Every family brought something. The wealthier members brought more and shared with those who could afford less. When all of the food and wine was put in place, no one knew who brought what. Everything was shared from that point on like one big family reunion.

The word *agape* refers to selfless, sacrificial, unconditional love—the highest of the types of love for which there is a term in the Greek language. Agape perfectly describes the kind of love Jesus has for his Father and for all people. Looking around, Mark could tell that everyone truly loved one another. And they already are showing it to me, he mused.

This kind of mutual sharing between rich and poor apparently had not been easily established in Corinth. While in theory followers of Christ adopt his example, the meal at times deteriorated into just an occasion for eating and drinking, or for ostentatious displays by the wealthier members. In one of his letters, Paul rebuked the Corinthians, but judging from what Mark could see, those problems were in the past.

"Sosthenes—I want you to meet someone." Longinus tugged on the presbyter's sleeve.

"Ah. You are the one who added to my prayer." The tall, slim leader looked dignified, clean-shaven with greying hair showing over his ears. His friendly smile and sincere eyes set Mark at ease.

"Peter used to say it when he prayed in Rome," Mark explained.

"Oh! So you knew Peter?" Sosthenes showed distress at the mention of Peter, but he sincerely wanted to hear about him.

Longinus cut in, "This man's name is Mark. He was an associate of Peter, but came here when Peter was put to death."

"That was terrible; we were all shocked. Were you close?"

"I worked for him."

"Oh really! What did you do?"

Mark gave a brief description of his duties with the head of the church.

"Ah. How fortunate we are to have you here. Will you be staying for a while?"

This time Longinus answered, explaining how Mark had arrived penniless and needed a job.

"Hmm. Can you come to my house tomorrow so we can talk some more?"

"Of course. What time?"

"How about mid-day?"

"I will be here."

Looking around, another person captured Mark's attention. Her cheerful face, though plain, was radiantly bright and locks of her short auburn hair were catching rays of light, sending them out like little beacons. "Who is that?" he asked Longinus.

"That is Agathe, one of our deaconesses."

"I thought that deaconesses were older." The woman was not much older than Mark.

"Agathe is a very special person. Her family came from north of the Bosphorus and became Christians in Athens. She is both intelligent and kind. She has been with us three years and serves everyone here very well because she has no husband or children."

"Don't deacons and deaconesses have to be married?"

"They usually are. But an exception was made on that too in Agathe's case. Would you like to meet her?"

"Yes!"

"Agathe." Longinus waved and got her attention. She came over to the men wearing a big smile. "This is Mark. He is from Rome."

"The one who spoke out during the liturgy? I thought they had better manners in Rome."

Mark blushed. Would he forever be labeled for that one mistake? "I—shouldn't have."

"Oh. That's all right. We are not that formal here. But don't try it in the main church with Onesiphorus!"

Not sure how to respond, Mark said, "I like it here. The people are nice."

"They are. I love them too. I'm also relatively new to Corinth. We should get along," Agathe added.

"Yes. We should."

"Good to meet you, Mark. I need to speak with those people over there. Let's talk again some time."

"Sure." Mark watched as Agathe bounced to another group. Laughing and joking, she gave them all little hugs, which although unconventional, were good signs of friendship. "This is a nice community," he said to Longinus. "I like it." But for the rest of the day, he kept catching glimpses of the intriguing woman from the north.

The next day when the sun was high, Mark walked up to the presbyter's door.

"Come in. Good to see you." Sosthenes greeted him.

"It is good to see you too."

"Shall we have something to eat?" Sosthenes motioned toward a table. The

MARK'S PASSION

home contained a few simple furnishings—nothing elaborate. Presbyters did not receive much compensation.

Mark picked up a piece of bread, but before he could take a bite, Sosthenes said, "Tell me more about what is going on in Rome."

Mark related several accounts about people he knew in the city and the persecutions they were enduring. The presbyter listened intently, sometimes asking questions. Then he turned his attention to Mark's situation.

"So you need a job?" he asked.

"Yes. I came here with nothing."

"I could use a secretary. It will be part-time, and I can't pay much."

"I'd like to do that, and anything will help." Mark replied enthusiastically.

"If you continue to stay with Longinus, then I can pay for your meals there." Mark nodded in agreement. "And maybe I can find two or three other men who could use your skills. That way you could get a little money and get back on your feet."

"That will be very helpful." This was everything Mark hoped for.

"Will you also help with our teaching ministry?"

"In what way?"

"Oh—helping with the catechumens. You would add a sort of 'eyewitness' presence to our teaching."

"Peter was the eyewitness, but I can relate what he told me."

"Good. I will tell the other catechist. Her name is Agathe. She is one of our deaconesses."

Mark's heart raced, involuntarily. "I met Agathe at the Agape dinner."

"Good. We had a man leading the group, but he moved away. Agathe is an outstanding teacher. She is good at everything and not bound by custom, but the men tend to relate better to a male catechist. Don't tell her I said that, but it is the way things are."

"I would love to work with Agathe. And I'll keep what you said in confidence."

"Fine, then. Come back tomorrow morning, and we will get to work. We also will talk to Agathe then."

"Sounds good." Mark was quite pleased with the arrangement. "May I ask one more question?"

"Yes, of course."

"I noticed that Longinus and Klea have no children. Can you tell me why, so I don't blunder with what I might say?"

"Very thoughtful of you." Sosthenes gathered his thoughts. A sorrowful expression gave away how troubled he was by what he was about to reveal. "It happened while they were betrothed. One day some Roman soldiers grabbed her near the market. They muffled her mouth and dragged her aside. Then one by one they raped her."

"Oh no! How terrible."

"And then one of them stuck his dagger into her opening."

"No!"

"Yes. She survived the ordeal, but she doesn't speak much to men, unless she really trusts them."

"I will be respectful. I don't want to be a cause of further hurt," Mark assured him.

"Good."

"And Longinus went ahead and married her?"

"Yes, indeed. Longinus is a good man and he loves her deeply," Sosthenes told him.

"A very good man. I could tell right away. And they had no children?"

"None. Apparently the dagger did what the soldier intended."

13

In the evening Mark related the news of his employment to Longinus and Klea. They both seemed pleased. After the meal he helped Klea tidy up, much to her surprise. The simple gesture spoke of his appreciation better than words could do.

The next morning Mark went again to the house of the presbyter. Sosthenes had some correspondence that needed a reply. Mark listened and made cursory notes. Later, when his employer heard Mark read the finished letters he exclaimed, "These are perfect. You even improved my Greek!"

At mid-day Agathe joined the men. She looked radiant, even though her features were quite plain. Her short auburn hair had more curl than Mark remembered. She was slender—almost skinny, but her beaming personality made up for any deficit in natural beauty. In fact, because of her deep, authentic love for people, she appeared quite attractive. He liked everything about her.

MARK'S PASSION

"Hello everyone!" She gave Sosthenes a warm hug. Mark felt a bit jealous.

"Let us have some food. There is something I want to speak with both of you about."

Mark broke off a piece of bread and poured a little olive oil in a small bowl. Agathe took some grapes and two figs.

"Agathe, you've met Mark and you know that he spent a lot of time in Rome with Peter. I thought he might add something to our catechumenate."

"Like what?"

"Well, he probably can tell stories about Jesus that he heard Peter tell. That might be very helpful to the inquirers."

"It might be." Agathe's subdued reaction surprised Mark.

But Sosthenes seemed to expect it. "I'd like for you to give it a try. You do the main part of the teaching and let Mark follow up with a story."

"All right. I will do that," Agathe agreed.

"When do we meet with the catechumens?" Mark should have let Sosthenes do the talking.

He cut in, "The group meets Monday evenings. Why don't you two start then. Is that agreeable?"

"Sure."

"Sure."

"Good then. Now I have to go. The bishop wants to see me."

When the presbyter left, the two sat where they were, eating in silence. Then Agathe spoke. "I know why he wants you to teach with me."

"Why is that?"

"Because men prefer to take instruction from men."

"Sosthenes told me you are competent," Mark assured her.

"I am competent! I have run a very successful class."

"He said the class has gone very well."

"I have nothing against you, Mark. You may be a fine man. But these others—they are so . . . gender conscious."

"Yes. Most men are. And so are women."

Agathe laughed. "So you are a philosopher too?"

Mark smiled, partly because his new associate's mood seemed to warm.

"Monday evening, then."

"Monday evening."

As people arrived for the meeting, Agathe greeted them with a round of warm hugs. Mark wanted her to take the lead, and she made the same assumption.

She spoke about the importance of putting our faith in Christ. Mark thought it was an excellent talk. When she finished, he began to applaud, but stopped when no one else joined him.

"Now, Mark—who worked with Peter in Rome—will share on this topic," Agathe told the group.

Mark was a little nervous, mostly because of the presence of Agathe, so he got right into it.

"I heard Peter tell about a time when Jesus was teaching near the shore of the Sea of Galilee," he began. "When evening came they got in a boat with him to cross to the other side. Part way across,

A great gale arose, and the waves beat into the boat, so that the boat was already being swamped. But he was in the stern, asleep on the cushion. They woke him up and said to him, 'Teacher, do you not care that we are perishing?' He woke up and rebuked the wind, and said to the sea, 'Peace! Be still!' Then the wind ceased, and there was a dead calm. He said to them, 'Why are you afraid? Have you still no faith?' And they were filled with great awe and said to one another, 'Who then is this, that even the wind and the sea obey him?'

"Most of us—if we found ourselves caught in a little boat on a stormy sea—would do about the same thing the disciples did. We would panic!

"Then we'd probably pray, 'God, help us!' That's an acceptable behavior for followers of Christ. In fact, it is an appropriate thing to do. Only later—with hindsight—could we check on the depth of our faith.

"And this, I think, is the essence of this story. Jesus is the Son of God. He *can* save us, and he cares enough about us to do it. The disciples asked, 'Do you not care that we are perishing?' And Jesus proved that he did care, by calming the sea.

"I would like us to think for a moment—in our memories—of times we felt afraid. Even the youngest of us here can do that. And us older ones, we've had more scary times. Think of one or two examples.

"I had to leave Rome suddenly because of the persecution. Then at the first port, a citizen attacked me and turned me over to the soldiers. That night in prison I prayed to Jesus. I had no one else to turn to.

"The next day a fire broke out, and two of us escaped. I wouldn't have known what to do, but the other prisoner led me to a ship that was just departing. We got on board. The captain knew the other man, but he did not care one bit about me, yet he let me stay on. I arrived in Corinth destitute, and here I found friends.

"Have you thought of a circumstance yet, where you were afraid?" he asked his listeners.

"Maybe it was a physical threat. Maybe you had no employment and wondered, 'How will I take care of my family?' Maybe there was an illness. Think of one or two situations where you felt seriously afraid.

"The dramatic story of Jesus saving the disciples from a violent squall that suddenly popped up on the Sea of Galilee is layered with meaning. This miracle of Jesus calming the wind is evidence of Jesus' divinity. It proves that he is the Son of God.

"On another level, Jesus' reaction and question to the disciples, 'Do you not yet have faith?' teaches us something about being his follower. Without faith, we are blind to Jesus' identity as the Savior of the world. Only with the eyes of faith can we see who he truly is.

"God is always with us. We may feel insignificant and powerless at times, but Christ is in the boat with us. That is why he came to earth as a human being—so we will know that he will take care of us.

"Just one word of advice: don't wait until the next storm before you seek out the Lord's help. It is better to get in the habit of inviting him into our lives when the wind is calm. Then, when the seas get choppy, we will turn to him naturally and readily, and we will see his hands at work.

"Every day pray, 'Jesus, I believe you are bigger than all my fears. I give these fears to you. Jesus—I trust in you.'

"Now . . . do you have an example of a time you were afraid clear in your mind? Can you picture the situation and how frightened you felt?

"Good.

"These situations were serious. You had every reason to be afraid. But wasn't there some mysterious assistance at your side? Were you not helped in some way? Maybe it appeared to you in a loving friend or relative. Maybe the circumstances eased up a bit for you. There are all kinds of ways that Christ can answer our prayers.

"You are not yet baptized, but Jesus has a plan for you. That is why he is beckoning you to join his Body and help spread his good news. He wants you, right here in Corinth, to be his followers too.

"We all are growing from the kind of disciples we are into the kind of disciples Jesus wants us to be. Just keep at it, and you will know Jesus definitely is—the Savior of the world."

No one spoke.

Everyone sat there stunned.

Clearly, the story and the talk had touched each one deeply. Mark had been neither eloquent nor dramatic, but the words of Jesus connected with their lived experience, and so had his.

They all left in silence. Even Agathe's parting hugs didn't break the spell. They just murmured a word of thanks and walked home.

When all had left, Agathe couldn't contain herself. She threw her arms around Mark's neck and embraced him warmly. "That was wonderful. We are going to make a great team." Then she kissed him on the cheek and patted it with her fingertips.

Longinus was still awake when Mark returned. They closed the door, and Mark lay down on the couch, but he didn't sleep.

He kept going over the last moments with Agathe in his mind. His whole body tingled when she embraced him. His heart leapt when he felt her kiss. He touched the spot on his cheek with his own fingers, but it didn't feel the same as the moment when she patted him with hers.

She is so slender, he thought; some would say too skinny. But I like how the curves of her body move under her clothing.

Is she too old for me? How many years? Three or four more, maybe. That isn't such a big difference. And we have so much in common. Agathe is more youthful than most women her age—in some ways like a twelve year old maiden. Yet, she is so mature—with the wisdom of one twice her years.

And bold! I have never met a woman who is so outspoken—or for that matter any man! She seems to transcend that distinction. With everyone, she is a 'person' not just a female. Yet she is so feminine. I was aroused by the first touch of her hand.

Mark allowed his mind to just savor the experience of her body close to his. He felt the brush of her hair against his face—her warm breath mingling with his—and he cherished the sweet scent of her skin. He pulled her even closer, and she responded—allowing her soft breasts to press against his chest. He felt her heart beating in precise rhythm with his. Then he lifted her face and kissed her lips—moist and parted and desiring. Through the dark night he held her close in his dreams.

14

The next two days were busy. Sosthenes had plenty for Mark to do, and he also found two merchants who needed his skills. It was not until Thursday that he again encountered Agathe.

She bounded into the room in the presbyter's home where he was working. "Hello Mark. How have you been?" His heart raced as he received her gentle hug.

"Great. It is good to see you." Mark had decided not to reveal how much he had been thinking about Agathe. He did not yet know if she had a similar interest in him. "What will be our next topic with the catechumens?"

"The Day of the Lord. With this group I have not yet talked about when Christ comes and the dead are raised."

"What do you plan to say about it?"

Agathe looked at him like she was thinking, what a queer question. Shaking it off, she continued, "The people know a little already. I like to begin with the part in Paul's letter where he says, 'the trumpet will sound and the dead will be raised.'"

Mark had read the letter, and he remembered the image, but he couldn't recall the details. "Wasn't he describing what the resurrected bodies will be like, or something?"

Agathe looked shocked. "Didn't you study these letters in Rome?"

"I wished that I had studied them and spent more time with Paul. He was living not far away, just outside of the city, but Peter kept me busy."

"Good God! What a missed opportunity. I would have given anything to talk with Paul. But Silas told us a lot."

"Silas was with Paul, and I was with Peter."

Ignoring this response, she quickly recited the passage from memory.

We will not die, but we will all be changed, in a moment, in the twinkling of an eye, at the last trumpet. For the trumpet will sound, and the dead will be raised imperishable, and we will be changed. For this perishable body must put on imperishability, and this mortal body must put on immortality. When this perishable body puts on imperishability, and this mortal body puts on immortality, then the saying that is written will be fulfilled: 'Death has been swallowed up in victory. Where,

O death, is your victory? Where, O death is your sting?'

"Yes," Mark commented, "When Christ comes, we all will be changed and the dead will be raised. But . . . ."

"But what?" Agathe couldn't understand why Mark was hesitating.

"I mean . . . I am not clear about when this will take place."

"When the trumpet sounds!"

"Yes," Mark added, "but when will that be?"

"Soon, of course. We thought it would have sounded before now, but the extra time has allowed us to gather in more saints."

"I know that everyone expected Christ to return soon. But it has not happened, and the apostles are getting old. Those who knew Jesus are dying."

"Well, then it is closer now than ever."

"I'm not sure. What if it turns out to be a long time? What then?"

Agathe cut him off. "That's impossible!"

Mark didn't like how the conversation was going. He wanted to make friends with Agathe—now they were bickering.

She spoke first. "Either you believe that Christ will come again, or you don't."

"I have no doubt that Christ will come again. He promised that he would. I just don't think we have a clear idea of when."

"Everyone knows it will be soon."

"How can *everyone* be sure? Before he was crucified, he told his disciples, 'Only the Father knows.'"

"Well Paul was sure. That's good enough for me."

"Early on, Paul felt certain. But later, when he wrote to the community in Rome, he made no mention of timing."

"Do you not have faith?"

"Look, Agathe. I have great faith, and you have great faith. I believe that Christ will come again just like you do. But I am open to the possibility that it may be later than we think. It may be past our lifetimes. It may be generations away. That's why I'm writing a narrative of his public years. Then, regardless of how long it turns out to be, people will have the truth about Jesus."

"You are writing a narrative—about Jesus?"

"Yes. I started it in Rome. I had gathered a great many notes before Peter was taken away. I think they are lost now. But I am passionate about completing the story, even if I have to write it from memory."

"That's amazing! I didn't know. You are a very forward-thinking man." She seemed genuinely sorry at the way she had bickered with him. "We must talk about this some more—before next Monday."

"Will you dine with me?" Mark was surprised at how quickly the words came out.

"Yes. Certainly. When and where?"

"Well..."

Laughing, she replied, "You don't have a place yet. So—you come to my house. How about tomorrow evening?"

"That sounds good."

"Good. See you then." Agathe explained how to find the house and again embraced him sincerely.

That evening Mark was quiet at supper. Longinus asked, "How are things going?"

"Oh, fine. Sosthenes found two merchants that are employing me." He held up three coins. "I already have three day's wages. I would like to buy a tunic that fits me."

His host laughed. "That is not yet enough."

"I know."

Then Klea spoke up. "If we purchase the cloth, I can make one for you."

"Really! That would be wonderful. You are so kind to me."

Klea blushed.

Longinus took two of the coins and handed them to his wife. "Yes. Let us make Mark more presentable."

Mark took a sip of wine and continued. "The class with the inquirers is going well. I am teaching it with Agathe."

Both of his hosts smiled. "Have you got into any *discussions* yet?"

"Do you mean with the catechumens, or with her?"

Both laughed out loud. "She is very strong in her opinions," said Longinus.

"Yes. But I love that about her. She has great faith and is an excellent teacher." Mark instantly was aware that he had used the word love, when he might have said like.

"She is very intelligent and has a heart for all people," Longinus continued. "We are fortunate to have her here in our little church."

"I—like her very much. We did get into a discussion today—about when the Lord will return. She was uncomfortable with my questions. But when I told her I was writing about Jesus, she seemed genuinely interested. Agathe is a remarkable woman. She definitely has been called by God."

"Yes. She wants to be a presbyter," Longinus added.

"A presbyter! No. Does she think that the bishop will ordain a woman?"

"She hopes so, but the Day of the Lord may come first."

Both men laughed. Klea laughed with them, but not as heartily.

That evening, as he lay on the couch, Mark thought of Agathe. But his musings were not as sweet as they had been the previous nights. He kept reviewing their conversation over and over, but there was no resolution. The mind of the woman he found so attractive, remained a mystery.

The next day, when he returned from work, Klea was smiling. "I have a new tunic for you. Would you like to try it on?"

"Really? So soon? You are very fast."

Klea beamed as she held up the garment.

Mark went into the next room and changed, returning with a big grin on his face. "It fits perfectly! How did you do it?"

"Oh. I just made it like I do for Longinus, only a little less in the shoulders and a bit more in length."

"Klea, I can't thank you enough. You are amazing!"

"Now you will look nice when you go out with people."

Mark gave her a gentle hug. "You and Longinus are so good to me."

On the way to see Agathe, Mark purchased a jug of wine. I need to bring something, he thought. I'm using my last coin, but it may be a good investment.

Agathe lived in two rooms above the house of a prosperous merchant, accessed by a steep flight of stairs. He bounded up the steps, but paused at the doorway thinking, I must keep my head this evening.

"Is that you, Mark?" Agathe called. "I heard your footsteps. Come in."

The apartment was neat and tidy—as he had imagined. The furniture in the living area was simple—a table for preparing food and one for eating, a couch, and one chair—just enough for a single woman. On one wall was a primitive painting of Paul, struck to the ground on the road to Damascus.

"Do you like my *Conversion?*"

"Yes. Where did you get it?"

"I saw it in a shop in Athens. The woman said it came from Jerusalem. I don't know anything about the artist, but the painting reminds me of my mission."

"Your mission is to bring people to Christ."

"Yes. It is my calling in life." Coming over to Mark, she gave him a little hug. "Oh, you brought wine!"

"And do I detect fish?"

Both laughed at how the other had done what they could to make the evening special.

As he opened the bottle he blurted, "I was surprised when you invited me to your home." Mark wished he had not said that.

"Why?"

"Well, it is not customary for a woman and a man to dine together without someone present."

"Oh, this is Corinth." Agathe patted him on the chest. "And will we *need* a chaperone?"

Mark blushed and took a sip of wine. "I got a new tunic."

"Yes. I noticed. You are coming up in the world."

He blushed again and took another sip of wine.

"Tell me more about what you are writing."

Mark welcomed the change of topic. "The concept is simple. I call it the Good News of Jesus Christ. I am taking what I heard from Peter and combining it with the Passion document to form a narrative story of Jesus—what he did and how people responded."

"That sounds great."

"Thank you. I want to emphasize how Jesus is the Son of God, but also show what we need to do to be good followers."

"That will be a big help with catechumens."

"Yes, but . . ."

"But what?"

"But when I lost my bag in Syracuse, I lost all my notes. Now I have to work for money. I'm not sure how I will finish it."

"You will finish it, if it is God's will. Christ will provide the way."

"Yes. I have to believe that. But it seems more elusive now."

Agathe came to him and caressed his cheek. "You will do it. I'm sure."

Mark was not accustomed to having a woman so close, looking right into his eyes as she spoke. It unnerved him, but he liked it. Yet he could only handle it for so long without changing the subject. "And you—I hear that you would like to be a presbyter."

"Who told you that?" she asked drawing back.

"Longinus. Was he not supposed to say?"

"Oh, it's not a secret. I do feel called to lead a community."

"Have you heard of women presbyters?" Mark asked, without showing bias.

"Phoebe was a presbyter right here in our eastside church before Paul sent her to Rome."

"Phoebe of Cenchraea? I thought she was a deaconess."

"Paul referred to her as a deacon and an esteemed leader. That's like saying she was a presbyter."

"I see. Well, I believe that you could do it, even though it's not the custom."

"The custom! Why does everything always have to be according to custom?" Agathe showed her anger. "Jesus constantly broke with the customs. How can the Holy Spirit guide the church to new horizons, if we always conform to custom?"

"But the men, and the women too . . ."

"Yes the men, and the women too, do not see how a woman can be a leader. Well, they just need to open up their imaginations!"

"I agree."

"Anyway—I'm only thirty-four years old. It can happen. If Sosthenes is elected bishop after Onesiphorus, then maybe it could happen right here."

"I do hope so. You will make an excellent presbyter."

Agathe softened. "You are so good with words."

During dinner the two talked about many things, including the topic of the Day of the Lord. When it was time for him to leave he said, "This was wonderful—a delightful evening."

"I like being with you Mark."

"Well, I will be going. I have three jobs tomorrow."

"Will you take the rest of the wine?" she asked.

"Why don't I leave it here? Then maybe there will be a reason to return."

Agathe blushed. Then she came over to Mark to give him a goodbye hug. As her arms circled his neck, he took her and pulled her to his chest. It was clear that he did not want to let her go.

"What is this about?"

"I want to hold you close to me."

"Oh, Mark. I am too old for you," she stated.

"Nonsense. We have a great many things in common."

"That's true, but . . ."

"But what?"

Pressing her hands against his chest and looking directly into his eyes, she said, "But I am not the woman for you." A single tear ran down her cheek.

"You could be."

"Let's talk about it another time." She kissed him gently on the lips and pushed a little harder with her hands. He let go and walked out the door.

15

Mark saw Agathe next at the Sunday liturgy. He wanted to speak with her at the dinner afterward, even though he had no idea what he would say. She seemed always to be busy, talking—laughing—hugging—instructing. He caught her eye, and immediately she came to him, but only for a quick hello. As she left, she touched his cheek with the back of her fingers.

He wandered from group to group, but he was not interested in small talk. Sosthenes spoke with him for a few minutes about his needs for the coming week. He put some bread and oil on a plate and sat with some children, but he didn't say much to them. His mind was on Agathe.

Monday evening, he again went to the class of catechumens. As he watched Agathe interact with each newcomer, he thought, she is so good with people. It is totally natural for her. She has so much love in her heart. That is a difference between her and me. I love people too, but my love is expressed in intellectual things. Her love comes forth in her sincere words and helpful actions.

Agathe brought the class together with a prayer. Then she said, "Tonight we will explore what will happen when Christ returns." She recited from memory the parts of Paul's letter that related to the raising of the dead and gave an excellent presentation.

Mark was impressed with her ability. He thought, she really would make an outstanding presbyter, if only people will accept a woman.

"Now, Mark. You were speaking with me about the question of *when* Jesus will come back. Will you share with us your thoughts on the subject?"

"Yes, I will," he replied. "When Jesus spoke about the destruction, most people assumed it would be soon. Peter asked Jesus, 'When will this be, and what will be the sign that all these things are about to be accomplished?' Jesus replied, *'Beware that no one leads you astray,'* and he talked about what the signs will be.

> *'Brother will betray brother to death, and a father his child, and children will rise against parents and have them put to death. And you will be hated by all because of my name. But the one who endures to the end will be saved.'*

"Jesus said many more things, describing the signs, but he never answered the question of when.

"Now, even though most people thought it will be soon, it has not yet happened—and those who heard Jesus speak are now dying. I believe it is best to remain open to all possibilities. The signs that he described already have been seen—we see them today—and they probably will continue always, until he comes again.

"Jesus promised that he will return, but we don't know when. It may be this week. It may be next year. It may be in a hundred years or a thousand years. It may be this very night. The important thing is to live our lives as he wants us to live them: devoutly, respectfully, generously, and doing our part in support of his command that the good news be preached to all nations.

"To be open to all possibilities regarding the timing does not contradict the messages of the prophets, or Paul, or Peter—or the words of Jesus, himself. To focus on living good lives today and passing on our faith does not contradict anything. It may actually be a better approach to following the Way than speculating about when Christ will return and wasting energy looking for clues in the day's events.

"So those are my thoughts. I believe that they are worth pondering. Jesus said, *'The one who endures to the end will be saved.'* Center your lives on being among those people."

The catechumens thanked Mark as they left. One summed up their feelings saying, "You gave us a lot to think about."

Agathe was quiet while they straightened up. Then picking up her shawl, she turned to him and said, "I would like for us to have dinner again."

Mark looked into her eyes and replied, "I would like that too."

"Friday evening again?"

"Friday evening."

And giving him a friendly hug with her free arm, she whispered, "We have the rest of the wine," and rushed out.

The days transpired very slowly that week. Mark tried to concentrate on his work, but he kept thinking of Agathe. *She is such a mystery,* he mused. *I can't tell what she is thinking. She seems to like me—but she loves everyone. Why should I expect her to have special feelings for me? Yet her touches are so tender, and she did kiss me on the lips. What am I supposed to think? How am I supposed to feel? I am falling in love with her, and she is holding back.*

On Thursday evening, Klea spoke about his mood. "Mark, we noticed that you are quiet. Is there something on your mind?"

He didn't know how to answer. Certainly there was one major theme on his mind, but he didn't know if he could explain it well.

"Is it Agathe?" she asked.

"You are so perceptive, Klea. Yes. I can't get her out of my mind."

"You are smitten with her?"

"Smitten and slain on the ground."

Klea smiled, but continued, "Other men have tried to gain her heart."

"Oh, I believe that!"

"She is different, you know."

"Yes. That is what I find so attractive about her. You see, I am different also. And we have many goals in common. I think we can have a good partnership. She said so too."

"Agathe can be a good partner. But are you looking for a wife?" she wondered.

"I am looking for someone to love, and who will love me."

"That may not be what she is looking for."

"I know. That's why I am so caught up in my thoughts," Mark admitted.

"She may reveal her feelings soon."

"I certainly hope so. We are dining together tomorrow evening."

"I will pray for both of you."

"Thank you, Klea. You are a dear friend."

On Friday evening Mark noticed that he was quite nervous as he walked to Agathe's apartment. He had no idea what the evening might bring. But Agathe had invited him; that gave him a reason to be optimistic.

"Hello dear," she said as he entered the door, but there was no hug or touch.

"Hello." Mark felt quite awkward.

"I have a bit more to do for our dinner. Go ahead and sit down."

Mark found the couch and waited.

"Would you like a little hummus?" She brought a plate of small flatbreads. He took one and dipped it into the spread, took a bite, and smiled.

"I have some lamb for us."

"Wonderful."

"It will be ready in a few minutes."

As Agathe turned back to the food, Mark noticed the outline of her hips beneath her clothing. She must want love, too, at this time of life, he told himself.

Finally, she poured two cups of wine and sat them on the table. "We are ready."

Mark sat down and took a bite of the lamb. "This is quite good."

Their sentences were short as they ate. Agathe didn't seem to be in any hurry to get into the topic of their relationship, and Mark didn't know how to bring it up. Finally she spoke, "About Monday night . . . I'm sorry that I pushed you away so abruptly. You see, I have certain ideas about my life."

"Yes."

"I am not going to have an affair with a man."

"I didn't intend that."

"And I'm not seeking marriage." Mark drew a sharp breath. "And you have no means of getting married, anyway."

"You are right about that."

"So." Now she became short for words.

"I just want to be close," he said.

"We are close. We are in a community together—we teach together—we dine together."

"I want to be closer than that."

"How close do you mean?"

"As close as we can be."

Agathe thought for a moment, wanting to choose her words carefully. "Paul's advice to the unmarried and widows was for them to remain unmarried, as he was. So you should feel that way too." Mark remained quiet. "Paul said, *'Only if they are not practicing self-control should they marry. For it is better to marry than to be aflame with passion.'* Is that what is happening with you?" she asked.

Mark was taken aback by her frankness. "I am not 'aflame,' but I do want love."

"I do love you—I love all people."

"I didn't mean only that kind of love."

Agathe began to cry, and Mark touched her hand. "From the moment I saw you, I knew that you are a very special person. And when you kissed my cheek that first Monday night, I felt something new come alive in my heart."

"Stop!"

"How can I stop? You are frank in expressing how you feel. Why can't I be?"

"You can be frank. We both must be honest." She sobbed some more and then took a deep breath. "Paul told us, *'Now concerning virgins, I have no command of the Lord, but I give my opinion as one who by the Lord's mercy is trustworthy. I think that, in view of the impending crisis, it is well for you to remain as you are.'"*

Mark began to hate how she could quote so well the missionary's letters. "But what if the *crisis* is not so closely impending? What if Christ's coming is delayed? Will you remain without marrying for the rest of your life?"

"There you go again, thinking about the future. I am thinking about the present!"

"But what if there is a future? Should we not be preparing for it?"

"I don't know." Agathe looked down, as if trying to find the right words. Then she looked straight into his eyes and said, "I can tell that you don't like for me to quote Paul. But I get much inspiration from his words, and there is an image he used that has become central to who I am."

"What is it?"

"He said, *'Do you not know that a little yeast leavens the whole dough? Clean out the old yeast so that you may be a new batch, as you really are unleavened. For our paschal lamb, Christ, has been sacrificed. Therefore, let us celebrate the festival, not with the old yeast, the yeast of malice and evil, but with the unleavened bread of sincerity and truth.'*

"Mark, I am yeast in this community. Whether or not I am ordained a presbyter, I am doing much good here. And just as Jesus is yeast for the world, I am yeast here in our assembly. He sacrificed his whole life for those he loved, and I want to do the same."

Mark was speechless. He had never met anyone—woman or man—who so clearly and courageously set such standards for their life. His eyes became moist like hers—not from a sense of loss, which was becoming more and more apparent, but from inspiration. This remarkable woman was showing him the kind of man he needed to be, at least until he completed the gospel.

"I am beginning to understand," he said.

"Good." She took his hands firmly in hers and kissed them.

"I . . . I . . ."

"Shh." Pausing, she released a sweet smile that revealed the depth of her feelings. After she kissed his hands again, he left.

16

The next weeks passed quickly. Each day Mark assisted Sosthenes and the two merchants, and each evening he visited with Longinus and Klea. He was accumulating a few coins in his pouch.

On Monday evenings he went to the catechumenate class with Agathe. She was as effervescent as ever with the people and always warm to him. He did his best to act as though nothing had happened, but deep inside there was a hole in his heart. He thought of apologizing, but what is there to apologize for? Falling in love with someone is not a crime. Yet—he could not get rid of feeling uncomfortable when he was with her. The happy lift that he felt whenever he saw her was gone.

He thought a great deal about his sense of purpose, wishing that he had the dedication Agathe had. He needed to find a way to complete his writing. But how? He purchased a blank codex and two reed pens, thinking that he would write as much as he could from memory. But as time passed by, very little was put on paper.

Then the bishop proclaimed a fast for the weeks leading up to Passover, which meant no Agape meals with the community and more modesty for meals at home. Sosthenes summed it up, "Having less joy in our lives for a few weeks is good for us. It reminds us of the sacrifices Jesus made and the suffering he endured for our sake. Our celebration will be all the more meaningful and joyful after the fast."

One Sunday after the Eucharist, two men approached Mark, asking, "Would you like to come to our prayer group? You seem kind of sad. This might help." They were Levi and Jacob, two brothers who had come to Corinth from Jerusalem when their older brother took over the family cloth business. Jacob appeared to bit older than Levi and more settled. Levi seemed anxious and hot-blooded. Both looked typically Jewish: lean with slender faces and curly black hair. Mark had heard that they were doing well in Corinth, with Levi handling the buying and selling, and Jacob taking care of dying and dressing the fabrics.

"A prayer group might be good for me. When do you meet?"

Levi answered, "Friday evenings."

MARK'S PASSION

Mark felt a jolt go through his body at the mention of the dates. Fridays had been times when he and Agathe had dinner together. Yet there had been no further invitations from her, and none were expected during the fast, so he replied, "Yes. That will be fine. I will come."

"Good," said Levi, who gave him directions to his home.

That evening Mark asked Longinus, "What can you tell me about Levi and Jacob? They invited me to their prayer group."

"Oh, they seem like fine men," he responded. "They came from Jerusalem. They were baptized there by James. I don't know how long ago that was. They were Jewish, but now they shave their beards and get along in the Greek world as well as anyone."

"I wonder if they knew Jesus."

"That's not likely. They are only a few years older than you. It was their father who first accepted Christ, but he is gone now. They might have known Stephen and James, though."

"That's a thought. I will ask them."

Mark could hardly wait for Friday evening. He approached Levi's house with renewed optimism. I won't ask questions this evening, he thought. I will do that later. Tonight I'll just pray with the group.

As he entered the door, Levi welcomed him. "Mark. Come in. Do you know everyone here?"

"Yes. I think I do."

"Good."

"Hello everybody," Mark said to the group. They smiled back.

"We pray in tongues. Do you?" Levi asked.

"Ah. . . Not yet, actually."

"Well, you will learn. We sit still for a while, focusing on the Lord, and when someone feels inspired, they just begin."

"That sounds natural enough. Sure."

"Good. So let us gather. . ."

Instead of emptying his mind, Mark quickly stepped through the possibilities. These are good people, following practices recognized by Paul in his letters; it might help me to join in. Or the evening could be a harmless distraction, in which case it won't matter. Or the whole thing could be of a great evil, so I should leave immediately. Regardless of how frantically he searched for answers, none came forth.

Then he heard a sound. It began with a low moan. Then picking up energy, it rolled into a series of well-articulated syllables, which no one in the room understood. But they all got in touch with the feeling and joined in the sound—although in differing languages.

Mark decided to take a peek at the others. Through half open lids he determined that they all had their eyes closed and lips moving. He would do the same.

Then they seemed to take turns leading the prayer, first one person, and then another.

Should I try? Mark wondered. And then, as though someone pushed him, he began a series of sounds like children make. *"Ini ano sube nuuu. Ini ano sube nuuu. Ini ano sube nuuu."* This introduction was followed by a lengthy rambling that every now and then returned to the opening line, *"Ini ano sube nuuu. Ini ano sube nuuu."* When he heard his voice begin to fall off, he was relieved.

When all the voices subsided, Levi took a deep breath, which the others copied. Then letting the breath out he proclaimed, "There. That was a good session." The others agreed.

"Mark. How did you like praying in tongues?"

"Oh. It was fine—actually."

"You did very well for your first time. Just relax and keep at it, and the next thing you know your prayer will become mature. The Holy Spirit will know what language to give you."

"Thank you."

"Will you be back next Friday?"

"Yes. Yes, I will."

After the Sunday Eucharist, the prayer group approached him. "We liked having you in our group." "You can become a great prayer." "Will you be with us this Friday?"

"Yes. Thank you." And to Levi he said, "Isn't it unusual for Jews to speak in tongues?"

Levi answered, "It is unusual, but Jacob and I are not your typical Jews."

"I gathered that."

"When we became Christians, we opened ourselves to new practices."

"Which is good. Thank you for answering. I will see you Friday."

A few moments later he felt a familiar presence at his side. It was Agathe. "Are you praying in tongues now?"

"Well. I went once. They seem authentic."

MARK'S PASSION

"So," with a coy smile she asked, "how did your language sound?"

Mark blushed. He didn't know how to take the question. "It was kind of childish, actually. But Levi says it will mature."

"I'm sure you will," laughed Agathe. Then more seriously, "They do seem authentic, and this community has a long history of praying in tongues. But there is something about those two. I can't put my finger on it. They make me suspicious, but I honestly can't tell you why."

"I will keep alert for your suspicions."

"Thank you." Then squeezing his hand in hers, she left.

The following Friday evening was similar to the first, and so was the Friday after that. Mark felt that his prayer was beginning to sound more mature, and except for the unusual languages, it was not unlike other forms of prayer that he was accustomed to.

Every now and then Agathe asked him about the group. His answers always were positive.

Then one Sunday, as Passover was drawing near, Mark decided to ask Levi about the Christians in Jerusalem. "Did you know James or Stephen or any of those in the Holy City?"

"Oh yes! We grew up in Jerusalem. James baptized us." Levi's eyes saddened as he mentioned James, the leader of the Jerusalem church. "We were here in Corinth when the chief priests turned against them. The *Sanhedrin*, the high council, first ordered the execution of Stephen. Then three years ago, when Festus died and Ananias II became High Priest, he had James arrested. He was interrogated by the council and stoned to death for blasphemy, but he was only insisting that Jesus had been the Messiah."

"You confirmed what I had heard."

Then Levi turned red. "Those imposters in Jerusalem say they have the right to lead the people. But they are no better than the Romans—they collaborate with them—against the people!"

"I'd like to talk with you more about what it is like there."

Seeing Jacob come up to them, Levi composed himself. "Is my brother giving you lessons in prayer or politics?" Jacob asked.

"Ah—today we were talking about how things are in Jerusalem," replied Mark.

"It is very uncertain there. We should speak about it someday."

As Jacob led his brother by the arm, Mark wondered, what is going on with them? Levi displays a great hostility toward the Jewish leaders, but Jacob wants to put off talking about it.

Two Mondays later Mark again went to the catechumenate meeting—the last session before those in the class were to be baptized. I will miss this group, he thought as he walked the familiar way. There will be no more Monday evenings with them. Then he also admitted, no more Monday evenings with Agathe.

Agathe brought the class to order. "Tonight we will discuss temptation, something every human being experiences. Even Paul knew its pull. He devoted many lines in his letters to the topic." She gave a well-prepared talk—a bit longer than usual—and the people listened intently.

"Mark, what would you like to add?"

"I will say just a few things. First of all, I want to thank each of you for accepting me into your group. From the first night when we talked about dealing with fear by relying on the Lord, it meant a lot to me to have your friendship. As you know, I arrived in Corinth destitute and on the run from the Romans. My belongings were lost, including my precious notes and sources for completing the narrative of Jesus. My life seemed to have reached an impasse, but your interest in the stories of Christ, along with Agathe's outstanding support, kept me going and gave me hope.

"You may not know it, but Jesus also was tempted. I remember writing just a few lines about it in my notes.

In those days Jesus came from Nazareth of Galilee and was baptized by John in the Jordan. And just as he was coming up out of the water, he saw the heavens torn apart and the Spirit descending like a dove on him. And a voice came from heaven, 'You are my Son, the Beloved, with you I am well pleased.'

And the Spirit immediately drove him out into the wilderness. He was in the wilderness for forty days, tempted by Satan; and he was with the wild beasts; and the angels waited on him.

"Jesus not only was tempted—just like us—but it happened immediately after his baptism. It happened even though he had just heard his purpose affirmed by the voice from heaven. We must never forget that Jesus was like us in all ways except sin. Even though he is the Son of God, when he chose to come to earth as a human being, he faced every kind of pitfall that we experience. But he did not succumb to them.

"Here in Corinth, you have an ideal living role model for dealing with these issues. She is right here among you. You have seen how dedicated she is to following the Way and how open she is to giving her love to each soul who needs comfort and support. She is an inspiration to you, and she has been an inspiration to me—a true leader in the ways of the Christian life. She embodies agape love better than anyone I ever have met. Of all the people I have grown to love in Corinth, I respect Agathe the most."

Agathe blushed bright red. Going over to where she was seated, he helped her to her feet and embraced her lovingly. With tears in their eyes, everyone applauded the two dedicated souls that the Holy Spirit had brought together for a common purpose right there in their midst.

Walking in the cool evening air back to the home of Longinus and Klea, Mark thought, I may be a luckier man than I think I am. I simply must put all my trust in Christ.

Mark also knew that he needed to find love. Becoming interested in Agathe had taught him something important about himself—he never would be happy and he never would feel fulfilled until he had true love in his life.

17

The Paschal feast was quite a celebration within the Christian community in Corinth. The weather was beautiful. The fast was over. The anxious catechumens finally were baptized. Sosthenes preached one his best homilies ever, and on top of everything else, the Agape meals resumed. By evening the entire assembly was exhausted from the heady day of laughter and storytelling.

The mood was quite different in Rome. Disgruntled senators and Praetorian guards had been talking of conspiracy against Nero. His excesses and theatrics of the previous months had sickened them, and some began saying that the time was ripe for his execution. They spoke of many candidates for the throne, including the aging philosopher Seneca or Gaius Piso, an aristocrat with no particular qualifications except for his acceptability to the various factions in the plot. When Seneca declined, the nod went to Piso.

The conspirators intended to assassinate Nero in public, during the games of the mid-April festival of Ceres. But too many were in on the plot, and on the evening before the coup an informant leaked word to the palace. Fifty-one men, including nineteen senators and eleven military officers, were charged—and twenty were convicted, including Seneca and Piso. They were executed by their peers or ordered to commit suicide. Seneca chose to open his veins and bled to death.

Nero was shaken by the stunning evidence of how low he had sunk in the eyes of the Roman aristocracy. A new wave of terror began, ostensibly to uncover further plots, and the Emperor retreated further into his fantasy world.

In Jerusalem, fear and violence also raged. An organized terrorist movement, called the *sicarii* for the curved daggers they concealed under their clothing, increased their attacks on the ruling class and wealthy landowners that were collaborating with Rome. They stalked their enemies in bold daylight, mingling with the crowd. Then, after stabbing their victims, they joined in the shouts of indignation over the killings.

Mark arrived a bit early for the Friday evening prayer group and caught Levi and Jacob arguing. "Now is the time," growled Levi. "I've been praying about it. This is the time for Jews to rise against Rome!"

"Hush," said Jacob. "I also have prayed. And I do not believe that the time is right."

Noticing Mark at the door, they cut short their conversation.

"I heard what you were saying—about Jews rising against Rome. Wouldn't that be doomed to fail?"

"Yes!" shouted Jacob.

"No!" interjected Levi. "The Jews are the people God has chosen to be a light to the world. When they take the lead, all nations will follow, and the tyranny of Rome will be put to death."

"I wouldn't know about that," said Mark. "But this doesn't sound like a Christian position."

"What do you mean, it is not a Christian position?"

"I mean that Jesus never advocated using violence against Rome. He was all about passive resistance and saving lives."

"So the world should lie down and endure the theft that is going on before their eyes?" Levi demanded an answer.

"For a time, they should. We are building a new world—a new world in Christ. It will take time—perhaps many years—but it will grow. I will bet my life on it."

"And I'll bet my life on a successful uprising—one that will teach all the rulers a lesson!" Levi insisted.

"That is a fool talking," said Jacob.

Mark wanted time to gather his thoughts, but Levi grabbed his brother by the throat. "Who is the fool?" Levi shouted. "Who is the fool? The ones who think God will do the fighting for them are the fools!"

With Mark holding Levi's arms, Jacob managed to free himself. "Brother. We must compose ourselves. Our guests will be arriving."

Levi did compose himself, just as the others came to the door. Mark did the same, but he wanted to speak with Jacob privately about the dispute.

At the Sunday liturgy, Jacob came to Mark saying, "Tomorrow my brother will go out of town to purchase cloth. Can you come by the shop?"

"Yes. I will."

"Good." Then just as suddenly, he walked away.

The next afternoon Mark entered the fabric shop, thinking that it might be without customers at that time. He was right.

Jacob came in from the back room. "Hello, Mark. Thank you for coming."

"Yes. Certainly."

"My brother, you know, he has no stomach for the way things are in Jerusalem—or anywhere else for that matter."

"I gathered that."

"I tell him, 'We are Christians now. We left violence behind.'"

"Yes."

"But Levi is an idealist—and he has our mother's anger. I am like our father—he was a man of peace."

"Your father was the first in your family to accept Christ."

"Yes. And I have tried to follow his wisdom."

"Where is this likely to lead?"

"I don't know. When we came to Corinth, I thought that Levi would mellow with time. But the events of the past few years have made him even angrier. When they arrested Paul, I thought he would go mad."

"What happened then?"

"Paul chose the wrong time to go to Jerusalem with the donation he had collected for the church in the Holy City. An Egyptian Jew who claimed to be sent by God to overthrow the Romans gathered up an excited mob on the Mount of Olives and vowed to knock down the walls of the city by performing miracles. The Procurator unleashed his troops killing more than six hundred in the slaughter.

"In the turmoil, some others who were suspicious of Paul attacked him and brought him before the leaders of the Sanhedrin. And you know Paul—he told the High Priest what he thought of him. The Procurator took over the case, but didn't know what to do with Paul. Well—I'm sure you know that Paul was a citizen, and he asked to have his case heard in Rome by the Emperor, so they shipped him to Rome."

"I know about the donation and the shipwreck on the way to Rome. But why did Levi get so incensed?" Mark asked.

"Levi got mad because the Jewish leaders, who should have accepted Christ but didn't, thought only of their own welfare and set themselves against the people. Levi sees them as the real culprits—the ones who got Jesus crucified and who turned on innocent people like Paul and Stephen and James."

"Oh. Now I understand. He is angry at the whole ruling elite—Jew and Gentile."

"Precisely."

"And he wants to do something about it."

"Exactly."

"And he believes that violence is the only method that will succeed."

"You understand completely."

"Oh my."

"Yes. Oh my. . . And usually I try to keep him under control. I say, 'You are a Christian now,' and things like that. Most of the time he calms down."

"It is good that you told me this. I don't know what I can do about it, but I will assist you when I can."

When Levi returned, nothing further was said. Jacob kept a watchful eye on his brother and Mark held his tongue.

This all changed when news of the April plot against Nero reached Corinth.

At the Friday evening prayer group, Levi announced that he felt he was receiving the gift of prophecy. "It is like the Holy Spirit is preparing me for a new epoch in my life. I feel it in my heart." When people asked when he would speak the words of wisdom, he replied, "I don't know. But I feel that it will be soon."

The wait was not long. One Sunday in June—during the quiet after communion—Levi began speaking in tongues. All eyes immediately were upon him. Then he shouted, "I am going to prophesy! Yes. I am going to prophesy! Hear me now! Hear me now! The time has come for the world to rise up against the Empire. Nero is weak. He has never been weaker. The Jews in Jerusalem must take the lead. God will be on their side. When the Jews strike, the whole world will follow. Death will be dealt to all of the oppressors. Death will be dealt!" His brother had him by the arm, trying to lead him outside. Sosthenes was aghast at the outburst. "Death will be dealt!" Mark and two other men helped Jacob get his angry brother outside. "Death will be dealt!" the voice trailed as the men took Levi home. Mark went back inside.

Sosthenes futilely attempted to calm the assembly. "Something unseemly has happened in our midst. We must not let ourselves be distracted by it. Levi probably will regain his senses shortly. Let us go on with our meal as if nothing has happened."

The plea did not work. The only thing people wanted to talk about was the outburst.

Sosthenes and Agathe kept circulating among the people trying to quell the speculation, but when the last family left they turned to Mark. "What is going on?" they wanted to know.

"I saw this coming; I should have told you."

"You saw it coming! Why didn't you tell us?"

"Well, after Passover I caught Levi arguing with Jacob about the role the Jews could play in an uprising against Rome. When Jacob asked to see me, I went to him, and he told me how his brother has been angry for years against the ruling elite in Jerusalem. But then Levi calmed down and nothing further was said until the news about Nero reached us. That seemed to set him off."

Sosthenes asked, "How can a peace-loving person like Levi want to take up arms against the Empire?"

"He is not as peace-loving as he appears to be. Jacob says that their father was a man of peace. He brought the family to baptism—the boys were not yet adults. But in the last few days I have seen his angry side."

"What does he want to do?"

"Exactly what he said during the liturgy: Levi believes that if the Jewish people rise up against their rulers, the whole world will follow their lead."

"And if they fail?"

"He doesn't see how they can fail, if God is on their side."

"But the violence—he wants to overthrow the ruling class with violence!"

"He feels it's the only way that will work."

"Oh my God."

"That's what I said."

Agathe, who had been silent, spoke up. "I am thinking about the community. Clearly this 'prophesy' was not from the Holy Spirit. Authentic prophesy would not involve the kind of drastic violence that Levi envisions."

Both men agreed. "So we will need to remove Levi from our midst," she added.

"You came to that conclusion rather quickly," Sosthenes replied. Mark was thinking it as well.

"Paul said in his letter, *'Drive out the wicked person from among you.'* We have a wonderful community here, and it is our job to keep it that way."

"There was a great emphasis in the letter about being one Body," Sosthenes assured her. "But the apostle wanted every effort made for the various parts of the body to get along and recognize one another's gifts."

"Paul was talking about true gifts," Agathe insisted. "These vary, and they need to be respected. But when a man says wicked things during the Eucharist, it flies in the face of everything Paul taught."

"Driving him away is an option, but first I would want to speak with the bishop about it. In the meantime, let's keep our eyes open and—especially you Mark—let's keep one another informed about anything new happening."

Just then Jacob came back into the room. "I hope I am not interrupting, but I want to convey my apologies on behalf of my brother. He has not been himself lately. I believe that when he settles down, he will feel remorse for this inappropriate outburst. I pray that you will give him that opportunity and will receive his apology with forgiveness."

Agathe started to say something, but Sosthenes touched her arm. "We will expect you to keep your house under control for the good of the community."

"I understand completely. I assure you that there will be no further outbursts."

"Very good."

"Oh, and one more thing: I told my brother that we must turn over the leadership of the prayer group to another member. I will see that he does. We only wish for our families to come to Sunday Eucharist. We will be on our best behavior."

18

For the rest of the summer, the brothers did as Jacob said they would. There were no further outbursts. Another member began to host the prayer group, and Mark continued to attend on Friday evenings.

Agathe acknowledged that the situation seemed satisfactory. "Levi seems to be behaving. How is the prayer group doing?" she asked him.

"Oh, fine. The prayer is a little less lively without Levi, but we are continuing, and I am getting better at praying in tongues. I am becoming more optimistic again."

"That's great. I've been praying for you too."

"Thank you."

"You are most welcome. I still think you are a fine man, you know."

Mark blushed. "So are you—you know."

At the Sunday meal, Sosthenes called to a man Mark had not yet spoken with, "Severianus! Come meet our talented member." They were approached by a well-groomed, middle-aged man with a short beard and greying hair. "Severianus, have you been on another business trip? I have not seen you for nearly a month."

"Five weeks and two days," the man replied.

"I want you to meet Mark. He is from Rome and speaks and writes in many languages. He might be able to assist you."

"You do not look like a native of Rome."

"No. I am from Antioch. I spent eight years in Rome. I know some Latin, but my languages are Greek, Syriac, and Aramaic," Mark told him.

"And you write in these languages?"

"Yes, I do."

"Hmm. Perhaps you can be of use to me. Come and see me when I get back. I am leaving tomorrow."

"I will do that. When do you expect to return?"

"I will be gone twenty-two days."

Sosthenes cut in. "Where are you going?"

"I am going to Larissa, Thessalonica, and Philippi to discuss trade."

"Did you say Philippi?" Mark immediately realized that he worded this stupidly.

"You heard me say Philippi. Why do you ask?"

"Oh, I should not have asked. I need to get a message to the bishop in Philippi."

"I possibly can deliver a message for you. What is his name?"

"Alexios."

"I do not know an Alexios in Philippi. How would I contact him?"

"Ask for the house of the bishop. But if it is out of the way for you . . ."

"I do not mind helping," Severianus assured him. "If I can locate Alexios, what shall I say to him?"

"Say that Mark from Rome has been detained. Tell him that I am in Corinth and may come to him later."

"I understand the message. I will see what I can do."

"I greatly appreciate it."

Mark hoped that Severianus could find Alexios. He didn't want his not arriving in Philippi to be a cause for worry.

The following Sunday Jacob and Levi approached Sosthenes and Mark. It appeared as though the two had something on their minds.

Jacob spoke. "We want to let you know that we will be leaving Corinth. We are very grateful for this community. Everyone has been most supportive."

Sosthenes asked, "Where are you going?"

"Back to Jerusalem. Our older brother has been very ill. We heard that he died, and we are returning to take care of his family and the business."

"But what about your business here?"

"We were very fortunate. We have a good buyer."

"You have a buyer already?" Sosthenes asked in surprise.

"Yes. We have received payment and are leaving for Jerusalem this week."

"So soon? We will miss you both."

"And we will miss you. We will pray for you and for this community," Jacob assured him.

"And we will pray for you."

Mark had been holding his tongue. "But is there not a growing danger in Jerusalem?"

"Yes, that is true. But we must do our duty for our family. We will pray for God's protection."

"Levi, may I speak with you before you go?"

"Of course, Mark, if you want to."

"May I come to your house tomorrow?"

"Certainly; we will be packing."

The next morning as Mark walked the familiar route to Levi's house, he prayed to the Prince of Peace for guidance. As predicted, the family was packing their belongings.

"Hello Levi," Mark greeted him. "Can you take a short break?"

"Certainly, Mark. Let's go outside."

Finding a place in the shade, they sat down and Mark explained why he wanted to talk. "Perhaps I should not pry into your affairs, but have you put aside your thoughts of joining in the violence that seems to stalk the Holy City?"

"The various options still circle in my mind. We Jews have a role in God's plan, you know."

"Yes. And we Christians have a role as well—a peaceful role."

"You speak of peace as though it will come about without human effort," Levi complained.

"No significant change can come about without both God's grace and human cooperation. But Jesus was very consistent in teaching the value of love."

"Until he got fed up and kicked the money changers out of the temple."

"Jesus did have that outburst—he was human. But no one was hurt that day. He was not like the sicarii," Mark explained.

"Yes. Jesus was not like the sicarii, and his methods did not produce results either," Levi grumbled.

"Have you heard about the fig tree?" Mark asked.

"What fig tree?"

"There was a fig tree near the temple that was not bearing fruit. When Jesus came to it he saw nothing but leaves. He said, *'May no one ever eat fruit from you again,'* and his disciples heard it.

"Then the next morning, after the incident in the temple, they saw that the tree had withered away to its roots.

Peter remembered and said to him, 'Rabbi, look! The fig tree that you cursed has withered.' Jesus answered them, 'Have faith in God. Truly I tell you, if you say to this mountain, be taken up and thrown into the sea, and if you do not doubt in your heart, but believe that what you say will come to pass, it will be done for you. So I tell you, whatever you ask for in prayer, believe that you have received it, and it will be yours.'

"The lesson for us is to not lower ourselves to the ways of violence. They are outdated. You saw how many were baptized at the Paschal feast—our numbers are growing daily. If we are patient and pray for God's kingdom to come and do all that we can in faith, then one day what you wish for will come to pass without violence and without war. Can you believe this?" Mark asked.

"I can believe it. But so far I have seen no evidence that it has worked."

"Can you be more patient, and continue to believe?" Mark persisted.

"Perhaps I can. You have given me a lot to think about. I will keep your message in my heart. Perhaps I can be patient for a while longer."

"For as long as it takes?"

"Well, we will see. I will take your message with me. Thank you. Now I must get back to the packing."

After a sincere embrace, Mark returned home.

Two weeks later, on Wednesday, Sosthenes said to Mark, "Oh by the way—that businessman, Severianus, sent a message that he wants to see you. Perhaps he has work for you."

"That will be excellent." As the presbyter explained where the merchant lived, Mark thought about taking on another job. *I can use the money, and working may keep my mind off of my losses.*

The house was easy to locate. Mark went through the doorway and entered a courtyard. Severianus was seated in the shade going over some accounts.

"Ah, Mark. Come in. Have a seat," he greeted him.

"Thank you. I was told that you wanted to see me. Do you have work?"

"I always have work. But what I have to tell you is perhaps more important. I found Alexios."

"Oh, good."

"Yes, and he was quite relieved to hear that you were alive."

"I didn't want him to worry."

"Yes. And he said something else. He said that a seaman named Timon brought your bag to him. Alexios now has all of your belongings. He looked inside and saw your codices and some pens. Is this important?"

"Is it important? Oh Jesus! I can't think of any news that could be more important. Thank God! Thank you God for creating loyal people like Timon!" Mark raised his arms in what was both a prayer of thanksgiving and an expression of jubilation. "Thank you—thank you—thank you God!"

"And thank you Severianus. You have given me a new cause for hope. I cannot express how grateful I am."

"You are most welcome."

Mark ran out the door, amazed at the goodness of God.

19

There was no question that Mark would go on to Philippi. He immediately knew it was what he should do, and so did everyone else. Sosthenes was elated—Longinus and Klea were happy for him—and Agathe, most of all, saw the hand of God at work.

He needed only a few days to finish his assignments with his employers, which provided just enough money to pay for the short voyage. He had hoped for another dinner with Agathe, but she did not invite him. On Sunday he said grateful goodbyes to the people who had befriended him. On Tuesday he sailed.

The ship left from the east bay, Cenchraea, which opens out to the Aegean Sea. If you leave from the main Corinth harbor, it takes another whole day to sail around the Peloponnesus peninsula when you are traveling east. It docked in Neapolis, the closest harbor to his destination.

Philippi is located on the via Egnatia, the Roman all-weather route connecting the Greek mainland with the provinces of Asia and Galatia, which lay east across the Bosphorus. The Roman engineers constructed the road a few miles inland, below the nearby mountains and above the hazardous marshes.

Philippi owes its name to Philip II of Macedonia, the father of Alexander the Great, who recognized the strategic importance of the location. He fortified the city, which flourished with the nearby gold mines and the abundant agricultural land that he claimed by draining some swamps.

About one hundred years earlier, on a late October day, Brutus and Cassius, Julius Caesar's assassins, waited near Philippi for the attack of Antony and Octavian, who had vowed to avenge the Emperor. Their battle positions were excellent, protecting both the city and the supply route from their fleet at Neapolis. But the bloody battle ended with Brutus and Cassius dead—choosing suicide rather than surrender—and Antony and Octavian victorious. The two victors faced each other a decade later, with Antony fleeing in Cleopatra's ships and leaving Octavian, soon to be crowned Augustus, as the sole *Princeps*, first among equals, of the empire.

After the ship that Mark sailed in docked, he walked toward Philippi. It was not raining, and he was glad that he made the voyage before winter. The road was better than Mark had imagined. Like the via Egnatia, it was wide enough for eight soldiers to march side by side with full battle packs. Today there were no soldiers, just a few carts going back and forth between the city and the harbor.

It felt good to walk on a solid road again after being on board the ship. Mark thought about the twists and turns his life had taken and wondered what new possibilities Philippi might bring. Perhaps the woman of my dreams will be here, he hoped.

After walking about an hour he saw shops and houses, a sign that the city was near. When he reached the intersection of the main road, he looked around wondering which way he should go. Finding the house of Alexios was not difficult. He simply asked at a shop, apparently the way Timon had done, and walked to it.

The door was open, and the bishop was meeting with a man and woman who looked like they might be contemplating marriage.

"I will be with you soon," said the bishop, pointing toward some cushions.

Mark sat down and waited. Alexios was quite tall—unusually tall. His abundant grey hair was neatly combed, and his face was shaven. His baritone voice was warm and friendly. The couple seemed totally at ease.

The wait was not long. "Hello, what can I do for you?" the bishop asked when the couple left.

"I am Mark. I was sent to you by those in Rome—after Peter was crucified," Mark replied.

"You are Mark! Wonderful. I was hoping you would come. I have your belongings."

"Yes. The merchant Severianos told me that you had them. I am very grateful."

"So you are a writer?"

"I have not yet completed any original writing. I was an aid and interpreter for Peter. I made notes of his speeches and sometimes spoke in his place. Then after the Great Fire, I began to visualize a more complete narrative of the public years of Jesus. I want to begin with his baptism by John and continue through his death and the empty tomb. In my notes I have additional facts that are not in the Passion document."

"The whole idea sounds excellent. It will be very useful."

"Yes. Many people have said so. But when I lost my bag, I thought it was over."

"The seaman told me you were missing. What happened?"

Mark related the story of the attack in the barber shop, the imprisonment, the escape, and the frightening voyage to Corinth. "I was greatly relieved at how warmly the brothers in Corinth accepted me." Realizing that he had not included the women there, he quickly added, "and the sisters too."

"We try to welcome people that way here, as well. Will you stay a while?"

"I have nowhere else to go. My first goal is to continue the writing," Mark assured him.

"Good! Stay here with me and Irana until you get your bearings. We have an extra room. Then we will find an appropriate place for you to live and work."

"That is generous of you. I am very grateful."

"Good. Now, would you like to see your things?"

Alexios led Mark to a small room behind the main living area. It was quite adequate, with just enough light coming in through a small window. There was both a chair and a couch. "Will you need a table? I have one in the storage area."

"Yes, that would be very helpful. This space will be excellent!"

"I will get it."

Mark's heart sang as he went through his bag. Everything was there: the clean tunic, the togas, even his razor. And every codex was just as he had left it—nothing was missing or damaged.

He studied each booklet carefully, one by one, fingering through the pages: his notes of the speeches of Peter, the Sayings source, the Passion document, the two unused booklets, and the one that started with the words, The beginning of the Good News of Jesus Christ, the Son of God. His eyes became moist as he pressed this last book to his chest, whispering, "I will complete the story of Jesus. I will not let anything get in my way."

Alexios reappeared with the table, assisted by a servant. It was larger than Mark had imagined. "Oh my! That's big enough for a professional writer."

"You have important work to do. In this house you are a professional." Both men grinned. "Mark, this is Ariston. He helps us here. If there is anything you need, just ask Ariston."

"Thank you." Mark extended his hand to the man, who received it in both of his and kissed it. "Oh! You don't need to . . ."

"Ariston is an equal in this house, but he keeps the customs of his people."

"Where are you from?" asked Mark.

"We believe he is from Bithynia," the bishop responded. "Ariston has been with us for eleven years."

Mark accepted the cursory information and smiled again. Ariston disappeared out the door.

"Ariston doesn't speak," explained the bishop. "He hears every word, but his tongue is frozen. It may have been the horror of a Roman attack on his city; we have heard him cry out in the night. We don't even know his given name. He is the best helper we could ever want, so we call him Ariston."

"Thank you for explaining. I don't want to blunder."

"Oh, Ariston understands. Now you get some rest. Then join us for dinner."

Mark didn't think he needed to rest, but when he lay down on the couch and closed his eyes, he fell quickly asleep.

When he awoke, he realized that he was being gently shaken by a man's hands. Looking up, he saw Ariston, smiling and beckoning. "Dinner?" Mark asked. "I will come right away."

Ariston appeared to be about thirty years old, with dark hair and skin a bit lighter than his host. He seemed quite fit, but carried a soft roll around his waist. He always wore the same simple smile. Mark supposed that he was happy with his lot in life, living with the bishop and his wife. He certainly seemed grateful and loyal.

Irana was a complete surprise—with very light complexion and cosmetically red cheeks. Mark had not expected her to be so short and pudgy. Standing near her husband, the top of her head didn't reach his shoulders. They make quite a couple, he thought. Irana, like the bishop, was warm and friendly, and when she had the opportunity, more talkative.

"Come and eat," she said, pointing to a large table. The three sat on one end. Ariston served. Mark discovered later that the servant also prepared the meals.

His hosts were anxious for information from Rome and Corinth. Mark related the terror of the persecutions, how Peter was crucified, and how his body was buried in an unmarked grave on Vatican Hill. After the meal they sipped wine and spoke about Mark's writing.

"Will the room be satisfactory?" Irana asked.

"Oh. Quite satisfactory. It is quiet, and I can spread out my things and concentrate. It's a better space than I had in Rome."

"Good. Then you may stay here."

"I would like to get a job. In Corinth I assisted two merchants with their correspondence and accounts."

Alexios replied, "You should be able to do that here, as well. But take your time. Let us put the Good News first."

"I greatly appreciate that. I really would like to focus for a couple of weeks. Then I will look for work."

"That sounds like a good plan." Irana agreed.

20

The next morning Mark broke a piece of bread, took some goat cheese, and hurried back to his room. Spreading the documents across the table, he pondered what he should do first, I'll put my mother's silver cross and Peter's medallion on the table, right in the center where I'll see them every day. Now this is a perfect place to write a gospel.

Then picking up the medallion, he gazed at the image of the Holy Spirit and prayed, Come Holy Spirit, fill me with your love. Set my heart on fire and guide me in this work. Make me faithful to the will of Jesus. Help me to keep the memory of him alive in the hearts of all. Grant me the wisdom to tell his story in the way you want it told. Keep me from sin and protect me from the evil one, so that I may finish this holy endeavor. Amen.

Then, not satisfied with the order in which he had copied the accounts on Minos's ship, he told himself, I need to put more of the mighty deeds up front so that people can be assured that Jesus is the Son of God. Filling a reed pen, he wrote,

Again he entered the synagogue, and a man was there who had a withered hand. They watched him to see whether he would cure him on the Sabbath, so they might accuse him. And he said to the man who had the withered hand, 'Come forward.' Then he said to them, 'Is it lawful to do good or to do harm on the Sabbath, to save life or to kill?' But they were silent. He looked around at them with anger; he was grieved at their hardness of heart and said to the man, 'Stretch out your hand.' He stretched it out, and his hand was restored. The Pharisees went out and immediately conspired with the Herodians against him, how to destroy him.

I need to get some more reed pens—these are getting dry, he realized, making a mental note to do so.

Mark never understood why the Pharisees were not accepting of Jesus. They were the best adherents to the Law of Moses—much better than the Sadducees. By any measure they were the most devout of all Jews, but their sin was pride. They had the time and the means to live in scrupulous conformity to strict standards, and they looked down upon the common folk who could not. I guess that's why Jesus and the Pharisees clashed, he thought. They had different ideas of right and wrong. Jesus lived by the law of love, and the Pharisees kept score on the unending list of commandments in their scrolls.

Leafing through his notes, he found the next story to copy.

Jesus departed with his disciples to the lake, and a great multitude from Galilee followed him; hearing all that he was doing, they came to him in great numbers from Judea, Jerusalem, Idumea, beyond the Jordan, and the region around Tyre and Sidon. He told his disciples to have a boat ready for him because of the crowd, so that they would not crush him; for he had cured many, so that all who had diseases pressed upon him to touch him. Whenever the unclean spirits saw him, they fell down before him and shouted, 'You are the Son of God!' But he sternly ordered them not to make him known.

This is an important account too, he told himself. It shows how Jesus was interested not only in the Jews, but also the Gentiles. And it shows how the unclean spirits knew who he was, even when the religious leaders didn't. That's why some people thought he was crazy. He was way too open-minded for their expectations.

Mark considered what he had written and said to himself, I am going to keep transcribing episodes that tell the story of Christ. Then when I've finished, I can see what accounts I have left out and add them in on the next draft. I can revise the order that way too, where I need to. I know what I will copy next.

Then he went home, and the crowd came together again, so that they could not even eat. When his family heard it, they went out to restrain him, for people were saying, 'He has gone out of his mind.' And the scribes who came down from Jerusalem said, 'He has Beelzebul, and by the ruler of the demons he casts out demons.' And he called them to him, and spoke to them in parables, 'How can Satan cast out Satan? If a kingdom is divided against itself, that kingdom cannot stand. And if a house is divided against itself, that house will not be able to stand. And if Satan has risen up against himself and is divided, he cannot stand, but his end has come. But no one can enter a strong man's house and plunder his property without first tying up the strong man; then indeed the house can be plundered.'

Jesus' family thought he was going out of his mind, and the scribes from Jerusalem accused him of being in league with the devil. But Christ was totally unique, Mark noted. Even the logic of his parables could not get through to many of their hard hearts. They wanted a mighty king, but he was the strong man who could protect them from their own sins. He was the one who could save them from the ruler of the demons, but they did not recognize him.

Leafing through the booklet, he found another passage. Those who did recognize him became the ones he felt closest to. They became his friends. He copied the account.

Then his mother and his brothers came; and standing outside, they sent to him and called him. A crowd was sitting around him; and they said to him, 'Your mother and your brothers and sisters are outside, asking for you.' And he replied, 'Who are my mother and my brothers?' And looking at those who sat around him, he said, 'Here are my mother and my brothers! Whoever does the will of God is my brother and sister and mother.'

Sitting back, he surveyed his work. I am on the right track. These few stories show that Jesus is the Son of God and they demonstrate both good response and bad. That is my goal.

Returning to the main part of the house, he found Irana and Ariston. She was directing the servant to put some food on a plate. "Hello, Mark. Will you join us? Ariston, dish something for Mark too. What would you like?"

Ariston placed some bread, cheese, and olives on a plate.

"That looks very good. Thank you," he said.

"Give him some figs, too," Irana added. Mark smiled and held up two fingers.

When he was seated, she asked, "Did you sleep well?"

"Yes. I was very comfortable." Ariston brought him a cup of wine. Mark nodded and smiled.

"And did you write today?"

"Oh yes. It's very quiet back there, and I spread my resources out on the large table. I got a lot done."

"Good. Alexios feels that your gospel will be a great help to the church."

"I need some new reed pens, though. The ones I have are getting dry."

"We should have those somewhere in Philippi."

Mark explained the concept of the written gospel as he ate, and shared an example of its usefulness from his experience in Corinth.

"Well you certainly are enthusiastic about it. I guess as time goes by more people will learn how to read."

"If only one person in a community can read, the rest can hear the stories of Christ."

"Yes, certainly."

Mark asked, "Is Alexios not here?"

"No. He is out at the farms, inspecting things with the tenants."

"Oh. You have land?"

"Yes. Enough. His grandfather did well expanding the holdings. So did his father. Now Alexios has to oversee both the farms and the church," Irana explained.

"When I arrived I saw him with a couple contemplating marriage. They seemed quite at ease with him."

"Alexios is good at overseeing things, but he loves his times with the people. He is a man with a big heart."

"I could tell."

Suddenly, his hostess changed the subject and asked a blunt question. "Are you married, Mark?"

"Who, me? No, not yet."

"Well, you should be—at your age."

"I had a girlfriend in Antioch. We were not betrothed, but our families expected us to marry."

"What happened?"

"One day Peter visited our city. My father knew him and introduced me to him. I had just completed my apprenticeship, and Peter asked me to go with him to Rome. So I went."

"And what happened to the girl?"

"Lydia? I don't know. She probably is married—she was very pretty. I was quite immature back then."

"I hear regret in your voice."

"Yes. Some regret. It was an exciting life with Peter. Every day was an adventure. But I miss not having a wife and children."

"And there has been no one else, since Lydia?"

Mark hesitated before answering. "One other. I met a remarkable woman in Corinth. Like me, she was devoted to serving Christ. I was very attracted to her, but it was not to be. She had different ideas about what she wanted to do with her life."

"So then you came here?"

"I learned that my books were here and I came. But I needed to leave Corinth—and Agathe too. I can finish my writing better here."

"Well, maybe here you will meet the right woman."

Mark blushed. He was thirty years old and blushing like a schoolboy. Yet in his heart, he hoped she was right.

The next day Mark noticed four fresh reed pens on his writing table. Who brought these? he wondered. It must have been Ariston. Alexios got in late, and Irana didn't go out. So Ariston does the shopping too—a servant with many talents. Nevertheless, it was very thoughtful of him. He simply heard what I needed and acted on it.

As Mark continued transcribing passages, he realized he needed to show how Jesus related to all classes of society. Selecting two stories from his notes, he combined them in a subtle way.

When Jesus had crossed again in the boat to the other side, a great crowd gathered around him; and he was by the lake. Then one of the leaders of the synagogue named Jairus came and, when he saw him, fell at this feet and begged him repeatedly, 'My little daughter is at the point of death. Come and lay your hands on her, so that she may be made well, and live.' So he went with him. And a large crowd followed him and pressed in on him.

Now there was a woman who had been suffering from hemorrhages for twelve years. She had endured much under many physicians, and had spent all that she had; and she was no better, but rather grew worse. She had heard about Jesus, and came up behind him in the crowd and touched his cloak, for she said, 'If I but touch his clothes, I will be made well.' Immediately her hemorrhage stopped; and she felt in her body that she was healed of her disease. Immediately aware that power had gone forth from him, Jesus turned about in the crowd and said, 'Who touched me?' He looked all around to see who had done it. But the woman, knowing what had happened to her, came in fear and trembling, fell down before him, and told him the whole truth. He said to her, 'Daughter, your faith has made you well; go in peace, and be healed of your disease.'

While he was still speaking, some people came from the leader's house to say, 'Your daughter is dead. Why trouble the teacher any further?' But overhearing what they said, Jesus said to the leader of the synagogue, 'Do not fear, only believe.' He allowed no one to follow him except Peter, James, and John, the brother of James. When they came to the house of the leader of the synagogue, he saw a commotion, people weeping and wailing loudly. When he had entered, he said to them, 'Why do you make a commotion and weep? The child is not dead but sleeping.' And they laughed at him. Then he put them all outside, and took the child's father and mother and those who were with him, and went in where the child was. He took her by the hand and said to her, 'Talitha cum,' which means, 'Little girl, get up!' And immediately the girl got up and began to walk about (she was twelve years of age). At this they were overcome with amazement. He strictly ordered them that no one should know this, and told them to give her something to eat.

Those are precious stories, he thought. Jairus was prominent, and the woman was poor, yet both realized that only Jesus could save them from what they feared the most. He leaned back with satisfaction, then rubbed his eyes.

The poor woman exemplifies all of Israel, who suffered under a series of foreign kings. They all knew that only the power of God could save them, but she recognized that such power was present in Christ. Jairus understood authority, as he himself was a leader; that's why he sought out Jesus. No one else could tap into the power of God, but the Son. And Jesus raised the little girl, proving that he is the divine Son. Yet he did so in a very human way. He was respectful of the woman, and of Jairus, and of the little girl. Seeing their faith, he granted their wishes, and he even made sure that the little girl was given some food.

Rubbing his chin, Mark wondered why Jesus so often tried to keep what he did from gaining publicity. He was not shy. Perhaps he didn't want his reputation to grow too fast too soon. His many healings had attracted widespread attention, and now he had raised someone from the dead. Maybe he sensed the danger in fame. The elite could get envious. Those in power would soon enough try to get him under control. He had to measure out his revelations—not overwhelm people with too much. I will keep that in mind as I determine the order of the passages.

It was getting late, but Mark decided to transcribe one passage more.

He left that place and came to his home town, and his disciples followed him. On the Sabbath he began to teach in the synagogue, and many who heard him were astounded. They said, 'Where did this man get all this? What is this wisdom that has been given to him? What deeds of power are being done by his hands! Is this the carpenter, the son of Mary and brother of James and Joses and Judas and Simon, and are not his sisters here with us?' And they took offence at him. Then Jesus said to them, 'Prophets are not without honor, except in their home town, and among their own kin, and in their own house.' And he could do no deed of power there, except that he laid his hands on a few sick people and cured them. And he was amazed at their unbelief.

Those in his home town simply could not believe that the son of a carpenter could be the Christ, Mark mused. Who did they expect—a mighty warrior—or some smooth-tongued diplomat from a noble family?

Nazareth was a small village, with a population of under five hundred—perhaps just large enough to have a synagogue. The village was about an hour's walk from the city of Sepphoris—the administrative center of Galilee. Following the death of Herod the Great, shortly before Jesus was born, some local fighters rose up and confiscated the city's treasury and weapons. In response, the Roman governor ordered the city to be destroyed and its inhabitants killed or sold into slavery. About two thousand were crucified.

Jesus was highly influenced by the memories and visible remnants of the slaughter. He and Joseph worked as *tektons*—artisans, woodworkers, or builders—as often or more in Sepphoris than Nazareth because of the extensive rebuilding of the city commissioned by Herod Antipas. He learned that the Romans meant business and, perhaps even more importantly, how violence and oppression were evils that most often devastated the poor.

21

When Mark joined his hosts for dinner, they were discussing the next gathering of the church. "Hello, Mark," greeted Alexios. "Will you come with us to liturgy tomorrow morning?"

"Yes. Certainly." Mark was looking forward to the time of prayer and communion with Christ, and he wanted to see how the bishop handled things in this city.

"Good. We will leave here early. I have much to get ready, you know."

"Where is the gathering?" Seeing no preparations at the house, Mark assumed that the community met elsewhere.

"It is in one of my barns. But it's a clean barn that we use only for this purpose."

"In Philippi you must need a fairly large building?" Mark commented.

"We have about four hundred, including the children. Not all come every Sunday."

"That's a good portion of the population. You have done well."

"Well, we continue to grow."

"Do you take precautions, regarding the Romans?"

"A community can never be too careful, but they don't harass us here. It's not like Rome."

Ariston came into the room and signaled that the food was ready. Mark went over to him and smiled. "Thank you for finding the reed pens for me. My old ones were getting very dry, and I greatly appreciate it."

Ariston made a low bow. He was not accustomed to such lavish praise—usually expecting no more than a simple thank you. He was only doing his job. Mark knew better than to extend his hand. Instead he placed his hands on the quiet man's upper arms and gave them a warm squeeze. He was quick to release them, however, not wanting to embarrass the servant.

At dinner Mark asked, "Will we have a meal tomorrow?"

Irana answered, "Not a full Agape meal. But we will socialize afterwards."

"That sounds fine. I meet people best in small groups."

"Well do look around. Maybe we can find you a wife."

Mark was shocked at her nerve. Why does she need to meddle in my life? he asked himself. But quickly gathering his wits he replied, "Let's not be in a hurry about those things. My first priority is working on the gospel, and then finding a job."

Alexios interrupted, "My wife is a gifted matchmaker. But there are some merchants that may want to employ you. I will ask around."

"I am very grateful."

Changing the subject, Mark asked if the couple had children. He learned that they had two sons and one daughter—all adults and married—a smaller family than average. The oldest son, Leonidas, was involved in the family business, and their daughter, Thaleia, already had gifted them with two granddaughters. Irana loved to talk about the little ones. Alexios expressed equal concern about Leonidas providing an heir.

The next morning Mark rose early, washed, shaved, and put on a clean tunic. Ariston appeared at the door, shaking his head. Going over to where the clothing was laid, the servant picked out the plain toga and held it up.

"Oh! Are we more formal here in Philippi? Thank you, Ariston, for keeping me on my toes. I want to dress appropriately and fit in. After all, I am the bishop's guest."

From the outside, the stone building where the Christians met looked like most any granary, but inside it was clean and welcoming. His hosts quickly got into making preparations for the liturgy, which gave Mark time to look around. In the center was a large table, on which Irana placed a white cloth. On one side of the altar he saw a high table for reading scripture, and the other side held a chair set above the floor on a raised platform. It certainly looked like a Christian church.

The people arriving were not all wearing togas, but he was glad that he had worn his. They were all ages—young mothers with babies, greying fathers escorting older parents, and noisy children greeting their friends. Mark noticed a few hugs, but not like at Corinth. The people seemed sincerely glad to see one another without making a production out of how they expressed it.

The liturgy was reverent, in part due to the authentic leadership of Bishop Alexios and in part from how dedicated the people were to the Lord. A man read the beginning of Paul's letter to their church, where the apostle said, *I am confident of this, that the one who began a good work among you will bring it to completion by the day of Jesus Christ.'*

The bishop's reflections were simple and encouraging: Each of us is growing in faith and our community is flourishing, just like Paul predicted. Remain committed, pray daily, and seek God's aid in any need. As Mark received the freshly baked, blessed, and broken bread of communion, he said to himself, it is good that I am here. Thank you, Lord Jesus, for taking care of me.

Immediately after the service Irana latched onto Mark's arm and led him around, introducing him to some of the families. Then she whispered, "Now Mark, do you see any girls that interest you?"

"Please give me a little time. I just arrived in Philippi."

"It's never too early. Now just point out to me one or two that you would like to meet."

Knowing that he was beaten in this skirmish, he nodded toward two fine-looking young women.

"Don't be ridiculous; they both are married. One has a child."

"Oh! Well, how about those four over there?" They appeared a bit younger.

"They are betrothed!"

"Really! I would not have guessed. Maybe I'm not prepared for this."

"Now look over there, at those three. They are nice, don't you agree?"

Mark looked in the direction Irana was pointing and said in shock, "They are so young! They couldn't be more than seventeen."

"More like fourteen—and the skinny one is two years short of that."

Just as the blushing bachelor was wishing he had slept in, Alexios appeared wearing a grin. "Come with me. I want to introduce you to two men who are interested in your services."

Glad to be free of Irana's grasp, he followed the bishop. The two were local merchants, and just like in Corinth, when Mark told them what he could do, they suggested times when he could meet with them. He told Alexios later, "It is sooner than I expected to be taking on jobs, but I need money, and as long as the hours don't mount up, I can continue writing."

That evening as Mark lay awake, thinking about the day's events, he pictured the girls who were taking on the interests of women. Is this the way Joseph felt, he wondered. Mary was no older than those girls when she was betrothed, and he accepted her totally. They deeply loved one another and provided a good home for Jesus. It was the custom; people didn't think about marriage in terms of age.

Then pondering his situation, he asked himself, is this the way it will be now that I am getting older? If I had stayed in Antioch and married Lydia, we would have matured together. Now I may have to take a wife who almost could be my daughter.

He closed his eyes and tried to sleep, but rest eluded him as he tried to picture what the girl he left behind might be like today. Reaching for the silver cross on the table, he rolled it in his fingers several times. Then, like he had done on many nights in Rome, he attempted to pray and think about his writing.

The next morning Mark immediately went to his table thinking, I need to get some work done, even though I'm tired from the restless night.

Leafing through his notes, he found the story that he wanted to include next and began to copy it.

The apostles gathered around Jesus, and told him all that they had done and taught. He said to them, 'Come away to a deserted place all by yourselves and rest a while.' For many were coming and going, and they had no leisure even to eat. And they went away in the boat to a deserted place by themselves. Now many saw them going and recognized them, and they hurried there on foot from all the towns and arrived ahead of them. As he went ashore, he saw a great crowd; and he had compassion for them, because they were like sheep without a shepherd; and he began to teach them many things. When it grew late, his disciples came to him and said, 'This is a deserted place, and the hour is now very late; send them away so that they may go into the surrounding country and villages and buy something for themselves to eat.' But he answered them, 'You give them something to eat.' They said to him, 'Are we to go and buy two hundred denarii worth of bread, and give to them to eat?' And he said to them, 'How many loaves have you? Go and see.' When they had found out, they said, 'Five, and two fish.' Then he ordered them to get all the people to sit down in groups on the green grass. So they sat down in groups of hundreds and fifties. Taking the five loaves and the two fish, he looked up to heaven, and blessed and broke the loaves, and gave them to his disciples to set before the people; and he divided the two fish among them all. And all ate and were filled; and they took up twelve baskets full of broken pieces and of the fish. Those who had eaten the loaves numbered five thousand men.

The crowds were hungry for Jesus' teaching, he thought, just like those here in Philippi. There are good people everywhere, who just want to live their lives in peace and grow closer to God. And Jesus fed them. He taught in parables how the kingdom of God is right here in our midst. People are like sheep without a shepherd, unless they know Christ. But when they hear how he loves them and cares for them, they begin to understand. Leaning back he vowed, I must finish the gospel so they can hear his words. He closed his eyes and pictured the scene of Jesus teaching in the deserted place and how attentive the people were—not caring about the hour or the empty feeling in their stomachs.

You give them something to eat. "That is our mandate," Mark muttered. "There is no one else to feed them. We who have been given the grace to follow Jesus, must accept the implications of this truth. Jesus set a fire upon the earth, and it is the responsibility of us all to fan the flames."

He knelt down beside his couch and prayed the words that failed to form the previous night—prayers of gratitude and hope and dedication.

Then getting up onto the couch he fell into a deep slumber.

That evening as supper was concluding, Alexios asked, "Will you read to us some of what you are writing?"

"Certainly," Mark replied. "When would you like to hear it?"

"How about now, while we sip our wine?"

"Yes. I'll get my book."

Returning with his manuscript, Mark sat down and opened to the page he had copied that day. "Ariston, please sit and join us." Surprised to be included in the family conversation, the servant found a cushion and sat down.

Mark read the last passage slowly and carefully. When he finished, he closed the codex and looked around. Alexios had lowered his eyes, Irana was speechless, and Ariston was crying. The impact of the simple story was profound.

22

Later that week Alexios confronted Mark with a question. "I was thinking about this Sunday. Could you read one of the stories at our gathering?"

"Of course. I guess there is no better way to see how people will receive them."

"Oh, I'm sure they will like them."

"I am too. Which passage do you want me to read?"

Alexios answered quickly, "The one about the multiplication of the loaves. I've been thinking about it, and I want to preach about maintaining our faith in God's care."

"Excellent! That is what the stories are for."

"I will need to listen to it a few more times before Sunday."

"Yes. Just ask, and I'll read it as many times as you want."

When Sunday morning arrived, Mark again put on the toga. Picking up his copy of the gospel, he walked with the family to the meeting place. It had rained all night, but it stopped just before they left the house.

"Maybe it will be dry when we walk home," Alexios stated.

Mark replied, "This is a nice day."

At the church, he recognized some faces from the previous week. But when he tried to introduce himself saying, "I am Mark," the people replied, "We know." Word gets around fast when there is a newcomer in the community.

He noticed that people were singing better this week, than the previous. It must be that leader of song, he thought. I don't recall him being here last Sunday. His strong voice is easy to follow. I will make it a point to speak with him after the liturgy. The musician was accompanied by a woman playing a seven string lyre. They looked like a couple. He was about Mark's age, the woman a bit younger.

After the scripture readings, Alexios stood up and announced, "We have something very special today. I am sure you have seen Mark, our new guest. What you may not know is that he came from Rome, where he spent several years with Peter. Mark is compiling a book of stories about Jesus, which he heard Peter tell. Let us listen to one of them today."

Alexios sat down and nodded. Mark went to the reading table, opened his codex, and said a silent prayer, Lord, help me to proclaim your word as you wish it to be heard. Then, with reverence and delight, he read the account of the multiplication of the loaves. When he finished, the room was as still as a cavern.

"Thank you, Mark," said Alexios. "I am reminded of the adage: Any good actor can deliver his lines well, but only a believer can proclaim God's word in a way that inspires belief."

Then the bishop spoke about the account of Jesus and the loaves, touching upon all of the important points. People were nodding in agreement as he encouraged them to place their faith in Christ and to be grateful for the good gifts they have in their lives.

After the liturgy the place was abuzz with conversations. Mark chose to just step back and watch.

He noticed that the men wearing togas tended to gather on one side and those in tunics on the other. Those who appeared to be servants clumped in the back, where they could talk with one another and keep an eye on those in their household in case they signaled a need. I guess it is only human nature, he mused. Even though everyone is equal in the Christian community, people mix more with those they know.

Then he noticed Irana coming toward him, so he moved over to where the musicians were gathering up their things. "Hello. I want to tell you how much I enjoyed your music this morning. You really got these folks into the spirit of the liturgy."

"Thank you," the man said. "We were not here last week."

"I certainly could tell the difference. My name is Mark."

"I know. I am Basil and this is Zosima." Basil was a handsome Greek with strong features, who appeared to be in his mid-thirties. The woman smiled.

"Good to meet you. Do you lead music every week?"

"Almost always. Last Sunday we were at a family reunion in Thessalonica."

"Oh. Do you know a seaman there named Timon?"

"No. I can't say that I do. A lot of people live in Thessalonica."

"Of course," Mark agreed.

"Do you know others there?" Basil asked.

"No, and I hardly know Timon. He once did me a great favor. I would like some day to thank him."

"Yes, that would be good."

"You two are a great team. Do you both play instruments?"

"Zosima is the best musician," Basil shared. Then holding up the seven-string lyre with a sound box he added, "She plays the cathara very well. It gives a stronger sound in large assemblies like this. She also plays the pan pipes and diaulos."

"What is a diaulos?" Mark directed the question to the woman.

Basil answered, "It is a double flute. Zosima can play almost any wind or string instrument, and she has a beautiful singing voice too." The woman blushed.

"Oh. I would love to hear you sing."

This time she responded. "I do not care to be in front of large groups. I sing with friends."

"Oh my; our loss. Well, I would love to hear you sing some time."

"Some time, yes," she said shyly.

Then Alexios came and interrupted saying, "It's good that you have met Basil and Zosima. Now there are others who want to speak with the famous writer from Rome."

"I am hardly famous," Mark retorted as he followed the bishop through the crowd.

That evening as the household gathered for supper, Irana could not contain herself. "So you met Zosima?"

"Yes. She is a wonderful musician."

"I am asking if you like her."

"Of course I like her, although she didn't say much. And I like her husband too."

"What? Did you think that Basil is her husband?"

"Of course."

"No! They are brother and sister!" Irana was laughing. So was Alexios, and Ariston displayed a big grin.

"Oh. Really?"

"Yes. Zosima is a single woman."

"I wouldn't have guessed—at her age."

"She is a widow."

"Oh. What happened to her husband?"

Alexios answered. "After they were married, he couldn't find work in Thessalonica, so he joined a caravan that was shipping goods. He was killed in an accident in Moesia—to the north."

"Over the mountains?"

"Yes. He is buried somewhere over there near the River Danube."

"How horrible! What a shock that must have been to her."

"She was devastated. So she and the children moved in with Basil."

"Oh. So she has children?" Mark asked.

"Two little girls—Anyte and Baubo."

Mark nodded.

Irana added. "They are darling, and little Baubo is walking now."

Again, Mark nodded his head.

"You must get to know them," she insisted.

The week was a busy one. The merchants had much for him to do, and he accomplished little writing. However, the sack in which he kept his coins was getting heavier.

On Thursday, he set aside a few hours to work on the gospel. *I want to continue to show how people misunderstood Jesus*, he thought. *This is crucial for us today, so we don't repeat their errors.*

Leafing through his notes he selected a passage and copied it.

The Pharisees came and began to argue with him, asking him for a sign from heaven, to test him. And he sighed deeply in his spirit and said, 'Why does this generation ask for a sign? Truly I tell you, no sign will be given to this generation.' And he left them, and getting into the boat again, he went across to the other side.

It must have been frustrating for Jesus, Mark guessed. He had healed a number of sick people and raised a dead girl to life, yet they still asked for a sign from heaven. What did they want, bolts of lightning?

He shook his head in disgust. Even if Jesus had made the sun stand still, that wouldn't have been enough. Those whose hearts were hardened simply could not bring themselves to believe. I don't blame Jesus for leaving them. They didn't deserve a sign.

Then he copied another story.

Now the disciples had forgotten to bring any bread; and they had only one loaf with them in the boat. And he cautioned them, saying, 'Watch out—beware of the yeast of the Pharisees and the yeast of Herod.' They said to one another, 'It is because we have no bread.' And becoming aware of it, Jesus said to them, 'Why are you talking about having no bread? Do you still not perceive or understand? Are your hearts hardened? Do you have eyes, and fail to see? Do you have ears, and fail to hear? And do you not remember? When I broke the five loaves for the five thousand, how many baskets full of broken pieces did you collect?' They said to him, 'Seven.' Then he said to them, 'Do you not yet understand?'

Mark reread the line, *'Beware of the yeast of the Pharisees and the yeast of Herod.'* The leaders in the villages and the rulers in Jerusalem were not yeast, but parasites. Those who were more educated should have encouraged the people—instead they lorded it over them. But apparently the disciples in the boat, who had only one loaf, also failed to understand the image. This is an excellent example of incomprehension, even among his closest followers. Mark liked how the story showed Jesus' frustration and the way he challenged them, *'Do you have eyes, and fail to see? Do you have ears, and fail to hear?'* He thought, no one who hears the gospel read to them will want to be among those who fail to take his message to heart.

That evening at dinner, Alexios brought up a question. "I have been thinking about this Sunday's liturgy."

Irana cut in, "Yes. Mark. You must get better acquainted with Zosima."

"I want to," Mark agreed.

"Good. Sunday will be an excellent time. Just go over to her and strike up a conversation."

"Yes. I will."

"Now don't forget. Zosima is shy; she will not come to you."

"I understand."

Alexios wanted to get back to his question, and Mark was relieved to hear him. "What I want to ask is, will you preach this week?"

"You want me?" Mark asked in surprise.

"Yes. I think it will be good for the people, and they will get to know you better."

"But you are the bishop."

"They hear me nearly every week. They need to hear a different voice once in a while."

"I am willing to do it, but . . ," Mark hesitated.

"But what?"

"I don't know. I was just trying to think of a reason why I should not. Don't you have deacons here?"

"We do, but this week I would like you. What do you say?"

"Well, of course. I am honored. What theme do you have in mind? Which passage shall I use?"

"You select it. I'll rely on your judgement."

Back in his room, lying on the couch with eyes wide open, Mark thought about the accounts he might use. I'll decide on the story tomorrow morning; tonight I'll just pray about it. But prayer did not fill his mind.

He found himself, instead, thinking of Zosima. He couldn't quite picture her. Images of Basil and others came to him clearly, but not the woman he had thought was someone else's wife. Was she younger or older than Basil? Thinner or heavier? Was her hair dark or light? He couldn't remember. Her smile was nice, and she seemed authentic. A bit shy, maybe, but then we only had just met. And I didn't show much interest in her, except for her music. Mark knew that he should just as well leave these questions for Sunday, but he could not get the talented woman out of his mind.

The next morning he had a very clear idea about which of Peter's stories he would read at the liturgy. Picking up the medallion of the Holy Spirit and rubbing it gently, he whispered a simple prayer of thanksgiving from his heart. "Spirit of God, you have guided me thus far, and I am learning to trust in you. Give me the words—please give me the words that you want these people to hear. I am the servant of Christ. Help me to be a worthy one. And thank you for all you have done for me. Amen."

On Sunday morning Mark realized that he was not a bit nervous. This is the Lord's work, he thought. Whatever is his plan for this day will be fulfilled.

When Alexios nodded that it was time, he picked up his book and went to the reading table. Opening it to the recently transcribed passage, he read,

Jesus returned from the region of Tyre, and went by way of Sidon towards the Sea of Galilee, in the region of the Decapolis. They brought to him a deaf man who had an impediment in his speech; and they begged him to lay his hand on him. He took him aside in private, away from the crowd, and put his fingers into his ears, and he spat and touched his tongue. Then looking up to heaven, he sighed and said to him, 'Ephphatha', that is, 'Be opened.' And immediately his ears were opened, his tongue was released, and he spoke plainly. Then Jesus ordered them to tell no one; but the more he ordered them, the more zealously they proclaimed it. They were astounded beyond measure, saying, 'He has done everything well; he even makes the deaf to hear and the mute to speak.'

Then Mark continued, "This was Gentile territory. Jesus' first concern was for the lost sheep of Israel, but in this account, that I heard Peter tell, he came from two cities in Lebanon and traveled to a region of ten cities east of the Sea of Galilee that had a strong Roman military presence. So the man he cured was considered a Greek—only he could not speak Greek or any other language because of his impediment and lack of hearing.

"Those who brought the man had heard of Jesus and had at least some confidence in him. They begged him to lay his hands upon him, and he did!

"This story very accurately shows the pattern of Jesus' cures. The person had faith, and Christ trusted in the power of his Father. He lifted his eyes and prayed. Then he made use of an outward sign—in this case a bit of spit on his fingers; sometimes it was only a simple gesture. He commanded the illness, *'Ephphatha', that is, 'Be opened,'* and the man's tongue was released and he spoke plainly.

"Can we approach Jesus with this kind of faith? Can we surrender our fears and allow his fingers to touch us—to touch us personally? That is all that Christ expects: nothing more, and nothing less. He is the Son of God. Just let go of your fears and trust in him. Do this, and amazing things will happen."

Mark paused at this point. He did not know what to say next. This pretty well summed it up. He did not know if he would say more, or if he was finished.

Then a voice from the back shouted, "Praise be to the Lord, Jesus Christ!"

All eyes turned to see who it was—it was not a voice they recognized.

"Praise be to the Lord, Jesus Christ!" came the voice again. "Praise be to the Lord, Jesus Christ!"

"It's Ariston!" several voices shouted at once. "It is the mute servant, Ariston!"

"Praise be to the Lord, Jesus Christ!" he continued shouting.

The bishop made his way to the formerly silent man and put his arms around him. Ariston began to sob.

Everyone gasped. It was beyond belief, but they had seen it with their own eyes. Mark had read how Jesus healed and gave a few short comments, and the man was cured.

Mark stood there looking on in amazement.

Restoring order, the bishop shouted, "This is a grace-filled day for us. Let us continue our prayer with gratitude to Christ."

The people settled down and entered into the prayers of Eucharist with renewed hearts. They received the Body and Blood of Christ with the greatest devotion of their lives. Some had tears in their eyes. Strong men knelt on the floor in humble adoration. Children, seeing how their parents were moved, had images of the day etched in their memories. Mothers clutched their babies and prayed that they might inherit the faith they treasured.

After the liturgy all of the people crowded around Mark. "You did it," some said. "You performed the miracle!"

"I did not," he replied. "What you saw was done by Christ!"

But they crushed in upon him. Regardless of how it happened, Mark was a hero.

He was glad to get back to his room after the exciting day. So much had happened, and he had several things to pray about in thanksgiving. Picking up the medallion of the Holy Spirit, he kissed it. But before he could pray he stopped short. "What about . . ?" He looked aghast. "Oh no!" And putting his hands to his head he exclaimed out loud, "Oh, God. I forgot to even speak with Zosima!"

23

The next morning Mark rose early and went to the living area to get a cup of water. Ariston was there, preparing the food as usual. Seeing Mark, he rushed to him, bowed down, and kissed his hand saying, "Oh Master Mark. I am so very grateful."

Mark allowed the kiss, knowing it was the man's custom, but protested, "You should not call me master. I am your friend. Jesus is the Lord." Then he pulled the servant to his feet.

"But I am so grateful."

"You have every reason to be grateful." Then he lifted Ariston's chin and looked straight into his eyes. "Christ freed your tongue. Now you can hold your head up high."

"Yes . . . Mark."

"You don't need to be frozen by fear any more. Jesus repeated over and over again to the people he met in Galilee and Judea, 'Do not be afraid.' As you hear more of the gospel, you will learn that."

"I do feel safe here with Alexios and Irana. It has been nearly twelve years since I spoke."

"That is a long time. Would you like to tell me what happened?"

Ariston hesitated—and then spit out, "The Romans . . ."

"You can speak now."

"The Romans came to our city—Heraclea in Bithynia. When we would not agree to their terms of peace, they slaughtered every one of us. I watched in anguish as they cut up my mother, my father, my brothers and sisters, and the little ones. I ran and hid in a cave. Then they burned our houses."

"Oh Ariston. You have lived through much horror." Embracing him tenderly, Mark told him, "You will see your family again one day. In fact, they may be with the Lord now. They may have been praying for you all these years—that you would be safe."

The servant drew back abruptly. "They were not Christians! I am the only one who has been baptized. The bishop, he baptized me just four years ago."

"We don't know all the ways of God. What we do know is that God is merciful. When God saw the evil that Rome forced on your city, how do you think he felt?"

Ariston looked at Mark in wonder, then fell back into his arms, sobbing. But the tears were mixed with laughter—the exuberant, grateful, redeeming joy of a man maturing in his faith.

Mark whispered, "Please be careful when you talk about your healing. I don't want attention drawn to me. Give all of the credit to Christ."

Back in his room, Mark immediately knew what he would copy next.

Six days later, Jesus took with him Peter and James and John, and led them up a high mountain apart, by themselves. And he was transfigured before them, and his clothes became dazzling white, such as no one on earth could bleach them. And there appeared to them Elijah with Moses, who were talking with Jesus. Then Peter said to Jesus, 'Rabbi, it is good for us to be here; let us make three dwellings, one for you, one for Moses, and one for Elijah.' He did not know what to say, for they were terrified. Then a cloud overshadowed them, and from the cloud there came a voice, 'This is my Son, the Beloved; listen to him!' suddenly when they looked around, they saw no one with them anymore, but only Jesus.

Mark sat back and studied the words on the page. There is an amazing transformation within a person, when they see the glory of Christ. They may know a little about him—maybe a lot. But when they clearly see how he truly is the Son of God, it can be an awe inspiring experience. Peter did not know what to say, he was so astounded. The one who constantly blurted out whatever came into his mind, was at a loss for words. That's why he mumbled something about building three tents. He knew that he was in the presence of ultimate holiness—something sacred beyond human understanding—which made him terrified as well as amazed because he knew he was a sinful man.

Then Mark remembered what Peter usually said after telling this story. It was not in his notes, but he heard it distinctly, like the great apostle was right in the room.

We went on from there and passed through Galilee. He did not want anyone to know it; for he was teaching his disciples, saying to them, 'The Son of Man is to be betrayed into human hands, and they will kill him, and three days after being killed, he will rise again.' But we did not understand what he was saying and were afraid to ask him.

He wrote the words, exactly as he heard them. Then—rereading the passage—he picked up his pen and changed Peter's 'we' to 'they' to preserve the flow of the narrative.

He thought, Peter did not connect the beautiful transfiguration he was blessed to witness with the terrible crucifixion that was to follow. Neither did

James and John or any of the others. In fact, Peter argued with Jesus about this prediction, and he was rebuked! They were in total denial about how immense divine love actually is—love vastly beyond what our human minds can comprehend. It took Jesus' willing surrender on the cross, to demonstrate the magnitude of this love. But in the years to follow, Peter finally understood, and he devoted the rest of his life to passing it on. Whenever he told the first eye-opening story, he followed it with the blunt truth of the second: how often humanity, when confronted by the power of the sacred, attempts to hold it in awe rather than enter into its goodness.

That evening just before serving dinner, Ariston made a little speech. "I want to say in words to you, Bishop Alexios and Irana, that I am very grateful for the many years that you have allowed me to be a part of your household. I came to you with nothing, and you took me in. I was so frozen with fear that I could not even speak, yet you welcomed me into the Body of Christ and baptized me. Before yesterday I could not say these words, but today I can.

"Jesus loosened my tongue. Jesus cut through my fear and said, *'Ephphatha', that is, 'Be opened.'* Praise be to the Lord, Jesus Christ. And Mark, even though you did not cause the miracle—Jesus did—you were the servant who placed me before him. I am grateful to you, as well. I thank you with all my heart."

Everyone applauded—it was the first time in his life that Ariston had been applauded for speaking out. He blushed and gave them a little bow.

Then Ariston served the dinner in the usual way. The only difference this evening was that when one of them said, "Thank you," Ariston replied, "You are welcome."

Irana brought up the first topic at the table. "So Mark. Did you get acquainted with Zosima?"

"Actually no."

"No! Why not?"

"Well, it just—didn't happen."

"What do you mean, it didn't happen?"

"The crowd—you know. I couldn't get to her." Mark wished that he had rehearsed his speech, like Ariston had.

"You couldn't get to her! Why didn't you just go over there?"

Alexios cut in. "Dear, there was a lot of commotion."

"So! For God's sake, Mark. If you want to have a wife, you do have to actually speak with her."

"Actually, Irana, I forgot. With all those people crowding around me, I simply forgot."

"Oh Mark. No one is that helpless."

"I . . . I'm sorry."

The bishop cut in again. "There is something else."

"Don't interrupt me until I'm finished. Now Mark, promise me that you will go to Zosima this Sunday. I will make sure that you do."

"Yes. This Sunday. I will do it."

"I will make sure that you do."

"May I bring up something else?" the bishop asked.

When there was no reply from his wife, he went on. "Another businessman told me today that he would like to use your services. Would you consider another client?"

"Yes. I could take on one more. The gospel is progressing well, and my coin sack is not yet full."

"Good. He said to come to his home tomorrow morning. I'll tell you how to find it. But you must know one thing: Gentilianus is in some sort of dispute with another merchant—Demetrios. I don't know what the dispute is about or the man—he is not in our Body. But I thought you should know."

"Yes. I'll be careful when I speak with him."

The following morning Mark went to the house of Gentilianus, who was very cordial. His needs were much like those of the other clients, and they agreed to begin the following week at the usual wage.

On Thursday, Alexios came to Mark's room. "Can we discuss another possible passage that I may preach on this Sunday?"

"Yes, certainly, this is a good time."

Mark made several suggestions, but the bishop kept shaking his head. He was looking for something different. "There must have been occasions when Christ spoke about his expectations for his followers. I'm looking for something with challenge."

The writer leafed through his notes. "Here is one. I have not yet folded it into the narrative. It sounds kind of harsh at first hearing." Mark read the passage.

Jesus said, 'If any one of you put a stumbling-block before one of these little ones who believe in me, it would be better for you if a great millstone were hung around your neck and you were thrown into the sea. If your hand causes you to stumble, cut it off; it is better for you to enter life maimed than to have two hands and to go to hell, to the unquenchable fire. And if your foot causes you to stumble, cut it off; it is better for you to enter life lame than to have two feet and to be thrown into hell. And if your eye causes you to stumble, tear it out; it is better for you to enter the kingdom of God with one eye than to have two eyes and to be thrown into hell, where their worm never dies, and the fire is never quenched.'

"Hmm. That does sound harsh, but I like it. It has the challenge I was looking for. I'll try to approach it positively."

"Yes, you can do that."

"Will you read it at the liturgy?"

"Certainly."

"Good. Then afterward I will leave you to see Zosima."

Mark smiled. He didn't want the bishop's wife to lead him by the nose.

When Sunday morning came, Mark decided to go to Basil and Zosima while people were gathering.

"Hello, Basil. Hello, Zosima. This is a beautiful day."

The song leader responded, "Will we have excitement, like last Sunday?"

"I don't know about that. The bishop told me that he will speak on the challenge of Christ in our lives."

"Well, that will fit the music we have selected. Won't it, Zosima?"

"Yes, it will fit very well." Giving Mark a little smile, she continued tuning her lyre.

Mark noticed the smile. "Good. Well, maybe we can visit more after the liturgy." He made his smile more obvious.

As the liturgy began, he kept glancing in the direction of the musicians.

She is an attractive woman, he mused, a little taller than most. Her black hair has more curls than I thought, and it looks nice. Her face is kind of plain, but Agathe's was more so. Of course Agathe had a vivacious personality, which gave her charm beyond her physical grace. This one is more subdued and a little thicker through the trunk, but that is to be expected in a woman with two children. All in all she seems like a fine person.

Oh! Did she glance at me just then? I'm not sure. It looked like she may have.

What am I doing, studying her features, when I am supposed to be concentrating on the liturgy? I must be out of my mind. He put his head down.

When it was time for him to read, Mark proclaimed the account reverently and gently. The words of Christ in the passage could be delivered harshly, or they could be read with a tone of encouragement. When Peter told the story early on, he spoke sternly, like a father warning a rebellious child. But later, as he grew older, his tone shifted. Then the story sounded more like it was coming from a loving, nurturing mother. Mark took the later approach, and waited to hear what the bishop would say.

"Last week we saw living proof that Christ loves us. The way he blessed our brother Ariston was amazing. After almost twelve years in fear, Jesus freed his tongue and allowed him to resume a normal life. We should thank God for this great gift. We all are aware that Mark had read an account of Jesus healing and was preaching at the time. But Mark gives all the credit to Christ. So does Ariston. So do I. And so should we all.

"In the account that we heard today, Jesus is speaking not about what he can do for us, but about what we should do for him. The challenge in this story is unmistakable. We must turn away from all sin and be faithful to the gospel. I chose this story because we are moving into weeks of shorter days. And we can make the most of these weeks, if we concentrate on living up to Jesus' expectations. If we do, then our celebration of the Paschal feast will be all the more joyful.

"Jesus loved to use images when he taught. They helped people to understand his message. Today I want to share a story with you that also makes use of images. Listen to it with an open heart, and see if it helps you to become more dedicated to the life you are called to live.

"There once was a king, who said to his servant, 'Find for me the most beautiful cup in my kingdom, so that as I drink from it, I may savor its beauty.'

"Upon finding a cup of exquisite beauty, the servant exclaimed, 'This is the most beautiful cup I have ever seen!' And hearing him, the cup replied, 'Once I was just an ugly, soggy lump of clay. But one day a man with dirty and wet hands threw me on a wheel and started turning me around and around until I got so dizzy that I cried, 'Stop! Stop!' but the man with wet hands said, 'Not yet.' Then he started to poke me and punch me until I hurt all over. 'Stop! Stop!' I cried, but he said, 'Not yet.' Finally he did stop, but then he did something worse. He put me in an oven, and I got hotter and hotter until I couldn't stand it any longer. I cried, 'Stop! Stop!' but the man said, 'Not yet.'

"'Finally, when I thought I was going to be burned up, the man took me out of the furnace. Then, a gentle lady began to paint me, but the fumes were so bad that they made me sick to my stomach. I cried, 'Stop! Stop!' but the lady said, 'Not yet.' Finally she did stop and gave me back to the man again, and he put me back in that awful oven. I cried out, 'Stop! Stop!' but he only said, 'Not yet.' And when he took me out and let me cool, a very pretty lady kissed me and put me on this shelf.'

"'You are no longer ugly,' the servant said to the cup. 'You now are exceedingly beautiful, and you are fit to take your place in the hand of the king.'"

The people again sat in silence. Mark was amazed. What a powerful way to put just the right touch on this challenging passage. And the Eucharist again was deep and devout, beyond everyone's expectations.

After the service, Mark went straight to the musicians. "Your songs were outstanding," he praised. "Our liturgies are getting more inspiring every week."

"Thank you for the compliment," Basil answered. "We are glad you like it, but we just do our part. When everyone does their part well, it enhances the experience for all."

"Yes, but good music is an important stone in the foundation," Mark insisted.

"Thank you," Basil replied modestly.

Turning to Zosima, Mark asked, "How did you like the bishop's talk?"

"Oh, I liked it. The bishop always hits the nail squarely."

"And today was no exception."

"Today was no exception. It made me want to do my best during these winter weeks."

"Do you have any special music planned?"

"We are practicing some things. I think the people will like them."

Changing the subject, Mark continued to keep his attention on Zosima. "I am told you have children."

"Oh yes. Two girls. Anyte, who I hope may be a poet, and Baubo, who likes to make sounds. I don't know how musical she is yet."

"Irana said she is walking."

"Her first steps. Everyone starts with small steps."

Basil cut in. "Mark. Will you come to dinner with us one evening? Then we can get better acquainted."

"I would like that," Mark said enthusiastically. "When do you have in mind?"

"What do you think, Zosima? How about Wednesday?"

Zosima smiled in agreement. So did Mark.

"Then it's agreed. Let me tell you how to find my house."

24

This will be a busy week, Mark realized, as he walked to the house of Gentilianus. This merchant is now my fourth client. I'll make his needs my first priority until I get them caught up.

The gate to the courtyard was open, and the businessman was pacing back and forth. He was not a big man, but he carried his body very upright and his movements were stiff and pompous. His greying beard gave him a distinguished look and marked him as a man of tradition. "Good morning, Gentilianus," Mark said as he stepped through the gate.

"Oh, good morning, Mark. Thank you for coming," Gentilianus greeted him.

"Certainly. Let us talk about the first things you need me to do."

"Yes. Umm. Well, the most urgent matter is . . . We'll get to that," the merchant muttered.

Mark waited to hear the instructions.

"Will you prepare letters to my suppliers? I need to tell them that the payment for their last shipments will be slightly delayed. Here are their requests."

Glancing at the invoices, Mark replied, "I can do that. May I ask how long the delay will be?"

Gentilianus furrowed his brow. "I don't know how to word that. You see, one of my largest customers has not paid for his last delivery."

"When did he say he will pay you?"

"Well . . . He . . . He said I would receive it two weeks ago, but that has not happened."

"Have you spoken with him?"

"I have gone to his house. His servant says he is not there."

"Is he on a trip?"

"I don't know. This is most difficult." Gentilianus obviously was very disturbed.

"I see."

The businessman suddenly turned to one side and threw up his hands. "Demetrios and I are friends. We have known each other since we were little boys. Our families dine together. I never thought he would do this to me." Turning back to Mark, he lamented, "I am sorry. I shouldn't bring my personal issues into this."

"If I am to assist you, I must know what we are dealing with. Go on."

"Well... Demetrios has been trustworthy. We have done business for years, but he lives beyond his means. He threw a huge wedding banquet for his oldest daughter. Everyone was invited. The wine, the food—it must have cost a fortune, and now I am suffering the brunt of it."

"You speak as though you are the only one affected. Do you know any of his other creditors?" Mark asked.

"Yes! And they all are happy with Demetrios!"

"That seems odd."

"It is not odd. I am the only one he owes money to, and I am the only Christian. He treats the others royally."

"Oh. This is something I have never encountered before."

"Neither have I." Gentilianus threw his hands in the air again. "I never imagined that after I joined the church, my relationships would change."

Mark had no idea how to proceed. Obviously, neither did his client. "Well, for now, perhaps we should say in the letters that your delay will be short. Can we state that you will remit when you receive their next shipment? That will give you time to work something out."

"I suppose. Yes, you can say that. Please prepare the letters, and I will sign them. Maybe something will change in the next few days."

Mark looked forward to the dinner with Basil and Zosima. On Wednesday the hours seemed like days, until he arrived at their home.

"Ah ha! Good evening, Mark." Basil led him into a cozy living area, which was neat and tidy, but a bit cramped for space. "May I offer you a cup of wine?"

"Of course." Mark glanced at Zosima, who was preparing food. She smiled toward him. *She looks good this evening*, he thought. *She fixed her hair nicely. And do I detect a bit of makeup? Her cheeks look rosy.*

"Here you are, Mark. Fine day," Basil said as he handed Mark a cup.

"Yes. Very fine." As he accepted the wine, he noticed her figure—round and full—though still a young woman. Mark wondered how he would handle the small talk. The children running into the room quickly solved that dilemma.

"Here is Anyte," Zosima introduced her oldest girl.

"The poet," Mark remembered and noticed that Zosima seemed pleased.

"A future poet, perhaps. And this is Baubo," she said, picking up the other child.

Mark looked at the smiling toddler in her arms and made a funny face. At first the girl laughed, but when he wrinkled up his face and snarled, she began to cry and turned toward her mother. "Oh no! I didn't mean to scare her."

"Oh. She can be that way with strangers. She will get used to you."

"I hope so. I like children," Mark said politely.

Basil changed the subject. "Were you ever married?"

"No, not even betrothed. There was a girl in our neighborhood—but just as I completed my apprenticeship, Peter came to our city and asked if I would go with him."

"Oh, too bad."

"Yes. I often have regretted waiting so long. It was a good life with him in Rome. I would like to have love, though—and children."

"I know what you mean," Basil agreed.

"Were you married, Basil?"

"Yes, I was. And we had a little one just about due when my wife got ill. I lost them both as she tried to give birth."

"Oh, no. How terrible. What a shock that must have been."

"Yes. I grieved for a long time. But I will seek a wife again someday, when Zosima remarries and the children have a home. Our family will take one step at a time."

Suddenly, Baubo screeched. "Here, come to Uncle Basil." Mark was relieved for the diversion. He wanted to keep the evening on a lighter note.

"Come to the table." Zosima motioned for them to gather. It was a squeeze with five, but they managed.

Zosima brought up a subject that Mark could handle. "Tell us about your book."

"Well, it is the Good News of Jesus Christ. I have many notes from speeches that Peter gave. I'm combining them into a narrative, starting with Jesus' baptism in the Jordan and continuing through the empty tomb."

"Will you put something in about Mary? I would like to know more about how she felt—as a mother."

"Peter didn't say much about Mary. She was there when they crucified Jesus. I don't know much more," Mark admitted.

"Who would know?"

The question left Mark dumbfounded. He had only felt inspired to write the gospel since the Great Fire, and it had not occurred to him yet to seek further sources. "I have the Passion document and the Sayings of Christ. I would like to speak with others who knew Jesus, but many have died. Mary, I hear, is no longer with us."

"Yes. They say that at the moment of her death, she was lifted straight up to her son," remarked Zosima.

"I hadn't heard that. How do they know?"

"The information comes from the east. They say she just disappeared. There was no grave—no marker."

"That's amazing!" Mark exclaimed.

"Mary was in Ephesus—with John."

"That she and John were in Ephesus, I heard... Maybe I could correspond with John, if he still is alive."

Basil cut in. "I think he may be. He was the last that I heard—blessed with a long life."

"You have given me a great deal to think about. Thank you, Zosima. You have great insight."

"I know what women want to know. The story should not be only about men."

"That is true. Unfortunately, most of what I have in my notes is about men. But I will try to do more research."

"Good. Now—please—eat your food while it is hot."

Mark laughed. "I will, if you tell me more about your music."

He took some bites while the two shared about their musical backgrounds and their plans for the coming Sundays. When her mother asked her, Anyte recited a poem she had memorized. The little girl had been quiet, but when given the opportunity with others listening, she spoke up confidently. Everyone enjoyed the lively conversation, including Baubo.

After dinner, while Zosima put the children to bed, Basil poured three cups of wine. "Zosima can be a very outspoken woman when she gets the chance."

"Yes," Mark answered. "I like that about her."

When she joined them, Basil gave his sister a challenge. "Will you sing a song for Mark and me?"

Surprised to be asked, she replied, "I wouldn't know which one."

Mark supported the idea. "Any song will be fine."

Basil made a suggestion. "How about the Song of Mary?"

"What is that?" Mark asked.

"Zosima will tell you."

"All right. The song is about Mary. After the angel announced that she would give birth to Jesus, she visited her cousin Elizabeth in Judea. And in

Elizabeth's womb, the unborn John the Baptist—on encountering Jesus for the first time—jumped for joy. The song came from the east—from Mary in Ephesus, we think."

Picking up a small lyre, she began to play and sing.

My soul magnifies the Lord, and my spirit rejoices in God my Savior,
  for he has looked with favor on the lowliness of his servant.
    Surely, from now on all generations will call me blessed.
For the Mighty One has done great things for me, and holy is his name.
His mercy is for those who fear him from generation to generation.
  He has shown strength with his arm;
  he has scattered the proud in the thoughts of their hearts.
He has brought down the powerful from their thrones, and lifted up the lowly;
  he has filled the hungry with good things, and sent the rich away empty.
He has helped his servant Israel, in remembrance of his mercy,
  according to the promise he made to our ancestors,
    to Abraham and to his descendants forever.
Holy is his name.

The house was still. Neither man said a word.

Mark was struck by the pure beauty of her elegant soprano voice. They just sat there in awe.

Finally Mark said, "That was so beautiful. Not only is your voice beautiful and your interpretation very authentic, but the words also are so moving. I felt like I was right in the room with Elizabeth and Mary."

"Perhaps you will look into putting more about Jesus' mother in your book."

"Perhaps I will."

That night as Mark lay awake, visions of Zosima singing kept circling in his mind. He loved her angelic voice. What a pure, sweet soul, he thought. What a fine woman and mother she is. But Zosima had given him even more to think about. Tomorrow I must revise my plans for what should go into the gospel.

At daybreak Mark planned to get a bit of food and return quickly to his room. Alexios and Ariston also were up.

"Good morning Mark. Ariston and I were talking about the rain. We are getting plenty of it, even for this time of the year."

"Is it good for the farms?"

"So far, I would say yes. I always watch out for the strong winds, though, this time of the year. Did you enjoy your dinner with Zosima and Basil?"

"Yes. Yes I did. She—they are remarkable people."

"And did you like the children?"

"They are adorable. Anyte recited a poem, and Baubo tried to imitate her."

"The man who marries Zosima will gain a fine family."

"Yes, I agree. And Zosima gave me some important ideas for my writing."

"Oh?"

"She said that I should try to find more information about Mary. I hadn't thought of that," Mark told him.

"John, in Ephesus, should know. Perhaps when the sea is calm again, you could make the trip and speak with him."

"That's an excellent idea. Yes, after the Paschal feast I would like to do that."

"What will you focus on between now and then?"

"I need to step back and look at that."

The bishop thought for a moment. "Perhaps this would be a good time to go through the Passion document. Didn't you say that you have notes from Peter to supplement that text?"

"Yes I do. I can weave the two accounts together in a fresh codex. Then I can go back through the whole text and combine it all."

"That sounds like a good plan. I would like to teach more on the suffering and death of Jesus between now and the Paschal feast."

"Fine. As I get the accounts completed, you can preach on them."

"You can preach on them too. I would like for you to continue. The community likes you."

"Well—when you want me to."

"Good. There is another matter I've been wondering about. We should have some special decoration in the church during this season."

"What do you have in mind?" Mark asked.

"I don't know, actually. Maybe some dry branches, signifying a time of sadness—maybe some color."

Ariston stood up. "I have an idea. I will be right back," and he headed out the door.

He returned beaming, holding up Mark's white toga with the red border. "How about this?"

"Hmm. Red would set off this special season," Alexios remarked.

Mark interjected, "We wore those when we met with important people in Rome. The color added a bit of dignity."

"But here, it could mark the season," Ariston added. "Red is the color of blood—of suffering."

"I like the idea," the bishop said. "Madder is an inexpensive dye. We could make the red borders and sew them on. I'll talk with the others about it. Thank you Ariston."

"You are welcome."

On Saturday, Mark had time to work on the gospel. He opened the Passion document and beside it put a fresh, unused codex.

He began copying the Passion text.

It was two days before the Passover and the festival of Unleavened Bread. The chief priests and the scribes were looking for a way to arrest Jesus by stealth and kill him; for they said, 'Not during the festival, or there may be a riot among the people.' Then Judas Iscariot, who was one of the twelve, went to the chief priests in order to betray him to them. When they heard it, they were greatly pleased, and promised to give him money. So he began to look for an opportunity to betray him.

Hmm. So far, so good.

Then he leafed through his notes of Peter's talks and found some on the Last Supper. So he folded that book open firmly and combined the sentences.

On the first day of Unleavened Bread, when the Passover lamb is sacrificed, his disciples said to him, 'Where do you want us to go and make the preparations for you to eat the Passover?' So he sent two of his disciples, saying to them, 'Go into the city, and a man carrying a jar of water will meet you; follow him, and wherever he enters, say to the owner of the house, "The Teacher asks, Where is my guest room where I may eat the Passover with my disciples?" He will show you a large room upstairs, furnished and ready. Make preparations for us there.' So the disciples set out and went to the city, and found everything as he had told them; and they prepared the Passover meal.

When it was evening, he came with the twelve. And when they had taken their places and were eating, Jesus said, 'Truly I tell you, one of you will betray me, one who is eating with me.' They began to be distressed and to say to him one after another, 'Surely, not I?' He said to them, 'It is one of the twelve, one who is dipping bread into the bowl with me. For the Son of Man goes as it is written of him, but woe to that one by whom the Son of Man is betrayed! It would have been better for that one not to have been born.'

He said to himself, this is going very well—just like I imagined. Then he remembered, there was a story about a woman with an alabaster jar of costly nard, who anointed Jesus lavishly, and he said, *'She has anointed my body beforehand for its burial.'* Where is that? He found the story in his notes. That should go in this section too. Peter didn't say when this happened, but it fits. Then he picked up his pen and wrote the words 'alabaster jar' beside the account of Judas going to the chief priests, so he could fold it in on the next draft.

Now—the Supper. As he copied the short account of the Last Supper from the Passion text, he thought about the contrast between Judas and Jesus. Judas chose to betray, and Jesus chose to forgive. Even though Judas had arranged to hand Jesus over, he ate with him. And even though Jesus foresaw what Judas was going to do, he handed him the bread. Many years earlier, when Mark first saw this contrast, receiving the Body and Blood of Christ took on much more meaning for him. He thought, this truly is Jesus that I am receiving into my body and into my life. If I can forgive in just a small portion of how Jesus forgave, then I may begin to be worthy to be his follower.

Mark went to the pantry, broke a piece of bread, filled a cup with water, and rushed back to his room.

"Now—the arrest," he muttered as he leafed through his notes. Peter was the first to admit that on that very night, he denied knowing Jesus. And Jesus predicted it.

Finding the account in his notes, he wrote,

When they had sung the hymn, they went out to the Mount of Olives. And Jesus said to them, 'You will all become deserters; for it is written, "I will strike the shepherd, and the sheep will be scattered." But after I am raised up, I will go before you to Galilee.' Peter said to him, 'Even though all become deserters, I will not.' Jesus said to him, 'Truly I tell you, this day, this very night, before the cock crows twice, you will deny me three times.' But he said vehemently, 'Even though I must die with you, I will not deny you.' And all of them said the same.

Mark pondered the dilemma, all of them said, 'I will not,' yet all of them fled.

He continued to combine lines from his notes within the structure of the Passion document—Jesus' agonizing prayer in the garden of Gethsemane, the kiss of betrayal by Judas, the arrest of Jesus, and his trial before the Jewish council.

That evening he asked Alexios which passage he wanted to preach on first. The bishop selected the betrayal. "This is for next Sunday; not tomorrow. That will give us plenty of time."

Before going to sleep Mark pondered the rest of the story of Peter's denial. The leader of the apostles had been quite frank.

While Peter was below in the courtyard, one of the servant-girls of the high priest came by. When she saw Peter warming himself by the fire, she stared at him and said, 'You also were with Jesus, the man from Nazareth.' But he denied it, saying, 'I do not know or understand what you are talking about.' And he went out into the forecourt. Then the cock crowed. And the servant-girl, on seeing him, began again to say to the bystanders, 'This man is one of them.' But again he denied it. Then after a little while the bystanders again said to Peter, 'Certainly you are one of them; for you are a Galilean.' But he began to curse, and he swore an oath, 'I do not know this man you are talking about.' At that moment the cock crowed for the second time. Then Peter remembered that Jesus had said to him, 'Before the cock crows twice, you will deny me three times.' And he broke down and wept.

Even Peter, the prince of the apostles, denied knowing Jesus when the hazards mounted. But Peter never denied him again. He went to his death professing his faith in Christ.

Can I be that steadfast? he asked himself. Can I get this done and leave Peter's legacy for the church, or will I falter also? It was a question that remained to be answered with the passage of time.

Putting his book down, he picked up the silver cross that his mother had put in his hand when he sailed to Rome. This must be where I get my strength. He closed his eyes and surrendered.

25

The next morning—Sunday—Mark again looked forward to the liturgy and seeing Zosima. Irana instructed him to be sure to speak with her, so right after the service, he went over to the musicians.

"Hello Basil—and Zosima," he said.

"Hello Mark."

"I want to thank you for the nice dinner the other evening. I enjoyed myself immensely."

Basil responded. "We enjoyed it as well."

"I wish I could invite you, but I have no house."

"Oh, we understand."

Mark turned his attention to Zosima. "The song you sang was beautiful. It keeps going over and over again in my mind."

"I am glad that you liked it."

"I did, very much."

They all seemed at a loss for words. Mark turned and walked away.

"You just walked away!" screeched Irana as she was seated for dinner. "A man who is looking for a wife doesn't just walk away. You keep talking with her until something happens."

Alexios and Ariston listened, but neither said a word.

"Do you not like her?" Irana demanded.

"Of course I like her. What is there not to like. Zosima is an ideal woman."

"Then act like you want her, for God's sake."

"Watch your language dear." Alexios cautioned, but Irana ignored him.

"When a man wants a woman, he courts her. You can do that; can't you?"

"I courted a woman in Corinth. But this is different."

"How is it different?"

Irana was not letting up, and Mark could not formulate clear answers to her questions.

"I don't know why it is different. It just is."

"Well you had better speak more with her next Sunday, or I'll have to take over."

"Don't do that!" Mark hated the idea of having another woman handle his relationship. "I will be more persistent next Sunday."

"You had better be."

The next day Mark went to see Gentilianus. He was hoping the businessman had resolved the delinquency matter with Demetrios. This was not the case.

"That scoundrel has singled me out. He has paid everyone else but me." The man was getting beet red as he explained his dilemma. Mark was at a loss for how to help him.

"I am weighing my options. I can take him to court. I can make the matter public and ruin his reputation. I can hire thugs to rough him up. I can . . ." Each option involved an escalation of hostilities.

Mark responded. "A follower of the Way cannot do those things. Can you not think of a peaceful manner to handle this?"

"A peaceful manner! When a man who has been your friend since boyhood turns against you, what can be a peaceful manner?" the merchant demanded.

Mark couldn't find the words to answer the question. "Try to remain patient."

"How can I remain patient? The whole bunch of them are laughing at me."

"Perhaps you should think about what Jesus might do, if he were in a similar situation."

"Jesus was never in a similar situation! He was a poor preacher, not a businessman."

Mark again was at a loss for words.

"Please come back next week, Mark. I can't think clearly today," Gentilianus told him.

"I will do that."

The week was not starting out well. Fortunately, Mark's other clients had plenty for him to do. It made the time go by quickly, but he made little progress on the gospel.

Thursday evening after dinner, Alexios selected the passage he wanted to preach about on Sunday. Mark agreed that it would be a good choice. "And don't forget. We are wearing togas with red borders," Alexios reminded him.

"I will remember," Mark assured him.

On Sunday morning as people arrived, they immediately noticed the little ribbons of red and the place was abuzz with conversation. Mark waved and smiled to Zosima. She waved, but did not smile back.

The bishop explained how the weeks leading up to Passover were a time to give thought to Jesus' sacrifice. "We will hear accounts from the Lord's passion, and the red color in our midst will help us to keep his martyrdom in our minds and hearts."

When it was time, Mark went to the reading table to proclaim the passage. "As we know, on the night Jesus was betrayed, after supper he went with his disciples to a garden on the Mount of Olives. There, he poured out his heart to his Father. He prayed that the crucifixion he foresaw might pass him by. But seeing no other way, he pulled himself up and went back to his disciples, who had fallen asleep.

Immediately, while he was still speaking, Judas, one of the twelve, arrived; and with him there was a crowd with swords and clubs, from the chief priests, the scribes, and the elders. Now the betrayer had given them a sign, saying, 'The one I will kiss is the man; arrest him and lead him away under guard.' So when he came, he went up to him at once and said, 'Rabbi!' and kissed him. Then they laid hands on him and arrested him. But one of those who stood near drew his sword and struck the slave of the high priest, cutting off his ear. Then Jesus said to them, 'Have you come out with swords and clubs to arrest me as though I were a bandit? Day after day I was with you in the temple teaching, and you did not arrest me. But let the scriptures be fulfilled.'

All of them deserted him and fled. A certain young man was following him, wearing nothing but a linen cloth. They caught hold of him, but he left the linen cloth and ran off naked.

MARK'S PASSION

The bishop's remarks were to the point. "Not one of us here would betray our Lord. We would not pretend to be his followers and then employ a kiss as a sign to those who hate him. No. None of us would do that.

"But the question for us—during these weeks leading to Passover—is, will we flee? Will we desert him when the threat of violence reaches our doors? It is happening, you know, in Rome and in other places. Persecution could come here to Philippi. They are leaving us alone now, but we don't know what may come in the future. We need to use these weeks to prepare our hearts for commitment. We need to examine our dedication and resolve to stay with Christ regardless of the threat.

"None of us wants to be like the young man who was wearing just a linen cloth. When he ran, he left the cloth and ran off naked. Can you imagine what it would be like to be caught naked when it came time to appear before the Lord? Not one of us wants to find ourselves in that position.

"Violence is not the only threat that we may face. There are other hazards that can throw us off our course. I am thinking of challenges like public opinion—pressure—exclusion—loss of friendship—loss of business. Some of our relatives may show disdain to us. We may even find ourselves in some form of persecution—like the Christians in Jerusalem have endured all along.

"Do not flee!

"Do not flee. Make a plan as a family for how you will stand steadfast. If we are firm in our resolve, then nothing can move us. Do not flee.

"These can be grace filled weeks, if we use them to examine our lives and our commitment. Use them well, and when the Paschal feast comes, we all will have great reason to rejoice."

As usual, when the bishop sat down, the room was still. Each in their own way pondered their hopes and responsibilities in light of the challenges the bishop raised.

After the liturgy Mark went immediately to the musicians, but Zosima was not there. Basil was packing up their instruments. "Where is Zosima?" Mark asked.

"She has gone."

"Oh, I was hoping to speak with her."

Basil straightened up and looked him in the eyes. "Zosima and I had a long talk last Sunday, after your short conversation where neither of you knew what to say. There are some missing ingredients here, you know."

"Missing ingredients. What missing ingredients?"

"Well—can you support a wife and two children?"

"Not right now, but when I finish writing the gospel, things will change."

"And do you want to marry a woman who has two children?"

"I haven't thought about it. Anyte and Baubo are fine children."

"You said that they are fine children, which they are. But you did not pick up either of them or speak to them personally."

"My mind was not on the children that evening."

"That was obvious. You are pursuing Zosima, but you have not looked at the practical details."

"This has not progressed to the point where I have to look at practical details."

"Maybe for you it has not, but for a woman in Zosima's position, such things must come first."

"But I am very fond of Zosima."

"She knows that you are fond of her. And she likes you. This makes it all the more difficult for her. That is why she ran out sobbing today."

"She ran out sobbing! Why? For whatever reason why?"

"Mark—you are not being realistic. My sister must have a husband who can take care of her and the little ones. You are in no position to do that. You have no home—you don't even have a steady job. She can't allow her heart to rule in such circumstances. She needs a husband who will provide a home for them."

Mark stood there stunned. "But . . ." He knew that there were no buts. Basil had spoken the truth, and there was no getting around it.

Mark was dreading dinner with his hosts. *Irana will give me a grilling like no other, and I'll have nothing to say.*

But they already knew. Alexios spoke first. "We were sorry to hear about the issue with Zosima."

"How do you know?" Mark asked.

"When I saw her rush away from the assembly, and then you too, I spoke with Basil."

"I have been a fool," he admitted.

"No one would call you a fool. Zosima is a wonderful woman. But perhaps you are not yet ready to seek a wife."

"I know."

Irana added her condolences. "I am sorry for you. Did I pressure you too much?"

"Oh, no." He felt he could not speak the truth.

Ariston came over to Mark, took his hands, and kissed them.

"You are a good friend, Ariston." Wiping his eyes, he said, "You are all good friends."

Mark sat there silently for a few moments, pondering how much he didn't know about life, yet how abundantly the Lord had provided friends to support him.

Then the bishop changed the subject. "Maybe tomorrow we can talk about a plan for you to finish the gospel."

"I can do that right now. Between now and Passover I will finish the Passion. Then I'll look through the Sayings of Christ, and in one more pass I will have it basically done. This summer, if I need to, I can seek out other witnesses, like John the Elder in Ephesus and others. That should do it. . . I will continue to work for the clients I have and get a little more money in my sack. I want to repay you for your hospitality."

"Well, we are happy to help you, and you are helping our community in return."

"Thank you. I will continue to assist in the church as best as I can."

"And you must pray," Alexios added. "We will pray for you too. This work of Christ must be completed."

Back in his room, Mark picked up the medallion of the Holy Spirit and from the depths of his heart he did exactly as the bishop recommended.

The next day Mark went again to the home of Gentilianus. He hoped that the businessman had taken to heart what the bishop said during the liturgy about not fleeing our responsibilities as Christians. When they spoke a week earlier, the merchant who had not paid his debt seemed to have singled Gentilianus out for nonpayment because he had chosen to follow Christ—the only one in their group who had done so. Gentilianus was considering options for retaliation with an ever increasing degree of severity.

The door was open, so Mark walked in. "Good morning, Gentilianus," he said.

"I will not need your services today, Mark. I am going to tell Demetrios that unless he pays me, his children will be slaughtered in front of his eyes, then his wife, and then his own life will end."

"Oh no, Gentilianus. That is not the way to resolve this," Mark insisted.

"It's the only way. I have thought about it day and night. This is the only language he will understand."

"But that is the language of pagans. Not of a follower of Christ."

"They are all pagans."

"But that doesn't make you one."

"I have no alternative," Gentilianus insisted.

"You do have an alternative. You can love your enemies."

"If that was possible, more people would be joining the church."

"But it is possible. You and I have seen many who have lived out this command."

"They did not face the issues that I face."

Mark knew that some faced bigger issues, but he chose not to say it. Instead he brought up a point from the gospel. "When the scribes asked Jesus, 'Which commandment is the greatest,' he answered,

The first is, 'Hear, O Israel: the Lord our God is one; you shall love the Lord your God with all your heart, and with all your soul, and with all your mind, and with all your strength.' The second is this, 'You shall love your neighbor as yourself.' There is no commandment greater than these.'

"Can you do that?" Mark asked.

"I do love God, and I love my neighbors, but Demetrios is no longer my neighbor."

"Everyone is our neighbor—even our enemies."

"That sounds good to the ears, but it does not make sense in the head."

"If we believe in love, then it makes total sense."

"Yes, and if one is abused to the point of hate, then it does not."

"You must find a better way."

The businessman turned and glared at him. "What would you have me do—throw a banquet and let them all feast at my expense?"

"That might be a good idea."

"Rubbish!"

Turning his back, he said coldly, "Get out of my house—and don't come back."

Having no other work that day, Mark sadly went back to his room and continued copying the Passion.

As soon as it was morning, the chief priests held a consultation with the elders and scribes and the whole council. They bound Jesus, led him away, and handed him over to Pilate.

The Jewish leaders were no different than Gentilianus, he thought. They saw only one 'solution' to the problems Jesus was causing—eliminating him. But to keep their own hands clean, they handed him over to the Roman governor. They wanted Pilate to give the order for Christ's death.

He copied the story of Barabbas, the insurrectionist, who was in prison for murder. On the occasion of the festival, the governor had to release one prisoner. The crowd wanted Barabbas, so Pilate asked the people, '*What do you want me to do with the man you call the King of the Jews?*' And they shouted, '*Crucify him!*' So Pilate had him scourged and handed him over to be crucified.

Peter had told a side story about how the guards carried out the order. Mark copied it from his notes.

Then the soldiers led him into the courtyard of the palace (that is, the governor's headquarters); and they called together the whole cohort. And they clothed him in a purple cloak; and after twisting some thorns into a crown, they put it on him. And they began saluting him, 'Hail, King of the Jews!' They struck his head with a reed, spat upon him, and knelt down in homage to him. After mocking him, they stripped him of the purple cloak and put his own clothes on him. Then they led him out to crucify him.

Sometimes it is easy to get a crowd moving in a single direction, he thought. Crowds love to follow, and when it comes to violence, the crowd gives shelter to the individual conscience.

The soldiers mocked Jesus for attempting to confront Roman power—which also was their power—a strength they gained when they enlisted. The army was a perfect place for those who had been abused. It gave them the right to dish it out at will. So they toyed with Jesus, like a cat pawing at a dying mouse.

He copied another passage.

They compelled a passer-by, who was coming in from the country, to carry his cross; it was Simon of Cyrene, the father of Alexander and Rufus. Then they brought Jesus to the place called Golgatha (which means the place of a skull). And they offered him wine mixed with myrrh; but he did not take it. And they crucified him, and divided his clothes among them, casting lots to decide what each should take.

This Simon, who came from the land of Cyrene in the west, was perhaps the most fortunate of all the unfortunates that day. He was only passing by, minding his own business, when the soldiers compelled him to carry the cross for Jesus. Mark wondered if Simon realized the significance of this simple act. He was the only person who did anything to lift the awful burden from Jesus' shoulders. I am sure he received his reward.

Mark quickly wrote how people continued to mock Jesus even while he hung on the cross—people passing by, the priests, the scribes—even one of the criminals hanging in crucifixion derided him.

Then pausing, he wiped his brow and wrote the account of the death.

When it was noon, darkness came over the whole land until three in the afternoon. At three o' clock Jesus cried out with a loud voice, 'Eloi, Eloi, lema sabachthani?' which means 'My God, my God, why have you forsaken me?' When some of the bystanders heard it, they said, 'Listen, he is calling for Elijah.' And someone ran, filled a sponge with sour wine, put it on a stick, and gave it to him to drink, saying, 'Wait, let us see whether Elijah will come to take him down.' Then Jesus gave a loud cry and breathed his last. And the curtain of the temple was torn in two, from top to bottom. Now when the centurion, who stood facing him, saw that in this way he breathed his last, he said, 'Truly this man was God's Son!'

My God, my God, why have you forsaken me? The very human cry of Jesus—who appeared totally forsaken, even by God—escaped from his lips. He looked to be absolutely abandoned. Yet the cry also was the first line of Psalm XXII, which began, as did many Jewish psalms, with a cry of lament—the psalmist pouring out his heart in anguish. But the psalm ended with praise of God, the master of all that lives, who has dominion over all the nations.

To him, indeed, shall all who sleep in the earth bow down;
  before him shall bow all who go down to the dust,
  and I shall live for him.
Posterity will serve him;
  future generations will be told about the Lord,
  and proclaim his deliverance to a people yet unborn,
  saying that he has done it.

Mark rubbed his chin and thought, how fitting that even at this God-forsaken moment, Jesus gave praise to his Father. That is amazing.

I also want to give prominence to the final remark by the centurion. He spoke out the realization, *'Truly this man was God's Son!'* I will put it at the end of the account, for emphasis.

Looking at his notes, he exclaimed aloud, "This must go in here, as well." The passage names some of the women who were at the cross, those who were more loyal to Jesus than the men.

There were also women looking on from a distance; among them were Mary Magdalene, and Mary the mother of James the younger and of Joses, and Solome. These used to follow him and provided for him when he was in Galilee; and there were many other women who had come up with him to Jerusalem.

26

The next week, Mark sent a message to Zosima's brother, asking him to meet privately. The conversation was brief. Mark simply told Basil the truth. "I have given this a lot of thought, and I've spoken about it with the bishop. You were correct to say that I have not acted wisely. The fact is that I did not, and I apologize.

"I am grateful to you for pointing my lack of discretion out to me. Now I can see with clear eyes. I must finish writing the gospel. Then I can begin to make new plans in my life. One priority must precede the other. I hope that Zosima will understand."

"She will understand," said Basil. "She already understands."

"I mean . . . I don't want her to be—uncomfortable—when she sees me."

"There will be some discomfort, because she likes you. But she must be cautious when it comes to matters of the heart."

"I know. . . And I hope we can remain friends."

"We are friends—all of us in the church are friends."

"Yes. So you will explain this to her?" Mark asked hopefully.

"I will explain it."

During the coming weeks there was no more rushing away by either Zosima or Mark, nor any visible signs of crying. But there also were no waves or smiles.

As the Paschal feast drew near, Bishop Alexios attended to the details of the central liturgy of the faith. "No more red! The Passion of Christ has come to its conclusion. Let us decorate for joy. This is the crown of our hopes. Make it look like a celebration."

At dinner he asked Mark to read the passage where Jesus was raised. Mark went to his room and returned with his notes from Peter's speeches. "I'm just getting to this point in my writing. This week I will bring the narrative to a conclusion and then step back and review what needs to be added or revised."

He read the text aloud.

When the Sabbath was over, Mary Magdalene, and Mary the mother of James, and Salome bought spices, so that they might go and anoint him. And very early on the first day of the week, when the sun had risen, they went to the tomb. They had been saying to one another, 'Who will roll away the stone for us from the entrance to the tomb?' When they looked up, they saw that the stone, which was very large, had already been rolled back. As they entered the tomb, they saw a young man, dressed in a white robe, sitting on the right side; and they were alarmed. But he said to them, 'Do not be alarmed; you are looking for Jesus of Nazareth, who was crucified. He has been raised; he is not here. Look, there is the place they laid him. But go, tell his disciples and Peter that he is going ahead of you to Galilee; there you will see him, just as he told you.' So they went out and fled from the tomb, for terror and amazement had seized them; and they said nothing to anyone, for they were afraid.

There was silence at the table, until Mark broke it. "They had to wait until the Sabbath was over before they could purchase spices or go to the tomb. That was the third day."

"We know," said Irana. "But are you just going to end the story with the empty tomb? It feels—abrupt. What about the appearances. Didn't Peter also speak about how Jesus appeared to some of his followers?"

"Peter did speak of appearances. I didn't write any of that in my notes, but he spoke of several occasions where Christ appeared. I just thought that I would end the story at the empty tomb because that is where our stories begin—we learn that the tomb was empty, and our own journey of faith begins at that point."

"That might be too subtle for some. People need to have things spelled out."

"I'll give that some thought."

Ariston asked the next question. "If the women didn't tell anyone about the man clothed in white in the tomb, how did anyone find out that Jesus had been raised?"

"Well, Ariston, that is a good point. Peter liked to dramatize how the women ran away in terror—that's the way he worded it."

"People today are not listening to Peter. They might need clarification," Ariston added.

"Thank you. I will do that. Alexios, what do you think about the ending?"

"I have been pondering how you handled it. A lot depends upon how the reader says the words, and on how the preacher interprets the message. You are correct in saying that we leave the earthly Jesus at the tomb. I'll emphasize this at the liturgy. In our lives we leave the empty tomb and go on with faith in the Risen Christ."

"That's the way I see it, but I can always carry the story further. Perhaps I will."

MARK'S PASSION

The Paschal celebration was all that the bishop had hoped for—faith-filled, joyous, positive—and all the people expressed how happy they were to have invited the Son of God into their lives. It was especially joyful for Mark, as well, because the weeks ahead appeared to hold the successful completion of his work.

At the end of the liturgy he noticed a man crying. It was Gentilianus, the businessman on the verge of taking revenge on the one who owed him money.

Mark went to him. "Gentilianus. Are you all right?" he asked.

"Oh. Mark. Oh, I must tell you. You were right!"

"I was right about what?"

"You were right about love! I did what you suggested. I held a feast last week, and I invited the whole circle. We ate and drank wine, and I saluted Demetrios for the excellent friend he has been since boyhood. Everyone had a great time."

"Outstanding."

"And do you know what? He paid me!" Gentilianus exclaimed.

"He did?"

"Yes he did! This week he paid me in full."

"How wonderful!" Mark said again.

"It is wonderful—and a great relief from a heavy burden. Your idea was amazing."

"It was not my idea to throw the banquet—it was yours."

"What?"

"I only suggested going the pathway of love."

"But did you not suggest the feast?" Gentilianus insisted.

"No. You brought it up. I only said that it sounded like a good idea."

"I don't know. I was out of my mind!"

"This is a happy day, Gentilianus. Let us give the credit to the grace of Christ."

The man threw his arms around Mark heartily. "A happy day to be in the Body of Christ!"

27

As the household was comparing stories about the wonderful events of the Paschal feast, Mark said, "I really should try to get a message to my family, but I don't know anyone who is traveling to Antioch."

"We might try the new process," the bishop answered.

"What is that?"

"I only recently heard about it. It's a way of forwarding packets from one bishop to another. They can be no larger than a codex. You just write the name of the city on the outside and send it with someone in the direction of the destination, and bishops keep passing it along until it reaches where you want it to go."

"Oh. How clever! So if I want to get a message to Antioch, we just send it part way and the process takes over from there."

"That is what I am hearing."

"That's amazing. May I use it to get a message to my family? I want them to know I am safe here."

"You may as well. I know a man who is sailing to Purgamum next week. We can send it with him."

That evening Mark wrote a long letter to his family, telling them how he had escaped the persecutions in Rome, his sojourn to Corinth, and his happy circumstances in Philippi. He outlined how he was working on the gospel and told about a few of the friends he had made, but he didn't mention any of the women. Then he folded the letter and sealed it, and wrote ANTIOCH in big letters across the outside. Then he kissed it as if to say, "Go with God."

This is wonderful, he thought. Even if they can't read, people will recognize the city by the familiar letters. After all, Antioch is one of the largest cities in the empire. I don't know if Evodius still is the bishop now, but whoever it is will find someone to read it to my family. Mark was a happy man.

The next day he spread his resources across the table and assessed the status of his writing. The first draft was finished, right up to the empty tomb. He thought, I have quite a few unused stories in my notes, and in the next draft I will fold them in. When the weather improves I'll try to see John in Ephesus about what else he knows, and maybe I can correspond with someone in the Jerusalem community. Then glancing through the Sayings of Christ he thought, there are many good things in here that Jesus said. I'll need to see where in the narrative some of them fit. And, oh! I must ask about Mary Magdalene. If I can find out where she is living, I also can send a letter to someone in her city. If all goes well, I can complete the gospel by the end of the year.

A few weeks later, at the beginning of the Sunday liturgy, Mark noticed some new faces—a middle-aged couple and a younger woman of striking beauty. He tried not to stare, but each time he looked away his eyes snapped back. Her light brown hair fell gracefully around her slender face, highlighting deep blue eyes that seemed to hold pools of mystery. Her full pink lips, which often puckered into a little pout, cast an inviting allure against her smooth light complexion. I've got to keep my mind on the liturgy, he told himself, but it was to no avail. He was completely taken in by her charms.

But when the bread was blessed and shared, she was gone! The entire family disappeared. Where is she? he wondered. One minute she was here, and the next moment she was gone. Am I dreaming?

He couldn't ask about the new household. People would think it was unseemly. Anyway, he reminded himself, she probably is somebody's wife. But for the next few days, he was haunted by her image.

"Mark. We're having guests for dinner this evening—some potential new catechumens. Will you join us?" Alexios asked.

"Yes, certainly," he responded. Then he thought, I wonder . . .

Mark didn't have to wonder long. When they came in the door, it was her!

"Irana and Mark, this is Ambrose and Sophia, and their soon to be daughter-in-law Kallisto."

Daughter-in-law, he lamented. Oh, no! How can this be? But he said hello graciously.

Alexios stated what Mark was thinking, "Your son is a lucky man."

"We all love Kallisto," said Ambrose.

"When is the wedding?"

"Well, Herodotos, our son, is at sea. The wedding must wait until fall. He loves the sea. In two to three years he will be ready to have his own ship."

"That's wonderful." Alexios said.

Mark's mind raced ahead. *How can I compete with that? He soon will be a successful sea captain, while I don't even have a steady job.* But he couldn't stop staring at her.

Kallisto noticed, and shot back a quick smile while tossing her hair, which again sent his mind spinning.

I've got to get control of myself, he insisted.

Alexios invited everyone to sit down while the wine was poured. Kallisto sat directly across from Mark, where he could see her shapely legs peeking out from below her tunic. *She is even more beautiful than I imagined, but I can't just stare at her. I wonder if she chose that seat on purpose.* She pulled her tunic up a tiny bit higher and slightly parted her lips. *She is so nubile*, he gasped.

"So," began Alexios, "you are wishing to look into our faith?"

Ambrose again responded, "Yes. We have friends who are Christians. What they have told us makes sense. If Jesus was the son of God, then we should learn more about him."

"The Son of God spoke about many things, and we will teach them to you. But most importantly, we are inspired by how he suffered and died for us and how on the third day, he was raised."

"It's hard to believe, but if it is true, then that is definitely compelling."

"Oh, it is true. Mark spent eight years with Peter, who was an eyewitness. Can you add anything Mark?" Alexios suggested.

"Yes," Mark replied. "There were many eyewitnesses besides Peter. He was the leader of the apostles, and I was fortunate to spend those years as his aid and interpreter."

"Did Peter not speak Greek?" asked Ambrose.

"He knew some Greek, but Aramaic was his native tongue. Most of the first followers were from Galilee."

"But how did these *Galileans* know that Jesus really was dead?" Ambrose obviously didn't hold Galilee in very high regard.

"It was witnessed not only by Galileans, but also by important people from Jerusalem. Peter told me about it.

When evening had come, and since it was the day of Preparation, that is, the day before the Sabbath, Joseph of Arimathea, a respected member of the Council, who was also himself waiting expectantly for the kingdom of God, went boldly to Pilate and asked for the body of Jesus. Then Pilate wondered if he were already dead, and summoning the centurion, he asked him whether he had been dead for some time. When he learned from the centurion that he was dead, he granted the body to Joseph. Then Joseph bought a linen cloth, and taking down the body, wrapped it in the linen cloth, and laid it in a

MARK'S PASSION

tomb that had been hewn out of rock. He then rolled a stone against the door of the tomb. Mary Magdalene and Mary the mother of Jesus saw where the body was laid.

Mark added, "So Jesus definitely was dead, and it was validly attested."

"Yes, I see."

Glancing at the others, Mark saw that Sophia was listening intently, but Kallisto was staring at the ceiling. "Do you have a question, Kallisto?" Perhaps he shouldn't have asked.

"Umm. Well. What difference does it make, if he was dead or not?"

"It makes a great deal of difference. If Christ was raised from the dead, it proves that he is the Son of God. And we, his followers, hope to follow him into eternal life. Do you see why that is important?"

"Well, I care more about living now, than what may happen after I die."

"We are happy now by being his followers, and later we will be even happier."

"But I hear that Christians have a lot of rules that you must follow. How can you be happy, if you can't do what you want?" she questioned.

Alexios took over. "You see, Kallisto, we are happy people. I am happy. Irana is happy. Mark is happy. Ariston is happy. Jesus gave us the Way to follow in order that we can be happy and fulfilled. We don't experience it as restrictive, once we make the decision with our hearts. And it helps to be part of a community where you are with like-minded people. Do you see?"

"I guess so."

"It will take some time. That's why we don't ask you to make a commitment while you are learning the faith. Only when you are satisfied and you wish to embrace Christ, will you be baptized."

"That sounds reasonable." Kallisto apparently didn't want to continue talking about it.

"So. Shall we eat?" asked Irana.

As they took their places, Kallisto removed her *stola* and made it a point to sit next to Mark. He kept glancing at her beautiful slender arms, which looked rather naked outside of her tunic. He wondered how it would feel to touch her smooth skin. He couldn't keep his eyes off of her, but he tried to keep it from being obvious.

The conversation continued at the table with Ambrose and Sophia asking questions and Alexios and Irana answering. Kallisto seemed bored, but Mark was so preoccupied with her presence that he hardly noticed. She often kicked her legs, and at times he could feel the motion against his own. It was driving him crazy.

As they were finishing dinner, Alexios asked, "Would you like to join our catechumenate class? There won't be many meetings during the summer, but starting in the fall we will meet every Tuesday evening."

Ambrose answered for his family. "Yes. I believe that will be perfect. And in the fall, Herodotos will be able to join us."

"Good!"

Kallisto had an additional idea. "Would it be possible . . . I mean—I probably am the one who is most in need of instruction, since I have so many questions. Would it be possible for Mark to come by and help me to get a better grasp of the faith?" Mark's pulse raced so fast he could hear it.

"You could do that. Couldn't you, Mark?" asked Alexios.

"Yes. Certainly I can," Mark replied. "I work for clients, and my days are flexible."

"Oh, excellent!" Kallisto grabbed his arm. "I am most grateful. I am slow to catch on, but when I get something, I have it down. Sophia, what day would you suggest?"

The future mother-in-law thought for a moment before replying. "I suppose Tuesdays. You and I usually are home on Tuesdays."

"Is that all right with you Mark?"

"Yes. I can come Tuesday about mid-day."

"Oh, thank you. I'm sure I can become a perfect Christian."

It was no use trying to work on the gospel. Mark had other things on his mind. He did go daily to assist his clients, but beyond that he could think only of Tuesday.

While it seemed like an eternity, the day finally arrived. Mark was incredibly nervous walking the short distance to the house. *She is betrothed*, he reminded himself. *So there is no reason why I should think that anything will come of this. Yet, she did seem interested in me. I guess I won't know until I see her.*

Entering the courtyard, he saw Kallisto and Sophia seated. She was wearing a lightweight linen tunic, and the first glimpse sent his heart racing, like it had at the dinner.

"Hello, Mark," greeted Sophia. "Thank you for coming."

"I am happy to be here," he replied.

Kallisto took charge. "Let's go inside. It's getting hot out here." Mark followed the women into the main living area, which was furnished with two comfortable couches that met at an angle. Kallisto took a seat on the end of one and motioned for Mark to take the other. The arrangement seemed incredibly close to him. "So—teach me about Jesus. Just assume that I know nothing. Start from the beginning."

"All right. Jesus was a Jew, from a town called Nazareth in Galilee," he began. Kallisto was staring directly into his eyes. "He lived at home with his mother until he was about thirty." She began kicking her legs. "When his time came, he began gathering disciples and going from village to village proclaiming the good news that the kingdom of God was near. That's how it started." He had never felt so awkward.

Kallisto studied him with her eyes as he continued the story. Sophia listened for a while and then began kneading some loaves. Mark kept talking, but Kallisto said very little. When Sophia went out to the courtyard to check the fire in the oven, Kallisto leaned forward, closer to Mark. He could detect the scent she wore, which kept him from giving intelligent instruction. He didn't know if she was teasing him or what.

Sophia came back inside, picked up the loaves, and took them out to the oven. Kallisto immediately stood up and jumped into Mark's lap, planting kisses all over his face. "Can you meet me tomorrow? Come at mid-day to the old shrine of Dionysos. No one comes there at that time. Meet me there."

"Yes."

Immediately, Kallisto was off of Mark's lap and back on her corner of the couch as if nothing had happened. Sophia came back inside, and Mark's face got so red that he was sure she would see and get suspicious. But fortunately, she was preoccupied with her tasks.

"Well, Mark. That was a wonderful lesson. I think I will like becoming a Christian," Kallisto exclaimed.

Mark took her outstretched hand, grasped it for a moment, and left.

28

Would he sin with a woman? Before this point in his life he had never considered it—his fantasies always were focused around love and marriage. But that night, as he thought of nothing else but her, he pushed the question out of his mind.

Kallisto, in Greek mythology, was a daughter of the King of Lykaon and a companion of the goddess Artemis. Kallisto swore to preserve her virginity for as long as she remained in the company of the goddess, but she was seduced by Zeus, who had disguised himself. She kept the fact hidden, but in a few months her condition was revealed while bathing, and Artemis, in her fury, transformed Kallisto into a bear.

Kallisto gave birth to a son, Arkas, and when the boy was grown, she one day inadvertently wandered into the sanctuary of Zeus. The king, not knowing the bear's identity, would have killed it for the sacrilege, but Zeus transformed both Kallisto and her son into stars, which can be seen in the constellation Ursa Major.

Mark felt like he was in the story, except it was she who was seducing him!

Even before mid-day, he went to the old shrine. The place was deserted. A new temple of Dionysos had been erected on the other side of the hill, and at this hour very few devotees were there either. Mark was nervous.

He paced the grounds for a long time before he caught the first glimpse of her. He knew it was Kallisto by her light brown hair, and as she slowly strolled up the hill he studied her every motion. "What a goddess she is," he uttered. Today she seemed even more beautiful.

"Have you been waiting for me?" she said coyly.

"Yes." He didn't know what else to say—he was so inexperienced at this.

"I know a place over near those trees. Let's take off our sandals." As Kallisto removed her sandals, Mark did the same. Then she took his arm and leaned her weight on him. "I love to walk barefoot," she said.

The place was secluded by bushes and shaded by the trees. She sat down on the grass and took off her tunic. "Are you going to just stare at me like a schoolboy who has never seen a woman before? Come here."

Mark did exactly as she said, mesmerized by her beauty. He lay down beside her, and feeling her smooth skin against his own, he savored the unfamiliar sensation, not thinking beyond the moment. He had waited years for this day.

Kallisto leaned over him, and with her hair brushing against his face, she pressed her lips to his. Each kiss, each touch, brought him more and more into her grasp. It was beyond his wildest dreams, like having a goddess from a Greek tale make love to him. He let all inhibitions go and gave himself entirely to her.

Time ceased moving. It only flowed around them and drew them tighter. The experience overwhelmed Mark. When they joined they were no longer two, but one. He felt a power within his limbs that he never knew he had. It was like they had been created precisely for one another and for this moment.

They lay there for several minutes as their breathing slowly quieted. It wasn't long before Kallisto began speaking. "Oh, Mark, I need a man in my life." He wanted to rest, but he tried to take in every word, afraid that he might miss something important.

"I need a man every day. I can't stand it when Herodotos goes out to sea. That's not fair to me."

"Yes." He didn't want to talk, but Kallisto did.

"A woman my age knows what she wants. In many ways he is like a little boy, seeking adventure in far off places."

"But you are betrothed."

"That's true. But I may not go through with it."

"What!"

"I said that I may not go through with it. The marriage won't be until late fall. By that time I want to have other options."

Mark didn't know whether to be elated or sad about what he was hearing. He simply was not ready to engage in heavy conversation, and Kallisto was showing no regard for the promises she had made to Herodotos.

"I want a man who will fulfill my every need. He must treat me like a princess and lay gifts at my feet."

"But life has its realities."

"I hate reality! I don't want to deal with reality. I just want one pleasure after another, with every day bringing a new experience."

"Is that possible?"

"Maybe. It certainly was not that way with Zethos."

"Who is Zethos?"

"Zethos was my first husband. He was strong and virile, and his family had money. I thought he would fulfill my desires."

Mark did not want to know any more. He already was having trouble absorbing what he had heard, but he asked, "You were married before. What happened?"

"Zethos divorced me," she said flippantly. "One day he just—divorced me."

"Why? You are a perfect woman."

"Not to Zethos, I wasn't—nor to his father. When I didn't produce an heir, they turned against me. It was only three years, but they turned against me."

"Oh."

"I asked his mother about it. I asked if there was another reason. She said I was selfish. Can you imagine that? She said *I* was selfish, when they were the ones who were thinking only of what I could give them."

"I'm sorry that you were hurt."

"Oh, Mark. You are such a sweet dear. Do you like me?"

"Of course I like you! Why would you ask after what we just had together?"

"I need to ask. I need a lot of reassurance. You see, I have no one else to go to. My parents are dead—my husband and his family have rejected me—my husband-to-be is gallivanting around the sea—Ambrose and Sophia seem to like me, but their values are oceans away from mine. Hold me, Mark."

He didn't say a word as he cradled her in his arms.

"Hold me close."

He pulled her even closer.

"Will you meet me here tomorrow at the same time?" Kallisto asked.

"Yes."

"Good. I'll see you then."

Mark lay where he was as he watched her saunter back down the hill, bewildered by her revelations. Then he put on his tunic and went home.

29

When he got to the bishop's house, Mark immediately told Ariston, "I won't be dining with the family tonight." Taking some bread and oil, he went straight to his room. He didn't want to face any of them.

Conflicting thoughts raced through his mind. Her husband divorced her. She cheats on her betrothed. It doesn't sound like she has much interest in the faith, and she is very self-centered. But oh, how I want to have her in my arms.

For every negative that called for caution, there was a memory of the wonderful afternoon shouting for attention. This was the most exciting day of my life, he told himself. I finally know what it is to be a man. It's like part of me had not yet been born—but now the beast has hatched, and it wants to fill the hunger in its belly.

For a few seconds, he thought about his mission for the gospel—how close he was to finishing. He even picked up his mother's silver cross, hoping to say a repentant prayer for grace. But just as quickly he put it down again. Prying himself away from Kallisto was hopeless.

The next day when he reached the shrine, he saw that Kallisto already had arrived. She was lying on the grass, staring at the sky. Little patches of light were peeking through the trees and dancing across her skin.

"I've been waiting for you," she purred.

"I came at the time you suggested."

"I know. You are such a dear." She motioned for him to sit down. "Sophia is eating with friends—I have lots of time."

He was pleased not to have to hurry. He wanted just to sit beside her and study her enthralling beauty.

"I've been day-dreaming," she announced.

"What about?"

"About being a beautiful princess in a great villa, with dozens of servants attending to my every wish."

"That's nice." A critique of such a self-centered daydream began to emerge in his consciousness, but he pushed it away.

"What do you daydream about?" she asked.

"You!" They both laughed.

"I mean, before you met me, what did you dream about?"

"Well . . . I guess mostly about love—finding a beautiful wife and making a life together."

"We all dream of such things. But in your wildest fantasies, what comes into your mind?"

"That is my wildest fantasy. I have been very busy since my apprenticeship and my travels to Rome. But my greatest desire now is to have true love."

"My greatest desire is to be totally free—like that graceful bird." Just then a brightly-colored bird darted through the branches and a single tail feather floated down to them.

"Oh, how beautiful." She picked up the feather and brushed it against her neck. He was mesmerized, watching her. He wished the feather was in his fingers.

Then suddenly, Kallisto jumped up and began dancing around on the grass. "Do you like to dance, Mark?"

"I haven't had much experience."

"Well, dancing is fun. You are so free. You just move in whatever direction you want, and your body follows. I love the feeling."

Mark watched her dance. He especially liked how she kicked her long, slender legs—childlike, yet graceful. She seemed a totally free spirit.

She came over to him and lay near him, kissing him deeply. "Let's just enjoy this magnificent moment."

After their passion, there was a long silence.

Finally Mark spoke, "Shall we meet again tomorrow?"

"Yes. But I never know what Sophia is going to do on Fridays. She is not predictable then. Come here at the same time—or a little later. That probably will work out."

Again that evening Mark avoided the family. And emerging from a restless night, he went through the motions of his morning ritual—shaving, washing, combing his hair, and getting a bite to eat. He was quite hungry.

At mid-morning, while he was staring at the booklets on his table, he heard a rustle at the doorway. It was Kallisto.

Coming over to where he was seated, she sat on his lap and planted big kisses all over his face. Then she giggled.

"Why did you come here?" he asked nervously, concerned that they would be overheard.

"I told you that Sophia can't be predicted on Fridays. So I came when I could."

"But how did you find my room?"

"You said it was in the back of the living quarters. This actually is nice and private."

"But Ariston will see you."

"I am smarter than you think. I know that the servants go out to shop at about this hour, so I waited until I saw him leave."

"But Irana is here," he cautioned.

"Yes. Doesn't that make it exciting?" she giggled, kissing his neck and ear.

"But this is not my home," he said in exasperation.

"Let's deal with that later." Then eyeing the table, she pushed the booklets off onto the floor and got on it.

He started to pick them up until she asked, "What's more important—those books or me?"

He stared at her, open mouthed.

"I hate this. Sophia is driving me crazy. It's like she is constantly spying on me," Kallisto pouted.

"But you can't just walk in here whenever you want."

"That certainly is correct. So Mark, you simply must get a place of your own. Wouldn't that be better?"

"Better than you sneaking into the bishop's house," he admitted.

"Well, think about it. I'll slip out just as quietly as I came in. Come to the shrine tomorrow."

When she left the room, he just sat there in amazement.

30

Mark picked up the books and placed them neatly on the table. But he wouldn't allow the image of her pushing them onto the floor to have access to his mind.

On Saturday they met again at the shrine, and Kallisto again brought up the subject of his living arrangements.

"Have you thought about getting your own place?" she asked.

"I might be able to do it, but I'll need a few days to work it out."

"Well do something. Sophia is driving me crazy."

Mark changed the subject. "Tomorrow is Sunday. Will you be coming to Eucharist?"

"Oh, I don't really want to go. Can we steal away while the others are there?"

"No. That won't work," Mark told her.

"Why not? After they are gone we can have either house all to ourselves."

"I can't meet you tomorrow. On Sundays I go with the bishop and we have dinner together afterwards."

"There you go again, thinking of other people instead of me. Don't I matter to you?"

"Oh Kallisto. You do matter. I can't express how much you matter to me." Drawing her close and looking into her eyes, he said, "I'll tell you what: Give me a few days to work something out. When we meet on Monday I'll tell you what it is. How does that sound?"

"But that's a whole day without my being with you," she pouted.

"And on Monday, we will be all the more excited about seeing each other."

"Oh, Mark. You can be so difficult."

Sunday morning he prepared to go to the liturgy as usual. He wondered if Kallisto would be there, but this was answered when he saw Ambrose and Sophia without her. Sophia waved and called to him, "Hello Mark. Kallisto is not feeling well this morning."

"Oh," he replied.

"We appreciate your giving her the extra lesson," Ambrose added.

"I was glad to do it," he said, hoping they wouldn't sense how embarrassed he felt.

"I wondered at first—when Herodotos showed interest in joining the Way—if Kallisto would come along. But with your help, she seems to be getting more attracted."

"Oh. With some it takes more time. Let's just watch and see." Mark stepped away, totally conscious of how he had sinned with their future daughter-in-law.

The liturgy began, and Mark found a place among people he didn't know. He hardly noticed the opening prayers, but somehow he mouthed the words.

Zosima led the psalm—her clear soprano voice reverently enunciating each verse. Everyone else focused intently on her melodious voice and how she captured the mood of the sacred prayer. That it was a voice he once longed to hear, fought for his attention. But his mind was too far away to notice.

When people began moving forward for communion, he instinctively went with them. And he received, even though he knew that he first should have prayed to God about his sins.

"You seemed preoccupied this morning," Irana noticed at dinner. "Is anything wrong?"

"Nothing—really," he stammered.

"You'd better not be having another woman on your mind."

Mark blushed.

Alexios changed the topic. "I told Irana and Ariston—I'll be going over to Thessalonica for a conference. You said you'd like to get a message to that seaman. What was his name?"

"Who?"

"The seaman who brought your things."

"Timon," Mark replied.

"Ah, yes, Timon. Well. . . I could ask the bishop about him, if you would like."

"Oh, yes. That would be good. Just say that I am grateful for his saving my belongings."

"Anything more than that?" Alexios asked.

"Oh, that I am very grateful."

"Are you wondering if he became a Christian?"

"Of course. Yes. Please ask about that, too," Mark added.

"I will do it."

"And oh, by the way," Mark blurted, "I've been thinking about moving. I should be getting a place of my own."

Irana reacted first. "Don't you like it here? We hope you have been comfortable."

"Of course I like it here. You have given me so much—and I am sincerely grateful. It's just that . . it's time for me to take responsibility for myself. I want to take steps toward having my own household."

Alexios responded. "You are welcome, Mark, to stay with us. But I can understand how you may want to begin making a transition. Do you have a place in mind?"

"I have not yet looked, actually. I've just been thinking about it," he admitted.

"Yes. Well, let us know."

"When are you leaving for Thessalonica?" Mark asked, wanting to change the subject.

"Tuesday."

"Well, I think I will retire to my room."

Walking into his room, Mark almost screamed. "How did you get in here?"

"Shh." Kallisto came up and kissed him.

"Someone is going to see you!" he hissed.

"And if they do, then our secret is out." She put two pats on his nose.

"No!"

"Well, anyway, guess what? I found an ideal place."

"You found a place. What do you mean?" he asked.

"I found a place. It's not far from where I am now. It has a private entrance and everything."

"Did you already inquire about it?" Mark was not happy.

"Of course. And do you know the best part?"

"What?"

"Guess," she teased.

"How can I guess? It could be anything."

"All right. Now hold your breath." Mark did. "It has a bed!" Kallisto squealed with delight.

"A bed!"

"Yes. And a couch and a table—it's perfect!"

"I told Alexios and Irana that I might be moving," Mark revealed. "I'll look at it tomorrow."

"No! Come now. Someone else might take it."

"How are we going to get out of here?"

"Very quietly. Follow me."

He did follow her, and he agreed to take the apartment. He told the owner he would bring the money in the morning.

Walking alone back to the household, Mark began wondering about the cost of the arrangement. Kallisto made a lot of demands. If there was to be a future, there also needed to be more income.

As he entered the courtyard, Ariston shouted, "There he is!"

"Where have you been?" asked Alexios.

"I was just out for a walk."

"Well—there is a man here who wants to see you. He said he would wait. We showed him into the living area."

"Oh, thank you. I'll go and see what he wants."

Ariston added one more fact. "He is an Egyptian."

The man was middle-aged, short and plump—with bronze skin, though he appeared to stay out of the sun. His head was completely bald, but his eyebrows were full and slanted up in a distinctively Egyptian manner. "Hello. You are Mark? I am Karpos. We have a matter to discuss."

"Sit down, please. Tell me what it is."

"I represent a large assembly in my country. We heard that you have a narrative story of Jesus, which you call the gospel."

"I am working on it. Yes," Mark admitted.

"Very good. Well, we believe that having a copy would enhance our evangelization. Can that be arranged?"

"When I am finished, you may have a copy. I am writing it for the whole church."

"Well—you see—we very much would like to have it put to work in our midst at this time," Karpos stated.

"At this time it is only a draft. There is much more to add," Mark told him.

"We would be happy to work with what you have."

"I have never considered that. I want it to be finished, you know?"

"Of course. Well. Perhaps we could have the draft now and receive the completed copy when it is ready."

"I don't know about that," Mark hesitated.

"We can pay—of course. I am authorized to be most generous," Karpos assured him.

"Oh, I've never thought about charging for the gospel. It has no price."

"But you deserve compensation—as a scribe—for making the copies."

Mark considered his point, saying, "I suppose that is true. Making copies should be worth something for the time."

"We could offer quite a sum. How long will it take you to make a copy? We must leave in a few days."

"When are you leaving?"

"Sunday morning—the first day of the week."

"I would have to work day and night to make a copy in that time," Mark explained, "and it wouldn't be perfect."

"We could pay up to one hundred denarii."

"One hundred denarii! That would be several month's pay."

"But your time is valuable. Will you do it for us?" Karpos pleaded.

"I guess so."

31

Mark wanted to stay in his present room until he delivered the manuscript, but Kallisto wouldn't hear of it. "That would be five whole days when I couldn't see you. That's money wasted." So Mark gave in. After making the deposit and wishing Alexios a safe trip, he brought his things to the apartment.

No sooner had he begun making the copy for the Egyptians, when Kallisto showed up. "Oh, Mark. You are such a dear for moving so quickly. Now I know you like me."

"You already know that I'm infatuated with you, and you use it to your advantage. But you must understand that if I am going to produce the copy on time, I have to work on it constantly."

"Well! You are just going to have to make some time for me," she pouted.

"I have to give them priority. They are paying one hundred denarii." Instantly, he regretted saying the amount.

"One hundred denarii!" she squealed. "Oh Mark, you are going to be such a success. Come here!"

She leaped onto the bed and struck a comic-seductive pose. The copy would wait a few more minutes, but after he satisfied her need, he pleaded to let him concentrate on the work.

The plea had some effect, but she came to his apartment on Tuesday and again Wednesday.

"When you get the money, are you going to buy me a present?" she asked.

"I suppose."

"You suppose! Let's have a little more enthusiasm. Tell me. What kind of gift will you buy me?"

"I haven't had time to think about it."

"How about a jeweled necklace? Would you like to see me with a new necklace? I will look so elegant."

Mark agreed with everything. He just wanted to complete the copy.

"You know, Mark," she said, "if you can make that kind of money, we should begin talking about our future."

"I will talk about anything . . . after I have delivered the copy." He pushed her out the door and got back to work.

There were two distractions on Friday. The first was Ariston, saying that Mark's clients had been asking about him. Their work was stacking up. "Next week!" he told him. The second was Kallisto. She wanted to talk, but Mark had too much to do. "I must finish the copy by tomorrow afternoon. You must stay away."

"Will you spend Sunday morning with me?" she pleaded.

"Yes. Just let me complete the transaction," he demanded.

Kallisto kept her promise, and Mark devoted himself to the copy. He hardly ate or slept, and did not shave, but by some unexplainable luck he managed to finish just as the Egyptians knocked at his door.

"Hello, Mark," said Karpos. "This is Draco, one of our elders."

"I am pleased to meet you. Come in." Draco seemed a bit older than Karpos, with a thin face and dark eyes. His straight hair was thick and black, and a small scar above the left side of his lip gave him a chilling appearance.

Karpos continued. "Do you have the copy for us?"

"I just finished. I have not yet had time to check it over."

"Hmm. What do you think, Draco?"

The older man began to speak in very measured words. "May I look at it, please?"

"Of course." Mark handed him the copy.

"The lettering looks good."

"It would have been even better, if I had had more time."

"And let's see . . . the pages . . ." Mark held his breath as the document underwent inspection.

"Does it meet your expectations?" he asked.

"We are leaving, so it must. Thank you for making it for us."

"You are most welcome."

The men stood up, as if to leave. Mark didn't think he needed to say it, but he did. "The payment?"

"Yes, of course." Draco counted out six denarii and laid them on the table.

"But," said Mark. "Karpos offered a greater sum."

"Karpos gets carried away. This is what we can pay."

"But . . ." Mark was speechless—his legs and arms were frozen. And he remained that way as the two men walked out the door.

Then he sat down on the bed and sobbed.

32

At some point during the fretful night, he must have fallen asleep. A fist banging on his door woke him. Still in a daze, he lifted the bar and opened the door. Kallisto was standing there beaming.

"Yuck! You are a mess. Why aren't you ready for me?"

"I had a bad night."

"I can see that. Well, let me in, and you get cleaned up."

Mark realized that he must be a sorry sight. "I will. Come in. What hour is it?"

"It's mid-morning. Ambrose and Sophia went to the church. I came right away, just as we planned."

"Oh, yes." The entire scenario raced back through his mind—the stress-filled week, his whisking her out on Friday, and the fateful meeting with the Egyptians on Saturday.

"Maybe when I see the money I will want you just the way you are."

"It's on the table."

Turning to the table, she picked up the six coins. "Where are the rest?"

"There aren't any more."

"What! What about the hundred?"

"They didn't pay a hundred."

"They didn't pay . . . Do you mean to tell me that this is all you got?" she screamed.

"That is what they gave me."

"And you accepted it! How could you?"

There was no answer.

"You let them have the copy for six denarii. I can't believe it. How are you going to pay for my jeweled necklace?"

He just stood where he was—in shock—like a helpless ass that had stumbled beneath its burden.

"You are so selfish sometimes. I was counting on you to take care of me." Then flinging the coins at his face, she stormed out the door.

He had all of Sunday to think his situation through, but he did not. Instead he just wallowed in a pitiful stupor. At one point he entertained the thought of severing the relationship, but the memory of having her body close to his ended that.

On Monday morning he got up and washed. *I've got to pull myself together*, he told himself. He did his best to shave, but cut himself twice—his hands were shaking.

I'll go to my clients, he thought as he found a clean tunic. *Their work is piling up.*

After combing his hair, he opened the door and prepared to leave.

"Mark. May I come in?" It was Ariston.

"Yes, my friend. Come in. Have a seat. I have nothing to offer you."

"I brought you some food." Opening a basket, the servant pulled out some bread and hummus.

"Oh, thank you. Actually I'm starving."

"Then eat."

Mark took two big bites and chewed them hungrily. Then he took two more. Ariston poured some water into a cup and handed it to him.

"Thank you." He took several gulps—then bit off another hunk of the bread.

"What is happening to you, Mark?"

"What do you mean?"

"I mean, what is happening to you? You have been a different person these past two weeks."

"I have been—busy."

"Yes. I have observed you. The woman is very attractive. And something has changed in you."

Mark wanted to deny the accusation, but he couldn't find the words.

After some silence, Ariston again spoke. "It might be best if you came back to the house."

"Oh. I couldn't do that."

"You could. And you should. This is not good for you here."

"But I need my own space."

"You only need your own space because of the woman. Before you met her you were satisfied."

"That is true. But I have new needs now."

"You think that you have new needs. But they are not your true needs. You have not been following your calling. You didn't even come to Eucharist yesterday. Irana asked if I had seen you, but I lied to her."

Mark was silent.

"This is not right for you. You were called to be a servant of the Lord. I am a servant; I know."

"But I must have Kallisto. I have never known such joy."

"Do you call this joy? Your face is bloody and your hands are shaking. You have cut yourself off from your friends. The fact is, Mark, you are a mess."

"But I need her so much."

"Do you not believe that I understand a man's needs? I see other men with their women, and I think, I would like that too. But I know my place. And with the bishop and Irana—and with Jesus—I have true joy."

"It is not just about sex. I have tasted love—and power."

"You can call it love, if you need to. And you can lust for power, if you choose. But it is not your calling."

Mark again was speechless. The truth was sinking in.

"You once told me about James and John—how they asked Jesus for power when he came into his glory. Do you remember the story?"

"It's in my notes."

"Will you please read it to me?"

Mark hesitated, but agreed. Then picking up the book and leafing through the pages, he found the passage.

James and John, the sons of Zebedee, came forward to him and said to him, 'Teacher, we want you to do for us whatever we ask of you.' And he said to them, 'What is it you want me to do for you?' And they said to him, 'Grant us to sit, one at your right hand and one at your left, in your glory.' But Jesus said to them, 'You do not know what you are asking. Are you able to drink the cup that I drink, or be baptized with the baptism that I am baptized with?' They replied, 'We are able.' Then Jesus said to them, 'The cup that I drink you will drink; and the baptism with which I am baptized, you will be baptized. But to sit at my right hand or at my left is not mine to grant, but it is for those for whom it has been prepared.'

Mark stopped reading and stared at Ariston. "Is this about me?"

"Perhaps. Is there more?"

"Yes."

"So continue."

When the ten heard this, they began to be angry with James and John. So Jesus called them and said to them, 'You know that among the Gentiles those whom they recognize as their rulers, lord it over them, and their great ones are tyrants over them. But it is not so among you; whoever wishes to become great among you must be your servant, and whoever wishes to be first among you must be slave of all. For the Son of Man came not to be served but to serve, and to give his life as a ransom for many.'

Mark sat down and began to sob from the depths of his being. Ariston sat beside him and put his arm around his shoulders. Mark turned toward the servant and placing his face against his chest, he allowed the floodgates of guilt and grief to burst open.

When the tears subsided Ariston asked, "Will you be coming home again?"

"Yes," Mark answered. "But first there is something I must do. And I will do it right away."

After walking the short distance to the home of Ambrose and Sophia, he saw Kallisto seated in the courtyard. "Pssst! Kallisto," he called to her when she saw him.

Putting his finger in front of his lips, he motioned for her to come out. "Can you come with me for a few minutes? You can tell Sophia you went for a walk."

She followed.

When they were inside of the apartment, he turned to her. "This is over. I don't have any nice way of saying it. But this is over. I am moving back in with Alexios."

"But Mark. We have such great possibilities ahead of us. We can be good for one another."

"It is not about you. This decision has nothing to do with you."

"Then what is it about? Have I not pleased you?"

"Oh, Kallisto. You have given me more pleasure than a man can hope for in a lifetime. But I have thought about my calling, which is to complete the gospel for Christ."

"For Christ! Do you mean to tell me that you are throwing me away for a dead man?"

"The Son of God is more alive than you will ever know. He is my Lord and my Savior. I can do nothing else, but to continue my service to Him."

"You've got to be joking."

"I am not. I've never been more serious. I know what I must do."

"You . . . You—Lion! You are not a man, but a lion. You wander around seeking a mate, and when you are finished with her you just fly away."

"That is not how I want it to be."

"Well, that is how I see it. You are just as selfish as Zethos. Only Zethos had a real reason—he wanted an heir. You just want to serve your son of god."

"That is what I want, and it's what I will do." He moved toward her to touch her hand, but she ran out.

"Maybe I am a lion," he thought. "But a lion does what he has to do."

33

Early Tuesday morning Ariston came to Mark's apartment carrying a basket. "Did you come bringing food, or are you checking to see that I am on my way home?"

"Both. I have bread, oil and figs."

"That sounds excellent. Come in."

"Did you finish with the—other matter?"

"Yes. It was awkward, but I believe that chapter in my life is over."

"You are a faithful steward, Mark."

After eating, Mark packed his bag and told the owner of the house he was not staying. The man was not happy. He and Ariston walked together back to the home of the bishop, where he placed the bag in his room.

"I need to go to each of my clients today. Don't expect me back until evening. Do you know when Alexios is coming home?"

"Probably today. The conference ended on Sunday."

"You can tell him . . whatever you want."

Ariston nodded, then Mark embraced him sincerely. "You are a good friend," he said, wiping tears from his eyes.

When Mark returned in the late afternoon, the tall bishop was sitting in the courtyard. Seeing Mark, he stood and opened his long arms. The rebellious writer immediately accepted the invitation and sobbed on his chest.

"Does Irana know too?"

"Yes. It will be all right, Mark."

"I have messed up my life. I have rebelled against God. I have deserted my calling."

The experienced bishop just let him speak.

"I have fallen from grace. God gave me the grace to live a Christian life, and with the help of that grace I was succeeding. But then I fell."

Alexios patted his back.

"She was so alluring . . . and I was so stupid."

"Now, there." He held Mark warmly in his strong arms.

"I have sinned against God and against the church. How will I ever be able to face those people?"

"Everyone makes mistakes in their life, including 'those people.' The important thing is to learn and not repeat the error."

"I sure seem to learn the hard way." They both laughed.

"Would you like to talk about it more?"

"Maybe in a day or two. I'm still sorting things out. I am very grateful that you are so understanding."

"I will not give up on you. I don't believe that Jesus gives up on us either. He forgives and forgives."

Mark sat down. The truth of the bishop's statement caused his legs to tremble.

Alexios gave him all the time he needed before speaking. "Are you all right now?"

"Yes."

"Good."

"And also . . . I also believe that there will be true love in my life one day. I need true love, and Christ knows I want to have true love. This never could have been it. The woman I marry will love Christ the way I do."

"Yes. I believe that real love is in your future."

Mark was grateful for the prediction.

At dinner the bishop said to Mark, "Oh. You may be pleased to know that your friend Timon became a Christian."

"Oh, really? That is wonderful!"

"He and his family attended the classes through the winter. They were baptized together."

"I am so glad."

"Timon also is grateful. I spoke to him briefly after the Sunday liturgy. He was in port, and said to tell you how much your encouragement meant to him. He says it makes the time at sea away from his family go easier now, since Jesus is at his side."

"That is beautiful. He is a fine man. I had hoped that he would contact the church in Thessalonica."

A little later the bishop sat back and added, "There is other news from Thessalonica—not as happy as what I told you earlier."

"What is that?" asked Mark.

"We bishops talked about it a great deal. We don't know what to make of it, but there appears to be growing rebellion among the Jews."

"Really? What happened?"

"Rumors are that Rome will make some sort of retaliation against the stabbings and banditry that have plagued the ruling class in the country. The Jews appointed a commander to organize the resistance groups in Galilee into an effective fighting unit. They want to be prepared to fight force with force."

"Oh no! They can't possibly win."

"Probably not. They are led by a twenty-eight year old—Joseph ben Mattathias."

"I haven't heard of him."

"He is from a high family, and he has been to Rome, so he should know better. Apparently he was dazzled by the wealth and power in the capital and shocked to see Judea falling into a state of anarchy."

"Is this Joseph a capable leader?"

"No one knows. The procurator, Gessius Florus, is faltering. He has been heavy-handed, but has failed to pacify the city. They say he took money from the temple treasury to recover a shortfall in Judean tax payments. The Holy City is in an uproar. There were riots, but the High Priest managed to persuade Florus to pull most of his troops back to Caesarea Maritima."

"This is likely to get bloody."

"It already is bloody. The tensions and frustrations of the decades of Roman rule are coming together in demands for freedom and justice. The bandits and raids have wreaked havoc in the agricultural areas. In Jerusalem, construction work has slowed because of reduced tax payments. Everyone hates the temple authorities for their collaboration, and on top of that, the Zealot party is pressing for an independent Jewish state."

"Rome will never allow that."

"Of course not. But that's not stopping the Jews from preparing for war."

Mark stood up. "I know exactly what you are talking about. There was a Christian in Corinth—Levi—who advocated just what you are saying. He even moved back to Jerusalem. His brother, Jacob, was more peace-loving. They went together, moving their whole families. I don't know what happened after that."

"And no one knows what will happen next. We bishops are wanting to stay abreast of the news."

"Of course. This can come to no good."

The next afternoon when Mark returned from his clients, Alexios had some different news. "Ambrose spoke with me today. He said that they are not going ahead with the catechumenate."

"Why not?"

"He said it's because you made advances toward his future daughter-in-law. If that is the way Christians behave, he wants no part of it."

"How could she have said such a thing?"

"When a woman feels scorned, she can say most anything. I told him I was sorry, and if they should wish to join later they will be most welcome."

"What did he say to that?"

"He seemed more concerned that I should punish you in some way. I didn't tell him the other side of the story."

"No. That would not have been advisable. I was complicit too."

"I know, but—I was not surprised."

"Neither am I."

That evening, after dinner as they sipped their wine, Mark told the family that he wanted to speak with them about the affair. They said it was not necessary, but he said he needed to talk it through.

"I have learned a great deal about myself through this episode," he began. "I was destined to blunder because I had no experience with sex. And she made me feel manly and powerful, beyond anything I had felt before. But there was an additional factor—that's what I want to talk about this evening."

They waited while he gathered his thoughts.

"I learned something about money as well. I've had no experience with that either." They laughed.

"There were these Egyptians. Did you tell them about them, Ariston?"

"I only said that you met with the man named Karpos. What happened?"

"He offered me a lot of money, if I would give them a copy of the gospel. I protested, saying it was not finished, and I would give it free to the church. But they were in a hurry because they were sailing back to their country. Karpos pushed a big figure at me for a copy—one hundred denarii—and Kallisto began pulling on me about ways to spend it. So I agreed. I managed to make the copy in only one week; I don't know how I did it. But when the time came for the exchange, their elder gave me only six coins."

"So you were cheated," observed Irana.

"Being cheated was not the problem. I didn't deserve that much, anyway. The issue was how I felt from the allure of easy money. It consumed me as much as the beauty of Kallisto—maybe more. I can see why people get caught up, chasing after ever increasing sums."

Alexios understood. "You are learning a great lesson in following Christ. The lure of wealth can be an obstacle to grace."

"Exactly! That's how I experienced it."

"That's why Jesus spoke so much about money."

"Yes! That's right!" After pausing for a moment Mark continued, "There is a story in my notes. I want to get it. Will you wait for me?"

"Yes." Alexios said. "Go and get it."

Mark ran to his room and came back leafing through his notes. "It's in here someplace. I haven't yet folded it into the gospel. Yes, this is it.

As Jesus was setting out on a journey, a man ran up and knelt before him, and asked him, 'Good Teacher, what must I do to inherit eternal life?' Jesus said to him, 'Why do you call me good? No one is good but God alone. You know the commandments: You shall not murder; You shall not commit adultery; You shall not steal; You shall not bear false witness; You shall not defraud; Honor your father and mother.' He said to him, 'Teacher, I have kept all these since my youth.' Jesus, looking at him, loved him and said, 'You lack one thing; go, sell what you own, and give the money to the poor, and you will have treasure in heaven; then come, follow me.' When he heard this, he was shocked and went away grieving, for he had many possessions.

"That's what happened to me," Mark admitted. "The lure of money was so seductive. It was enticing me away from the kingdom of God."

"And you learned your lesson without walking away sad," noted the bishop.

"Yes, but there is more.

Then Jesus looked around and said to his disciples, 'How hard it will be for those who have wealth to enter the kingdom of God!' And the disciples were perplexed at these words. But Jesus said to them again, 'Children, how hard it is to enter the kingdom of God! It is easier for a camel to go through the eye of a needle than for someone who is rich to enter the kingdom of God.' They were greatly astounded and said to one another, 'Then who can be saved?' Jesus looked at them and said, 'For mortals it is impossible, but not for God; for God all things are possible.'

Alexios spoke again. "Nothing is impossible with God. What seems beyond human comprehension can be achieved with the help of God's grace. Money is not the evil, but money can be an obstacle to our being open to receive grace."

"Exactly."

"One thing I don't understand," said Ariston. "How can a camel go through the eye of a needle? It is so big, and a needle is so small."

"That is how Jesus made his point," replied the bishop. "Only with grace is any achievement possible."

They all laughed.

Mark added, "And with God's grace, I will complete the gospel."

34

Later in the week, when the work with his clients was caught up, Mark went back through his notes of Peter's speeches. Beside every passage that he had not yet transcribed, he made a symbol showing how he might use it within the gospel. Then he began working on a new expanded draft, making progress each day.

In July there was news that Menahem ben Judas had captured the mountain fortress of Masada. How he managed to trick the Roman soldiers stationed there to open the gates, was anybody's guess. But in the process he garnered vast stores of weapons, which he distributed to those Jews who would use them. In addition, Eleazar ben Hananiah, the son of a former High Priest, was convincing the council to not accept any more sacrifices from foreigners. This bit of intrigue would mean that the temple could no longer accept payment and perform the twice-daily sacrifices for Nero. In August the council approved the measure, and Rome considered it an open act of rebellion.

Also in August a packet came to the bishop's house. Alexios asked, "Is this for you, Mark? It is from Antioch, and this looks like your name."

Opening the packet Mark sat down and looked through the contents. There was a letter from his brothers and one from the bishop, Evodius.

"I'll look at the family letter first," he decided.

Habib and Palut, your brothers in Christ, who have kept the faith and the memory of our beloved father—to Mark, his youngest son and our flesh and blood: peace, hope, and love in our Lord, Jesus Christ.

We were very grateful to receive your recent letter and are joyful that you are safe in Philippi. Our mother has worried about you since your previous word. She is getting on in years and is growing weaker all the time. If it is possible for you to visit soon, it will mean a great deal to her. And we would love to see you also.

She is very proud that you served Peter well and are writing a gospel from his teachings. Peter was a good friend to her and father.

We now have fifteen offspring between your sisters and us. Our homes are close together, and while mother lives with Habib, we all see her daily. She especially enjoys the grandchildren, and they all love her.

Have you married? Have you children? Since you did not mention them, we assume not. Antioch is a fine city—the church is flourishing. The family business is doing well—everyone wants more varieties of cheese. Should you wish to settle here and help us with the business, we will make a place for you.

Please write. And if you can come for a visit, we will make it a celebration.

We pray that the Lord, Jesus Christ will look after you and keep you safe. Grace be with you.

After kissing the letter and pressing it to his heart, he read it aloud to the household.

"Did you say there also is one from the bishop?" asked Alexios.

"Yes. Apparently Evodius still is bishop. He was bishop when I left Antioch ten years ago." He read the letter out loud.

Evodius, a bishop of Christ Jesus by the will of God the Father—to Mark, my child in the Lord: grace, mercy and peace.

I am grateful to God for the many years that he has permitted me to preside in this city. I pray for your family daily. If you have only half of the faith of your father, you are indeed a worthy man.

The memory of the day you sailed away with Peter is etched in my mind. And I have heard such good reports about you. Habib and Palut showed me your recent letter. The project of composing a narrative of our Lord Jesus Christ sounds promising. I hope to see it while I am still here. It will be so helpful for instructing our inquirers and for sharing Christ's wisdom in our liturgies. The church is expanding rapidly; we now have six presbyters and nine deacons. Most of them have learned to read, and having the gospel narrative will help us to preach a consistent message. Should you wish to work on the text in Antioch, I will do all that I can to assist you.

With the growing unrest in Jerusalem, you may wish to come closer to the unfolding events. Antioch will stay out of this conflict. It is up to the Jews to determine their own path. So you will be safe here, even though our streets are full of troops. I am concerned about the Christian community in the Holy City. It would be terrible, if they got caught in the middle.

I am getting old now. Perhaps I will go to the Lord soon. My prayer is that Ignatius will succeed me in the episcopacy.

Greet Alexios and his family. Tell them that I send my love. The Lord be with your Spirit.

When he finished reading, the room was silent. They were pondering what the coming months might bring.

35

Everyone agreed that Mark should go to Antioch before winter.

The goodbyes were emotional—people had been very good to him. But even though the voyage cost almost all that he had saved, Mark felt assured that this leg of his journey was right. He was going home.

The trip took several days. He didn't try to write while on board; the new, expanded draft was complete, and he simply wanted to use the time to reflect and pray.

As the ship passed Rhodes and began heading east, he thought a great deal about his family. It had been ten years since he had seen them. Each time he reread the letter from Habib and Palut, images from his youth fluttered through his mind. He did his best to imagine what those he knew might look like today, especially his mother. Unfortunately they had said nothing about Lydia and her family, and the total absence of information about the former friends left him anxious.

It was foggy as the ship passed Cyprus. He was getting very close.

Perhaps because of the monotony, he pulled his original notes out of his bag and studied the remaining passages that he had not yet folded into the story. What am I missing? he wondered. These little episodes mostly are about healings and casting out demons. And there is continuing conflict between Jesus and the authorities. Peter thought these were important. But I don't quite know how they fit.

He hoped that he would find the solution in Antioch.

Since ancient times there had been a city on the Orontes River, along the Silk Road and the Persian Royal Road, with geographic, military, and economic importance in the spice trade.

Alexander the Great once camped on the site and dedicated an altar to Zeus. After Alexander's death, when his generals divided up his territories, Seleucus I Nicator founded Antioch on a spot where an eagle—the bird of Zeus—carried a piece of sacrificial meat.

The new city was laid out in a grid plan, like Alexandria. Two great colonnaded streets intersected in the center. The external appearance of Antioch was impressive, but the city needed constant restoration because of the many earthquakes that continuously shook the area.

Antioch was populated by a mix of Greeks, Macedonians, and Jews. During the late Hellenistic period and early Roman period its population reached a peak of over a half million, and it became the third largest city in the Empire, after Rome and Alexandria.

The Romans favored the city right away, seeing it as a suitable hub for the eastern part of the Empire. Julius Caesar visited the city and confirmed its importance. Tiberius built two long colonnades on the south, and Agrippa enlarged the theatre.

Antioch also was a chief center of early Christianity. Because of the large Jewish population, the city attracted missionaries—first Peter and later Paul. Its converts were the first to be called Christians.

When Mark got off the ship the first thing he did was kiss the ground. He stomped his feet loudly on the stone pavement as if to say to the city, "I am home!" and he danced for joy.

He was a bit nervous as he walked the familiar streets to his boyhood home. No one knew of his arriving. His heart raced as he peered in through the gate. A lone figure was seated in the courtyard, his mother.

After studying her face for a few moments, he quietly stepped toward her; she appeared to be napping. Then kneeling in front of her, he gently said, "Hello mama."

The woman opened one eye, then the other. Then she let out a shriek and jumped to her feet. Shouting his name in Syriac, then in Greek, then again in Syriac, she threw her arms around her son. Big tears flooded from her eyes.

Mark attempted to hold back his, but they poured out like gushing springs. "Oh, mama—mama—I have missed you so."

His mother managed to shout his name again through her sobs, and soon other faces appeared, all of them shouting his name and smothering him with hugs. "Go," she said to one of her grandchildren. "Go tell all the others that Marcos is here." The child of about twelve immediately ran out. Mark did not know the girl. "Don't you recognize Lysandra? She is Habib's. She was just walking when you left. They all have grown big now."

Within minutes the courtyard was filled with excited voices. "You have grown older!" "You look good!" "You still like to shave, I see." "Do you have a wife?" Habib asked, "Are you staying? We can use your help in the business."

Mark tried to reply to each person as best as he could in the commotion. When Palut arrived, he asked the same question as his brother. "I have no reason to leave again," Mark answered.

"Wine! Bring some wine! Our long-lost brother has returned."

Word traveled fast. Soon the space was so crowded with neighbors that no one could turn around.

Each child needed to be introduced. They had heard stories about their uncle Mark, and they just stared in amazement as he suddenly became a real person in their midst. He couldn't possibly remember their names.

Then, at the gate, appeared the woman he had been wanting to see—Lydia. Her long black hair cascaded around her cheeks and to her shoulders like a gentle waterfall. Her figure was full and mature. She looked like a sweet angel sent by God to create happiness for a few select souls. Could he be one of them?

When he saw her, she smiled and made her way toward him. He stepped toward her with a great smile, and she gave him a warm and affectionate embrace. He returned it with the hug he had been too naive to give on the day he sailed away. Drawing back to where she could get a good look at him, she pinched his cheeks. "You look so good—such a handsome man! You are thirty-two now?"

"Yes, and you are reaching a perfect ripeness too. You are more beautiful than ever."

"I was only a child then."

"A child, blossoming into a woman."

She blushed and paused. "Mark, I would like you to see my little ones? Sharbil is working at this time. Children, this is Mark, who used to live here."

It came as a shock. He had not expected her to be without marriage. Yet, the words jangled in his brain, too disconnected from the image he had hoped for. He had nothing to say in reply.

"I waited for you for a long time. But you did not sail back or send a message. You only sailed away."

"I should have . . ."

"Shh." Her fingers were on his lips. "There is no reason to speak about it. You are happy with your work. And I am happy with these little ones—and with Sharbil."

When she said his name a second time, Mark recalled Sharbil, a vegetable merchant who was old enough to be her uncle—a man older than either of his brothers. Suddenly, he felt jealous. "I would love to meet him again. Perhaps at Sunday Eucharist."

"Yes. Perhaps."

More people wanted to speak with Mark. He was relieved when they pulled him away. He needed time to wrap his mind around the sudden news about Lydia. Should I have expected anything different, he wondered. But the answer left him in total dissonance.

It took a few days for the hubbub to settle down. On Friday he decided to pay a visit to the bishop. Overseeing the church in the metropolis had aged Evodius. Mark guessed that he was in his last years, grey and balding, plump and somewhat stooped over with pain. He greeted Mark warmly. "Mark, Mark. How good it is to see you."

"And to see you, bishop."

"Sit down. Sit down. Tell me how Alexios is in Philippi."

"Just as tall as ever, but handling things quite well. He and Irana are in good spirits."

"They are fine people. Was it hard to leave them?"

"They were very good to me. When I arrived in Philippi I had very little. They let me live with them for almost a year so that I could continue with the gospel."

"Yes, the gospel." The bishop suddenly got serious. "What stage is it in now?"

"It's a completed draft, but I still have a few more things to insert—a few healing episodes and some sayings of Christ. And, if possible, I would like to speak with other eyewitnesses. What I have is only from Peter."

"Well, there could not be a better source." Then pausing, he asked, "Have you distributed any copies?"

"Copies? No. Well . . . Yes. I gave out one copy."

"Was it to Egyptians, by any chance?"

"Yes! They pushed me to release one codex to them, even though I said it was not ready."

"Well." The bishop stroked his chin. "They were *Carpetians*. Did you think they were Christians?"

"They wanted the gospel of Christ. Are they not Christians?"

"They say they are Christians, but some of their beliefs vary from ours. They give little emphasis to how Jesus is the Son of God and how he saved us from our sins. They seek mystical knowledge as a means of salvation."

"I never should have given them a copy."

"No. Did you describe a young man in the Garden of Gethsemane, wearing nothing but a linen cloth?"

"Yes. When the guards came, he slipped away and ran off naked."

"And what else did you say about him?"

"Nothing. I don't know anything more about him."

"You didn't say that he was planning a liaison that evening with James and John?"

"Of course not! How could anyone think such a thing?"

"Well, the Carpetians like to justify their unconventional practices."

"Like . . ?"

"Yes. Like that."

Mark was dumbfounded.

"Bishop Anianus wrote to me about it from Alexandria. It is not the first time that they *revised* one of our documents."

Mark was speechless. It had never occurred to him that anyone would alter a text about Christ.

"I tell you what, I will write back to Anianus explaining what happened. Let us not say anything about it here in Antioch."

"Certainly not." Mark was relieved that Evodius was not angry, but he felt terribly guilty about the incident.

"But could you do this? Could you come back on Tuesday with your gospel document? We have an outstanding presbyter here from Galilee. Would it be all right with you if he read it over and gave his comments?"

"Yes, certainly. That would be very helpful. I want people to check my work."

"Amos was just a boy when his family accepted Christ. His expertise is more about what is going on in the region today, but he might be of help in assessing where you are with it."

"Yes."

"Can you come at mid-morning?"

"I will be here with the document and my notes."

"And will you be at Sunday liturgy?"

"Of course."

"Please wear a toga."

36

By Sunday, the whole *Kerateion*, the Jewish and Christian neighborhood, was buzzing with news about Mark. He wore a toga, his plain white one, and the bishop had him sit where he could be introduced for all to see.

"Welcome back." "You were so young when you left." "Were you really with Peter?" Questions rained down upon him. He did his best to answer each one.

Then he saw Lydia with her children and a slender, aging man. "Sharbil. Is that you?"

"Ah, Mark. Lydia told me that you are back. Welcome home."

"You are a man of good fortune, Sharbil, to have such a fine wife and children."

"I am indeed lucky. It took four years to convince Lydia to marry me. But she said yes."

Mark winced as he heard the number. "I am pleased that you are happy together."

Sharbil looked at his wife lovingly. She returned the gaze to him. "Will you be helping your brothers with the business?"

"They want me to, but we haven't yet talked about it."

"Well, Antioch is growing. And people always want cheese."

"And vegetables."

"And vegetables."

Mark sat down with his brothers on Monday to talk about the business. It was true—everybody wanted cheese, and they were busy. The help they needed most was what he had done for clients in Corinth and Philippi, handling correspondence and keeping accounts. He started right away.

On Tuesday he kept his appointment with the bishop, bringing the gospel text and some of his notes.

Amos, the presbyter, was only a few years older than Mark and looked like a Galilean—a bit rounder in the face than most Judeans, and with curly black hair. He had shaved his beard when he began studying Greek and writing in Sepphoris.

Bishop Evodius made the introductions.

"I am pleased to meet you, Mark. I'm looking forward to reading the gospel."

"I am glad to meet you also," said Mark, handing the presbyter the text.

"Why don't I go into the next room and start reading, while you and Evodius chat."

"That is fine," said the bishop. Amos left.

"Is there a lot to look after in a big city like Antioch?" Mark asked.

"Every day there is something. It never stops. But soon I will be passing it along to someone else."

"You are not that old."

"But I am ailing. I don't have all that much longer. It is in the Lord's hands."

"I will pray for you."

"Thank you."

The bishop asked, "Did you enjoy seeing your friends?"

"Very much! They have all matured so greatly."

"You were interested in a woman once—Lydia."

"Yes. Everyone assumed we would marry."

"And when you left, she waited for you for quite a while."

"I think about four years."

"That shows her love," the bishop noted.

"But she is happy now."

"We each find our happiness in what we can have. There is no happiness in what we cannot attain."

"That is true; I only recently learned that. I had hoped for something new with Lydia, but it is not to be."

"No. It is not. She is married now, with children."

"Yes. That is that."

The bishop stood up. "Perhaps you would like to join Amos now."

"Yes, that would be good."

The Galilean was pouring over the manuscript. "This is very accurate," he commented. "You have captured the essence of Jesus very well."

"I just wrote down things that Peter said. It was he who got them accurately."

"May I continue reading?"

"Certainly. I will sit here, and if you have any questions, just ask."

The presbyter continued reading, occasionally nodding his head. "Yes, yes, yes," he exclaimed on two occasions. Then he asked, "Do you have any more on Jesus' teachings?"

"Not much. I have stories where he cast out demons and healed people, and there are some episodes where he got into conflict with authorities."

"May I see them?"

"Here." Mark handed him the other codex. "The stories with the omega beside them are not yet folded into the narrative."

The older man glanced at the notes and smiled. Then he read more and smiled again. "These are stories in which only a Galilean would see the full significance. Was Peter energized when he told them?"

"Yes. I know they are important, but I don't know why."

"Let me explain. Take these two, for example—about the man in the synagogue with the unclean spirit and the demoniac among the Gerasenes. Galileans recognize these demons as representative of their sources of oppression. They undoubtedly are true stories, but on another dimension they also are symbolic."

He read the first aloud.

They went to Capernaum; and when the Sabbath came, he entered the synagogue and taught. They were astounded at his teaching, for he taught them as one having authority, and not as their scribes. Just then there was in their synagogue a man with an unclean spirit, and he cried out, 'What have you to do with us, Jesus of Nazareth? Have you come to destroy us? I know who you are, the Holy One of God.' But Jesus rebuked him, saying, 'Be silent, and come out of him!' And the unclean spirit, throwing him into convulsions and crying with a loud voice, came out of him. They were all amazed, and they kept on asking one another, 'What is this? A new teaching—with authority! He commands even the unclean spirits, and they obey him.' At once his fame began to spread throughout the surrounding region of Galilee.

"There was no question that Jesus could cast out demons," continued Amos. "But in this case the demons were right in the synagogue. The demons were the scribes and the Pharisees in their villages, who were keeping them suppressed. And this played into the hands of the rulers in Jerusalem."

"I see," Mark said with interest.

"And then look at this story about the Gerasenes. They were in the eastern part of the region, where there was a strong Roman military presence."

They came to the other side of the lake, to the country of the Gerasenes. And when he had stepped out of the boat, immediately a man out of the tombs with an unclean spirit met him. He lived among the tombs; and no one could restrain him anymore, even with a chain; for he had often been restrained with shackles and chains, but the chains he wrenched apart, and the shackles he broke in pieces; and no one had the strength to subdue him. Night and day among the tombs and on the mountains he was always howling and bruising himself with stones. When he saw Jesus from a distance, he ran and bowed down before him; and shouted at the top of his voice, 'What have you to do with me, Jesus, Son of the Most High God? I adjure you by God, do not torment me.' For he had said to him, 'Come out of the man, you unclean spirit!' Then Jesus asked him, 'What is your name?' He replied, 'My name is Legion; for we are many.' He begged him earnestly not to send them out of the country. Now there on the hillside a great herd of swine was feeding; and the unclean spirits begged him, 'Send us into the swine; let us enter them.' So he gave them permission. And the unclean spirits came out and entered the swine; and the herd, numbering about two thousand, rushed down the steep bank into the lake, and they drowned in the lake.

"Do you see the similarity?" Amos asked. "In this case it is the Romans who are oppressing—they are Legion, and they go into the swine. They are not Jews."

"So Jesus was identifying the sources of oppression and casting them out?"

"Exactly!"

"But he didn't get rid of all of them. They are still in the land, firmly in control."

"That is true. Jesus wanted the people to be patient, not to rise up in armed rebellion and be crushed. But he was showing them that the victory already was won when these demons were cast out."

"That is amazing. I always wondered why those stories were important."

"They pinpoint the source of the people's problems, and they show that God cares."

Mark sat in silence, absorbing the implications of what he had heard.

"You see, that is why we are watching so closely the growing unrest in the region. The people are rushing headlong into a storm of great proportions. They are moving in the opposite direction from what Jesus recommended."

"How do you mean? I have not heard the latest news."

Amos paused and gathered his thoughts. "Have you heard that in the temple they have ended the sacrifices for Nero?"

"Yes, but nothing beyond that."

"The Holy City is split in two. The priests have control of the upper city, and the rebel Eleazar's faction has the lower area. The priests asked Agrippa to talk sense to them. He told them, 'War, if it be once begun, is not easily laid down again, nor borne without calamities coming therewith.' He asked, 'What do you pretend to? Are you richer than the Gauls, stronger than the Germans, wiser than the Greeks, more numerous than all men upon the habitable earth? What confidence is it that elevates you to oppose the Romans?'"

"Did they answer?"

"Yes. They said that God would intervene on their behalf and smite the Romans, just as he had overcome Israel's enemies before."

"But there were plenty of times that God did *not* strike down their enemies," Mark stated.

"Precisely! But Eleazar isn't looking at those scriptures."

"No."

"And in addition, he just set fire to the city records office, destroying the debt records there. He figures he will garner the support of the Judeans who are struggling under the crushing load of debt."

"He really did that?" Mark asked.

"Really. But you have not yet heard the latest. The freedom fighter Manahem, who was garrisoned at Masada, rode into Jerusalem with the pomp and glory of a king—if not the Messiah. He has control of at least one faction of insurrectionists. He and Eleazar are rivaling for power, and no one knows who will prevail."

"That's terrible!"

"It is terrible, and I am convinced that in the coming weeks, governor Gallus will send his forces into Galilee and then to Judea. They have a full legion here in Antioch and detachments from other areas, with several thousand cavalry, archers, and infantry supplied by Agrippa. They will mow through there like locusts eating through fields of ripe grain."

"Oh my God!"

"That is what we are saying here, and we worry about the Christians in

Galilee and Jerusalem."

"What will happen to them?"

"They are not likely to join in the fighting, so people like Eleazar and Manahem will call them traitors. The brothers there are in a very tight spot."

"What options do they have?" Mark asked.

"I fear that their best option is to leave their homes and flee while they can get away. At some point the Romans will close off that avenue as well. If they stay where they are, they will be caught in the middle of a conflagration."

37

Habib made space in his home for Mark to settle in, a small room with a couch and a table. He liked it, for a temporary arrangement, because it put him close to his mother and he could continue his writing. It didn't take him long to get caught up with the correspondence and accounts in the business. He even learned how to serve customers and trade remarks about the fine points of cheese.

As he began the next expanded draft of the gospel, he chose two healing stories—one about a leper and one about a paralytic—and placed them near the beginning. They showed both Jesus' divine power to heal and how much he cared for the downtrodden.

After studying the episodes where Jesus got into conflict with those in authority, he decided to spread them out, so that they showed an ever increasing tension. Following Amos' suggestion, he tried to present them from a Galilean perspective.

Now John the Baptist's disciples and the Pharisees were fasting, and people came and said to him, 'Why do John's disciples and the disciples of the Pharisees fast, but your disciples do not fast?' Jesus said to them, 'The wedding guests cannot fast while the bridegroom is with them, can they? As long as they have the bridegroom with them, they cannot fast. The days will come when the bridegroom is taken away from them, and then they will fast on that day.'

Jesus said, 'No one sews a piece of unshrunk cloth on an old cloak; otherwise, the patch pulls away from it, the new from the old, and a worse tear is made. And no one puts new wine into old wineskins; otherwise, the wine will burst the skins, and the wine is lost, and so are the skins; but one puts new wine into fresh wineskins.'

In Galilee there was a shortage of food, he remembered. Even those who grew grain had most of it taxed away from them. It made no sense for the poor farmers to fast like the elders in the villages who had plenty. And Jesus' analogy about the bridegroom was apt. They would not always have Jesus with them. This goes near the beginning, he decided. Jesus came to proclaim something new. It could not fit into old containers.

He placed a similar story of conflict a little farther along.

Now when the Pharisees and some of the scribes who had come from Jerusalem gathered around him, they noticed that some of his disciples were eating with defiled hands, that is, without washing them. (For the Pharisees, and all the Jews, do not eat unless they thoroughly wash their hands, thus observing the tradition of the elders; and they do not eat anything from the market unless they wash it; and there are also many other traditions that they observe, the washing of cups, pots, and bronze kettles.) So the Pharisees and the scribes asked him, 'Why do your disciples not live according to the tradition of the elders, but eat with defiled hands?' He said to them, 'Isaiah prophesied rightly about you hypocrites, as it is written, 'This people honors me with their lips, but their hearts are far from me; in vain do they worship me, teaching human precepts as doctrines.' You abandon the commandment of God in order to keep your tradition!'

Forcing people to keep unnecessary traditions was a way of keeping them subjugated. The Pharisees and scribes had the time and the means to follow all the customs, while the poor did not.

The stories of confrontations continued to escalate until Jesus arrived in Jerusalem. There he staged a dramatic act of disobedience, cutting into the foundation of the economic system at its core.

Then they came to Jerusalem. And he entered the temple and began to drive out those who were selling and those who were buying in the temple, and he overturned the tables of the money-changers and the seats of those who sold doves; and he would not allow anyone to carry anything through the temple. He was teaching and saying, 'Is it not written, my house shall be called a house of prayer for all the nations? But you have made it a den of robbers.' And when the chief priests and the scribes heard it, they kept looking for a way to kill him; for they were afraid of him, because the whole crowd was spellbound by his teaching. And when evening came, Jesus and his disciples went out of the city.

Jesus only shut down the temple for one day, Mark noted. But it demonstrated how the entire sacrificial system had become a burden on the poor, a tax supporting the elite. Those who got ahead within the system were bound to retaliate. But Jesus made his point, and the crowds saw it.

Two other short episodes fit right before Jesus predicted the destruction of the temple.

As he taught, he said, 'Beware of the scribes, who like to walk around in long robes, and to be greeted with respect in the market-places, and to have the best seats in the synagogues and places of honor at banquets! They devour widows' houses and for the sake of appearance say long prayers. They will receive the greater condemnation.'

He sat down opposite the treasury, and watched the crowd putting money into the treasury. Many rich people put in large sums. A poor widow came and put in two small copper coins, which are worth a penny. Then he called his disciples and said to them, 'Truly I tell you, this poor widow has put in more than all those who are contributing to the treasury. For all of them have contributed out of their abundance; but she out of her poverty has put in everything she had, all she had to live on.'

Mark liked how the two short stories contrasted, but came to a similar point. The temple scribes were the agents of the high priests in making the system function smoothly, and they benefitted from it greatly. The poor widow came to the temple not just to pay her tithe, but from her faith in God, and she showed how great her faith was by giving all that she had.

When Mark finished the last draft, he showed it again to Amos and Evodius. "I love it," exclaimed the Galilean priest. "This is looking like a masterpiece!"

"I don't know about that, but I now have combined everything I got from Peter and the Passion source into one narrative. I am pleased with it too."

"What do you feel you have left to do?" asked the bishop.

"The things I have left to do involve travel. I believe it is essential that I get some additional perspectives. When winter passes I hope to go to Ephesus and speak with John. I would love to see Mary Magdalene, or write to her. Do either of you know where she is living?"

They shook their heads.

"And of course, the Christians in Jerusalem and Nazareth could have much to offer," Mark added.

"That is getting to be out of the question now," Amos noted. "The hostilities continue there. Gallus' forces overran Galilee without much trouble, and they didn't meet much resistance in Judea either. The Roman columns reached the outskirts of Jerusalem, but then suddenly stopped. I guess he didn't want to subject his troops to a wintertime siege of the walled city. Then, just as suddenly, he ordered his armies to withdraw to Caesarea Maritima for the winter. And on their way, the rebels showered a deadly rain of missiles from the hilltops. The troops broke ranks in a terrible rout; he lost about six thousand."

"So what will happen now?" Mark inquired.

"The Jews say that the victory shows undeniable evidence of God's favor. They believe they cannot be defeated with God on their side. The priest Ananias II has assumed power again in Jerusalem. He is calling for freedom. I fear that the whole miserable situation will reverse again in the spring."

"Evodius asked, "Do you suppose that this is why Nero has recalled Gallus and appointed a new governor?"

"A new governor! Who is that?" asked Mark.

"I just heard about it. Our new governor is Gaius Licinius Mucianus."

"I've never heard of him."

"No one knows much about him yet."

"He will need a good general," Amos added. "I bet that Nero will appoint an experienced general, who will wrap up the siege in short order."

"Will this be a good time for the Christians in Jerusalem to escape?" Mark wondered.

Amos quickly came back. "They have had plenty of chances to leave, but they stay. I fear that this winter will be no different."

In January Mark asked to see Amos again.

"May I talk with you about the end times? With what I have from Peter, I'm not sure of exactly what Jesus meant when he spoke about the last days."

"In what way?"

"Well, you read how when they came out of the temple, Jesus predicted that 'not one stone will be left upon a stone,' and his disciples asked, 'when will this be?'"

"Yes."

"Do you suppose it could be this winter? Or when the siege begins?"

"No one knows."

"I understand. But I have this one remaining passage where Jesus speaks about it. It seems to fit these times, right now.

When you see the desolating sacrilege set up where it ought not to be, then those in Judea must flee to the mountains; someone on the housetop must not go down or enter the house to take anything away; someone in the field must not turn back to get a coat. Woe to those who are pregnant and to those who are nursing infants in those days! Pray that it may not be in winter. For in those days there will be suffering, such as has not been from the beginning of the creation that God created until now, no, and never will be. And if the Lord had not cut short those days, no one would be saved, but for the sake of the elect, whom he chose, he has cut short those days. And if anyone says to you at the time, 'Look! Here is the Messiah!' or 'Look! There he is!'—do not believe it.

False messiahs and false prophets will appear and produce signs and omens, to lead astray, if possible, the elect. But be alert; I have already told you everything.'

Amos rubbed his chin and gathered his thoughts. "The daily sacrifices to the Emperor certainly could be considered a desolating sacrilege. The prophets Ezekiel and Daniel made predictions, and the Jews anticipate that God will sum up his wrath in one day and turn the tide on all of the enemies of Israel. That is what is feeding this fever. But Jesus announced a kingdom that would spread like yeast in dough. The kinds of events he described could be this year or any year. They could continue for generations."

"That's what I explained to the people in Corinth. They were expecting Christ to return soon," Mark added.

"Christ will return, but how soon, we do not know."

"That's what I said."

"And how Christ will promulgate his reign, we do not know. I can only imagine it to be peaceful," Amos added.

"I feel the same way. But how do you account for these specific images and words?"

"The images and words may have more to do with the Jews than with Christians. Many more should have followed Jesus. They are the people chosen to be a light to the world. They should have championed his cause, but they did not."

"Are you saying that the end times for the Jews and the Day of the Lord for Christians could be different?" Mark questioned.

"I don't know, but there is no inherent reason why they must be the same. I am a Christian because I want to look to the future, not to the past."

"That's the way I feel."

"Our job is not to speculate about when Christ will come again. Our mission is to pass along the good news, and keep his reign spreading."

"That's true. I will include the passage," Mark assured him. "During these winter days I'll be making several copies. I 'll give one to you shortly."

"Thank you. I look forward to reading it."

38

In February, Mark received word that Evodius and Amos wanted to see him. He was not feeling well, but he went anyway.

"Thank you for coming, Mark," said the bishop. "Amos and I have read your latest draft, and we like it very much. You have done well."

"Thank you. The basic gospel is complete, but I would like to gather more and add to it."

"Yes," the bishop paused. "Amos has more news. Tell Mark what you heard."

"It is about the war. Nero is leaving Mucianus here in Syria. He is not a military leader. General Vespasian has been appointed governor of Judea and commander of the Roman forces. He just arrived here and was welcomed by Agrippa. They plan to march south and join with Vespasian's son, Titus, who is coming from Alexandria. They will have at least three legions."

"Three legions. What an awesome force!"

"Jerusalem does not have a chance."

"I thought they would have waited until spring."

"There has been some unseasonably good weather, and they are taking advantage of it."

"If only the people could hear the gospel!" Mark blurted. "If they would listen and heed the words of Christ, they could be saved!"

"That hasn't happened yet, and it doesn't look like it is going to happen now."

"When are people going to learn that war only destroys lives? The only way to make a better world is through the ways of Christ."

"Yes, that is why we proclaim those ways," said the bishop. "And we will continue proclaiming them."

Mark left the meeting feeling very sad.

Mark's illness got worse.

In the first week his body temperature rose. He had headaches with a cough, and an occasional bloody nose.

In the second week Mark was too tired to get up. His forehead was very hot.

Habib sent for a physician.

"The rose spots on his chest confirm my suspicions," the physician explained. "It's Typhoid Fever."

"Oh my," gasped his mother. "What can we do?"

"Keep him comfortable. We have to wait and see what happens."

During the third week his constipation changed to diarrhea. At times he was delirious.

The physician shared the prognosis with the family. "The Fever is one of the leading causes of death in our time. It once killed a third of the population of Athens."

"How did he get it?" asked his mother.

"Anyone can catch it in these crowded conditions. We believe that the disease is spread from person to person by the inadvertent touching of particles of the infection."

"Can he recover?" asked Habib.

"It is possible. Only time will tell. Someone should watch over him at all times. I will send a nurse to help."

"We don't need no nurse," Mark's mother retorted. "We will take care of my son."

"I know a nurse who is experienced with these cases. You will need her at the end."

During the fourth week the fever subsided a bit. The nurse sat near Mark, kept him comfortable, and prayed for him along with the family.

But as the fourth week drew to a close, he got worse. The nurse told them it was time for family and friends to gather for the end.

"I have failed. . . I have fallen from grace. . ." Mark moaned in his searing hot brain. "I have so much more to do. . . I must see John. . . I must find Mary Magdalene. . . I need to speak with those in Jerusalem. . . And I have done nothing with the sayings; they have such power to inspire. . . I have not yet fulfilled my calling."

But it was to no avail. He floated up—to the ceiling—and saw his body lying still below. It was eerie. He knew it was him; he could see his own face. And the circle of people were speaking about him.

"He has succeeded well," he heard Evodius say. "The gospel will serve the church for all time."

"He understood Jesus, perhaps better than anyone," added Amos. "I am amazed at his insights."

"He was a fine brother," said Habib. "I'm sure our father is proud of him."

"I loved him," agreed Palut. "If only we could have had more time together."

"He was a perfect uncle," cried Lysandra. "Because of him I will always be a Christian."

"My son—my baby," sobbed mama. "Don't go. Stay with us, at least for a while longer."

His breathing subsided. The nurse did not say a word. When the others left the room, she took a bowl and washed his body carefully. Then going through his clothing and noticing the toga with the red border, she dressed him in it. Tenderly, she positioned his arms and smoothed the fabric. And after gazing down at his still form and praying for him for a few minutes, she bent over and kissed him lightly on the cheek.

39

Out in the courtyard there was great weeping. During the third week when Mark got better, their hopes went up. Now all hopes were dashed. The whole family was in a daze.

Mama was sobbing. It is so tragic to see your baby lying still on his deathbed. Habib and Palut were doing their best to comfort her, but to little avail. They, too, had hoped to enjoy many long years with their brother.

"I don't want you to take him yet!" Mama shook her fist toward the sky. She didn't expect the gesture to do any good, but she wanted Christ to know how she felt. No one attempted to stop her. Even God in heaven understood the depth of her pain.

Lysandra caressed mama's hair. "I will give you a new baby, grandma. I will be a grown woman soon."

"Oh, no!" Mama was no more ready to have her oldest grandchild grow up than to have her youngest son die.

Habib also did not want to hear such talk. He only recently had begun giving thought to Lysandra's coming of age. "Shh! We will talk about those things some other time."

They knew only one way to distill their grief—cry it out.

Then Palut began telling a story about when they were boys. "Do you remember how Mark tried to stop us when we were fighting? One time Habib and I were wrestling on the ground, and Mark, who couldn't have been more than three years old, came right up to us and shouted, 'You boys quit fighting! You'll get your tunics dirty!' It was so funny. We had to stop fighting just to laugh. But he was totally serious."

"Mark was always the peacemaker," remembered Habib. "He had to be; he was too thin to fight. He would sit watching and taking it all in. Then he would speak with such adult wisdom that we all had to stop and listen."

"He got the brains in this family," added Palut.

"He got the heart, too," said mama. "He loved Jesus with his whole heart." Everyone agreed.

When Mark saw the kiss he returned to his body.

His eyes opened slightly. The nurse had her head down, praying for him, and didn't notice.

"Who . . ."

The nurse screeched.

"Who are you?" he asked.

"I am a nurse—Maryam. We thought you were . . ."

"Oh. . . I remember. Yes. I was very sick."

She felt his forehead with the back of her hand. It was not as hot as it had been.

"What did you say your name is?"

"Maryam. You may call me Mary."

"I like the name Maryam. Are you Jewish?"

"Both my mother's and my father's families followed Jesus. They spoke Aramaic."

"That's a beautiful language. Where are you from?"

"From Gennesaret in Galilee."

Mark grabbed the nurse's hand and squeezed it so hard it frightened her. "Did you say Galilee? Are you a Galilean?"

"Yes. I am a Galilean Christian."

"I want to go to Galilee!"

"Right now you must stay in bed."

"But I need to go!" He started to get up, but she pushed him back.

"You can go to Galilee later, but today you must get some rest."

MARK'S PASSION

"It is very important!"

"It also is important that you rest."

"But I want to find . . ."

She put her fingers on his lips. "When you get well, we can talk. Now you must sleep."

"Don't go away."

"I will be right here."

When he closed his eyes to sleep, Maryam went out to the courtyard and shared the news with the family. They were overjoyed. They thought he was dead and couldn't believe he had recovered.

"What did you do?" mama asked the nurse.

"Nothing unusual, just what I usually do with patients. I washed his body and dressed him in his toga. Then I prayed for him for a few minutes and bent over and kissed him farewell. It is my way of saying, 'Go with God.'"

"Oh! You prayed for him and kissed him. That's how he was healed!" mama shrieked.

"No! No! Only the Lord heals. I did what I have done for others before. But they were not healed."

"You healed him! You healed my son!" Mama was screaming.

"I did nothing unusual. Maybe Jesus has something more for him to do in life. Perhaps that is why he healed him."

While the nurse's logic made sense, the family concluded that she had been instrumental in some way to the miraculous healing. In a matter of hours the news spread all over the district.

Maryam asked to see the bishop.

"I don't know what to do," she told him. "People are saying that I have a special gift or something. But I did nothing out of the ordinary. I just prayed for Mark and kissed his cheek."

"Maryam, it is true that only the Lord heals. Let's be grateful for that. But we cannot deny that something very extraordinary has happened. I agree with the possibility that Christ may plan something more for him. While the basic gospel is complete, Mark feels that he has more yet to do. We should just wait and see."

"But how can I stop all of this talk?"

"I doubt that you can."

"But it is so embarrassing," she lamented.

"The talk will subside. But while you find it embarrassing, others find it inspiring."

"I wish it would subside soon."

Bishop Evodius thought for a moment. "I must add this: the Spirit has brought you and Mark together in a remarkable way. His family didn't even think they needed a nurse. Christ may have plans that involve both of you."

"Like what?"

"I don't know."

"But how can that be? I have never been married, and am not seeking a husband," Maryam stated.

"I didn't mean it necessarily involves that. I just feel that there may be more yet to unfold."

"I don't understand."

"Neither do I; it is just a feeling I have. Maybe you should simply be open to the possibility and see what transpires."

"I can do that."

"Good. I will pray for you."

Maryam came daily to the house to check on Mark, and as usual, the patient, as he recovered, liked to talk. Mark told her his life story, including his time with Peter, the sojourn to Corinth, writing the gospel in Philippi, and his return home to Antioch. He even told her about the women: Lydia, Agathe, Zosima—and the blunder with Kallisto. Maryam listened to it all, which is part of what she liked about nursing. She found Mark intriguing.

He noticed her sweet, caring style. Maryam had a cheerful round face and deep green eyes. She wore her black hair shorter than most women. Long hair sometimes got in the way when she needed to move or handle a patient. She was in her late twenties, and while her face and figure were maturing, she certainly was what most people considered good looking. Mark especially liked her smile. When the corners of her lips curled up they displayed the sincerity of her compassionate heart.

Then, as he was feeling better and the visits were becoming less necessary, he asked her to share more about herself. "When did you come to Antioch?"

"When I was twenty."

"What brought you here?"

"My father and mother moved here when they heard about the prosperity in Antioch. And we have had an easier life here."

"Do you still live with them?" he asked.

MARK'S PASSION

"Yes. It is a good arrangement, for now."

"Is the house very far away?"

"Not far. We live in this district. I walk here. It only takes a few minutes."

"Were you not betrothed before you were twenty?" Mark may have been too blunt, and Maryam blushed. "I'm sorry, if I asked too much. I was just wondering."

"I was not betrothed." When she hesitated, he simply waited to see if she would go on. "There was a boy who lived near us. We noticed each other, and we wanted to be close."

"What was his name?"

"Samuel."

"Samuel. That's a nice name. I imagine that he was a fine young man."

"Oh yes. A very fine young man. But it was not to be."

"Why not?"

"Well—he was Jewish, and we were Christian."

"Oh. So that got in the way?"

"Yes. We spoke about it when we could. Our families were opposed to our friendship. They both said it would be impossible."

"Nothing is impossible when two people are in love."

"That's true. But he was determined to remain a Jew, and it was clear in my mind that I had embraced Christ and would stay that way."

"So it was not to be."

"No." Her deep sadness was apparent to Mark, and he waited for her to ponder the dilemma, knowing from experience what it feels like to lose a love. But he wanted to know more.

"And what happened after that?"

"There was no—after that. We moved here and I became a nurse."

"But other men must have been interested in you. You are very pretty."

She blushed a bit, then got a serious look on her face. "This is not the day that I wish to talk about it."

"That's all right. I didn't mean to pry into your life."

"It is very personal. I don't talk much about those things."

"And I will respect that. It's just that . . ."

She put her fingers on his lips. "I will be back in two days. Now, you get plenty of rest and drink lots of water."

Mark thought a great deal about Maryam during the next two days. He had nothing else to do lying there. Strength was returning to his limbs, and he got up for short walks within the house. Any day could be the last time she needed to come to check on his condition.

He knew every detail of her face from picturing her in her absences—her full pink lips, her deep green eyes, and how a little lock of her black hair seemed to always brush across her face even when the air was still, which highlighted her smooth light complexion. She was friendly toward him, but there seemed to be a barrier, a wall that enclosed her soul, which left him wondering if she ever would let him have even a glance inside. He was grateful for all that she had done for him, but his interest began to grow beyond gratitude. She seemed to dislike it when his questions became personal. So, unless she volunteered the information, how could he know more about her?

The sun was beaming into the room when she next came to see him. "You are doing well," she said. "You should begin taking longer walks within the neighborhood. Soon you will be back to work."

"Thank you. And how have you been?"

"Fine. Is your energy returning?"

"I'm getting tired of just lying here. I think too much when I am alone."

"You have your family. Do they not spend time with you?"

"Yes, of course. But I am a man of action. I like to be busy."

"I am the same way. And nursing keeps me busy."

"How did you learn to be nurse?"

This was a topic Maryam enjoyed talking about. "When we arrived in Antioch I met an experienced nurse. She lived next door. It seemed like an occupation that fit my personality, so I asked her a lot of questions and she helped me to get my first employment. I learned through practice, asking very little in payment at the beginning. But over these six years I have become skilled. Now I consider myself a professional and am not afraid to face any medical situation."

"The physician recommended you highly to my family."

"Yes. I learned that your mama didn't want a nurse to come here at first."

Mark laughed. "Well mama likes you now. She still talks about how you saved my life."

"I did not save your life!" Maryam frowned. "I only prayed for you. It was the Lord who saved your life."

He laughed again. "I know. There is more that I want to do with the gospel. But mama says the Fever left when you kissed my cheek."

"I was sending you to God with that kiss. I did not for one moment expect that you would return to life."

"Well, I am glad that I did."

"I am glad too. My gift is caring for people, and I believe that Christ helps me. But that does not include raising anyone from the dead."

"I will never say anything like that again."

"Thank you. You see, I am a very practical woman."

"Which is good."

"It is good. Nursing gives meaning to my life—I love it. But it won't help to have people getting high expectations about how I might heal them. In almost all of the serious cases, the people die. I only help them to be more comfortable in their last days."

"And that's a precious gift that you are able to offer. It is a beautiful gift—to the living and the dying."

"I am glad that you understand. You see, I am not looking for a husband."

Mark was surprised at her sudden frank change of topic. "I was not implying anything about your seeking a husband."

"That is correct, you did not. But I just want you to know. You are a very fine man, Mark. Many women would want you for their husband, but my spouse is nursing."

"You have made that clear."

"Thank you. I will come back again on Friday. That probably will be my last visit," she stated.

"All right. I'll see you then."

That evening at dinner the talk among the family mainly was about the movement of troops. From all over the territory soldiers were breaking camp and beginning to march south.

"I'm glad to see them go," Habib said. They bought a lot of cheese, but quite frankly I'm tired of having thousands of extra men in our city. I say good riddance!"

"I worry about the Jews, though," Mark admitted.

"They started this fight."

"Yes. But there are a great many Christians in Palestine. They will get caught in the middle."

"That's true."

"Which way are the troops going?" Mark asked.

"It appears that they will march along the coast. Those camped along the Orontes River are coming this way and turning. They won't be going through Damascus."

"Has anyone talked about more soldiers coming in from Egypt?"

"Titus' forces? There is no word yet, but they probably are moving too."

"So the armies likely will be in Galilee in March."

"That's what people are saying. With this big of an operation, there are no secrets. Vespasian is bringing enough troops to go in and mow through there like a vast army of warrior ants."

Mark pondered the image. The Romans had engaged in this kind of operation before and they would do it again. Part of their strategy was to show the world that you don't rebel against the Roman Empire without suffering a disproportionate cost.

"I want to see the bishop on Thursday," he said. "Will you arrange a time?"

"Certainly," replied Habib. What do you have in mind?"

"It is about the gospel. I need to tell him some things."

The appointment was for mid-morning.

"Ah, Mark," greeted the bishop warmly. "I am glad to see that you are getting well enough to come here."

"Thank you. I am feeling much better."

"That was a close call."

"Too close. And that is what I want to speak with you about."

"Yes. Go on."

"Well, before I got sick, I gave you a copy of the gospel."

"Yes, and both Amos and I feel it is most excellent."

"I don't consider it finished," Mark told him, "but under the circumstances I feel it is time for me to give it to the church. Anything can happen in these times. I had a close brush with death, and the political situation is getting quite volatile. I don't want to keep the gospel within my possession any longer. It should be in the possession of the church. That way if anything happens to me, the gospel will be safe."

"That is very prudent."

"There still is much more that I want to do, and given the time and some good luck I will do it. I can always add more detail to the text when I get it."

"So what I hear you saying is that we may make copies and begin using it," the bishop said in reply.

"Exactly. I will help make some of the copies as I have time."

"Work with Amos on that. We have some very fine scribes in Antioch."

"I will."

"This is an excellent plan. I want to begin using the gospel in our liturgies and with the catechumens right away."

"It is yours, bishop," Mark assured him.

"It is the church's gospel. You received the stories from the church, and after writing them into the continuous narrative you are giving it back to the church."

"Precisely."

"And anyway, nothing is mine. I, too, am getting weak. I may not be bishop much longer."

"You will serve as long as God wills, bishop."

"Thank you." Evodius paused. Then he said, "There is one more thing, Mark."

"Yes."

"It is about the woman, Maryam."

"What about Maryam?"

"Are you interested in her?"

"Yes, to some extent. She is a very capable nurse and a sweet person. But she told me that she is not seeking a husband."

"I wonder why she said that."

"I don't know. Perhaps I was too forward in my conversation. When I asked her to tell me more about herself, she shared about her nursing, but closed up about anything else. Then she simply told me the truth about her intentions. She was quite blunt."

"I am not surprised. I shared something with Maryam that I also will share with you. I told her that I have an intuition that Christ may have kept you alive because he has something more in mind for you."

"That may be correct."

"Yes, and I told her that she also may be part of God's plan."

"In what way?" What the bishop was saying surprised him.

"I said that I don't know. It is simply a feeling in my heart. I can't explain it nor offer any further speculation. But I want you to know about it."

"Thank you bishop. You are a very wise man, and I will keep what you said in mind,"

"Good! Keep me informed, if anything happens."

"I will."

When Maryam came to the house on Friday, she was in a serious mood. "You are well now, Mark. Don't do anything too strenuous for a while, but continue to get some exercise and plenty of rest."

"I will. Thank you for everything you have done during my illness."

"You are welcome. You were a good patient."

"Have you heard about the troop movements?" Mark asked.

"Yes. Everyone is talking about it."

"I fear for the Christians in the region, and also for the Jews."

"I fear for them too." She paused before continuing. "I have been thinking about going there to care for persecuted Christians."

"What? The war will be disastrous!"

"Yes. And there will be many wounded needing care."

"But you don't want to be caught up in it."

"I would go right now, if I could. But that would not be wise. I've been thinking about going when the troops move on."

"How do you mean?"

"Galilee is my homeland. Since Vespasian is heading south, he most likely will go through Galilee first and then move on to Jerusalem."

"That is the likely scenario."

"So I could go into the region after the main army has left for Judea. It would not be as dangerous then. But there will be many wounded and sick among my people. I can help them."

"That is an outstanding plan!" Mark exclaimed.

"Do you like it? No one else agrees with my going. They say I am crazy even to think of such a thing."

"No. I think you are very brave, and you are pursuing your calling."

"No one in my family understands what it is like to feel called."

"Oh, Maryam, I understand. I too have pursued a calling. I have not pursued it perfectly, but I've done my best—at least for the most part."

"Then you don't think I am crazy?" she asked shyly.

"Not at all."

"You are so different from most people, Mark. Most just want a secure life. But I want to do something helpful."

"Just like me."

"Well, you have finished your work. You've completed the gospel."

"I spoke with bishop Evodius just yesterday about that. I turned the gospel, in its present form, over to the church. If anything further should happen to me, it is not in my possession. But I have more to do. I said that if I can come up with more to add, I will write it later. I don't consider my calling complete. Not yet."

"That is amazing!"

MARK'S PASSION

"What?"

"You have your passion, and I have mine."

"A calling is a passion. We have more in common than we thought."

Then he added, "What would you think, if I told you that I want to go to Galilee with you?"

She looked shocked. "Why do you want to go?"

"Because the people who personally saw Jesus are growing old, and with the war many of them will die. I want to speak with them before it's too late and hear what they can tell me about Jesus."

"You would expose yourself to danger for that?"

"I will expose myself to danger for the sake of the gospel. I might come back with many more stories about Jesus, which otherwise would be lost."

Maryam stared at Mark in unbelief. "You are a most remarkable man!"

"I don't know about that, but I have a passion to gather all that I can for the gospel. We can go together."

"But how would we go together?"

"What do you mean?"

"How would we go together? We are not husband and wife."

The bishop told me what he shared with you—that he feels that Christ may have a plan in mind that involves both of us."

Maryam suddenly looked perplexed. "But I told you . . ."

"I know what you told me. You are not seeking a husband. And I told you that I will respect that. But we must be open to what Christ asks of us."

She looked down, pondering his words.

"We could go as brother and sister," he suggested.

"You mean . . ."

"I mean that I will accompany you and provide a degree of protection for you. A woman cannot travel alone. But I will respect you in every way—the way a brother respects his sister."

Maryam was bewildered at the proposal.

"I promise you—even if some people mistake us for husband and wife—I will not do anything that you do not wish me to do."

"And I believe that you will fulfill that promise." Her face lit up like she was hit by a sudden ray of sunshine. "Then we can go now!"

"Now? The troops are on the road."

"The troops are along the coastal route, but we can go around to the King's Highway. We can arrive in Galilee not long after they do!"

"How brilliant! Then I can speak with people before they are all destroyed in the slaughter."

"And I can nurse those who need care!"

They suddenly threw their arms around each other. Mark was elated that Maryam was opening to him. She clung to him tightly, realizing that this was the first time she had been this close to a man and was not frightened by it. She did not push away.

40

Vespasian's armies continued their deliberate march south. Nearly fifty-thousand men marched eight abreast carrying sixty-pound battle packs on roads that had been built primarily for this purpose, traversing an average of twenty miles per day. Titus' forces also were making their way north from Egypt.

Mark's family pleaded with him not to go, even by the alternate route. They understood clearly how brutal the fighting in Galilee would be.

"I lost you twice," mourned mama. "Once when you go to Rome and once more when you got the Fever. Now I don't want to lose you again."

Mark felt terrible. Everyone wanted him to stay. He knew they were right, but he also knew he would go.

Maryam's family also thought she was crazy.

"I forbid you to go!" stormed her father. "You are not going!"

"Papa, I'm not a little girl anymore. I am a grown woman, and a nurse who can care for the wounded. I don't expect anyone to understand."

"You can't go with a man you hardly know," said her mother. "It just isn't done."

"I trust Mark to treat me like a sister."

"Oh, baby. Men promise many things."

"He is a good man. I will be safe with him. And anyway, if Christ wants me to go and care for the wounded, then someone must accompany me. Mark is the ideal one."

Her father became enraged. "No! No! No! We have cared for you for twenty-eight years. You must obey us on this."

The next day the two went to see bishop Evodius. They explained their plan and shared their families' reaction.

"They think we are crazy," Mark told him.

"My father forbid me to go," added Maryam.

The bishop pondered the situation before responding. "I really don't know what to say. Your families are absolutely correct. It is insane to go into the war zone, and it is outside of the norm for two such as you who are unmarried to travel together. But I cannot tell you not to go. Christ may have a plan that none of us understands."

"Then you think we should go?"

"I did not say that. What I said was, I cannot tell you not to go. Please pray about this before departing. Let the Lord be your guide. And if you do go, you will need his guidance every step of the way."

Mark did pray, more seriously than ever in his life. Then he packed.

He put in his bag two togas, two extra tunics, a blanket, his razor, two blank codices, some pens, his copy of the sayings source, and a copy of the final version of the gospel. Then he put in two extra pair of sandals. It was going to be a long walk, and with food and water to carry, the load would be heavy.

He put strings on his mother's silver cross and Peter's medallion of the Holy Spirit, and placed them around his neck. He was as ready as he could be.

Maryam also prayed sincerely, and grew more confident in her decision.

Her father threatened to chain her to the house. That seemed kind of archaic in a modern city like Antioch, but it showed the extent of his desperation.

She hated to leave secretly, yet it seemed like the only way. Fortunately, when she left with her pack early Monday morning, her mother saw and followed, but her father was unaware of her leaving.

At Habib's house a crowd gathered. Everyone gave the travelers hugs and heartfelt goodbyes. Maryam's mother, knowing that further pleading was hopeless, embraced her daughter and through her tears wished her safety. Maryam was forever grateful for these last moments.

Even Lydia was present. Mark didn't know how she heard that he was leaving, but when he saw her he gave her one of the biggest hugs of all. It didn't make up for the time he failed to do so ten years earlier, but it expressed the bond they felt and how they both had become more mature.

Finally, after Mark kissed his mama for the eleventh time, they left.

They headed south and east. The planned route went up the Orontes River, then over a mountain pass and down toward the via Regia, the King's Highway, an ancient trade route from Egypt to the cities along the Euphrates River. They would meet the highway and proceed south to Damascus and then walk southeast through Caesarea Philippi to Bethsaida on the northern tip of the Sea of Galilee. The route was longer than the one taken by the Roman troops, but much safer under the circumstances. And since the troops were in better condition for going long distances on their feet, the two Christians expected to arrive after the army.

After walking for about an hour they stopped for a drink of water. The sun was getting high in the sky.

"We must start earlier tomorrow," Mark said, "to avoid the heat of the afternoon."

"At first light we will begin." Neither were experienced at the ancient method of human travel, but they had been given good advice.

"Are you doing all right?" Mark asked.

"Yes. Let's keep going."

With their late start, they covered only nine miles the first day. The Romans had placed mileposts at intervals along the roads, which served as good measures of distance. A mile was one thousand paces, counted each time the right foot met the ground.

The second day they did better—nine miles in the morning and six in the evening before dark. They were feeling the stress in their legs and hips, and their feet were taking a beating.

Mark laughed as they spread out their blankets. "By the time we get there we will be good at this."

"Hey. I'm keeping up with you." Her years of nursing actually made Maryam better prepared for the long walk than Mark.

"Shall we say a prayer together before sleeping?"

"Yes. Let's do that every night."

They held the tips of each other's hands and asked the Lord for his care. Then each one pulled their blanket around them tight.

"Mark."

"Yes."

"Thank you for coming with me."

"I said I wanted to come."

"I know, but I want to tell you that I am very grateful."

"And I am thankful that you let me join you."

"I wasn't sure at first."

"I know."

"But I trust you now."

"I know."

"When I was a little girl, the boys threw rocks at me."

"What! Why did they do that?"

"It's just what little boys do."

"I never threw rocks at girls."

"I'm sure that you did not." She paused a moment. "May I share one more thing?"

"Yes."

"After I told Samuel that there was no future for us, a number of men took an interest in me."

"I am sure that they did. You are very pretty."

"One of them tried to rape me."

"Oh, no! How terrible."

"He tried on four occasions. I fought him off, but he kept trying. He scared me."

"Oh, no."

"The last time he grabbed me I bit his hand so hard it left a scar."

"I am so sorry for you. You were so young."

"He thought I was old enough."

"Did you tell your parents?"

"Of course not! My father might have killed him."

"But your father is a Christian."

"Yes, but even that might not have stopped him. I was too frightened to tell anyone."

"What happened?"

"Then my father said he was thinking of moving to Antioch. He said it was more prosperous here. I said, 'Yes! Let's go!' and that helped them to move ahead with the decision."

"Well, you got away from that horrible man."

"Yes. And I became a nurse."

"Which is your gift." Mark added.

"It is my gift. And in many ways it has been a great blessing. I love nursing. But in some ways it has been a curse."

"How is that?"

"Giving my life to nursing has kept me away from men. I was very afraid of men, and in a strange city I wanted to stay away from them."

"I can understand that."

"Do you? I hoped that you would. I guess that is why I am telling you this. It is unlike me to reveal so much about myself."

"I am very flattered that you trust me enough to reveal so much." He reached his arm and took her hand in his.

"You are a good man, Mark. Good night." She did not remove her hand until after they both fell asleep.

A few days farther up the river road, a group of scraggly looking men suddenly jumped in front of them from both sides. They had been warned about bandits, and kept a wide berth when they saw a possible group. Turning around they were confronted by a wild-eyed man with a ragged beard.

"Hand over your bags, and you may save your lives!"

Mark and Maryam quickly looked at one another and held out their bags.

"And give me the jewelry I see around your neck."

"This is a keepsake my mother gave me years ago," Mark pleaded.

"Give it to me! It looks like silver."

"It has a little silver, but it is not valuable to anyone but me."

Noticing that it was a cross, the bandit moaned, "You are right about that. I have nothing to do with crosses or those who wear them."

Mark stood where he was while the bandit looked into their bags. His heart was pounding, but he managed to send a prayer for help to Jesus.

"What are these books?"

"They contain stories about people from Galilee. I am writing about those who lived there."

"You are heading to Galilee to write about people? Don't you know that Vespasian will kill them before you get there?"

"He will not kill them all. I'll talk with those who survive."

"You are a braver man than I am—or simply more crazy. Who will hear your story?"

"All who are interested. I want to preserve the memories of the older people—before they are gone."

"You will risk your lives against the Romans, just to preserve memories?"

"Someone has to do it."

"You are insane. But I see nothing of value in your bags. Go! Get out of here! Be gone with you."

Without hesitating, the two picked up their bags and moved a few steps up the road.

The man shouted at their backs. "You are insane, you know? I should kill you quickly. If Vespasian sees your books, he will nail you to a cross!"

They continued walking. The men laughed at them, but they did not look back.

That evening, shortly before dark, they reached Emesa, the last town before descending to the Arabian plain.

They had not said much since the confrontation with the bandits, and they ate in silence. But as they pulled their blankets out of their bags, words came pouring forth.

"That was a close call today," Maryam admitted.

"Too close. I prayed and prayed. Did you feel the hands of Christ around us?"

"I was too afraid to pray. But as we walked on, I told our Lord how grateful I was."

"The bandit was right, you know. We are crazy to be doing this."

"I agree." Taking his hand in hers Maryam added, "I thanked Jesus for sending you with me."

Mark smiled. "I want to go, and I am glad you are here, as well. I don't feel like we are either crazy or brave. It's more like we are being led."

"That's how I feel too. We are going to make it, Mark. If Christ wants us to get there, we'll make it."

They each wrapped a blanket around them for the night and lay down with their bodies angled, so that their heads were close—as had become their custom. Maryam said, "Do you know what I was thinking?"

"What?"

"We could have been killed today."

"Yes. I thought of that," Mark told her. Then he added, "But our chances were improved by not putting up a fight. Two lone people traveling like us, don't look very powerful."

"We looked power-less!" she laughed.

"That's what I'm saying. When we look powerless, we don't seem like a threat. The leader didn't even draw his sword."

Maryam chuckled. "Do you suppose that's why Jesus told his disciples to take nothing with them?"

"Certainly. When they went to the villages, he wanted them to be non-threatening—so people would be open to listening to their message."

"That's you and me, Mark. We are about as non-threatening as you can get."

"That's you and me," he agreed.

Both were silent for a moment, pondering the image of two helpless souls, alone on the road.

"Life is fragile—isn't it?" she whispered.

"Oh, yes."

"I see it when I care for people. We are not far from dying every day. Some heal, and some die."

"Death is all around us. I had many narrow escapes when I left Rome. I know what the hand of death feels like."

"We are going to Galilee, even though we may die," confided Maryam.

"That's right. We both know the risks."

"But with me, it's not about calculating the risks. I chose what I would do with my life. I am doing it, and I feel good about it, regardless of the risks."

"That is why we are together. I feel the same. I accepted the call to put the gospel in writing, and I may die doing it. But if that is what is to be, then it is what will be."

"You really trust Jesus, don't you?"

"I really do. Christ has brought me safe this far, and I hope to see him in the end."

"I trust like that, too; maybe not as much as you, but I am learning."

"We are learning from one another."

She reached and took his hand. "The Jews have a saying. Let's go to sleep with it in our minds."

"What is it?"

"Choose life!" She let the words sink in. "Moses did not make it to the Promised Land, he only saw it from a distance. God commanded Moses, who was getting old, to climb up Mount Nebo where he could look out over the Jordan valley and see the Land. God said, 'Then you shall die there.'"

"Did he go up the mountain?"

"Yes, he went—and he died on the mountain. They buried him there. 'Choose life' is not about avoiding death. It's about choosing to live each day in faith, following our calling. It is an exhilarating way to live!"

"The apostle Paul said, 'We walk by faith and not by sight.'"

"Precisely! That's you and me, Mark." She squeezed his hand.

"That's you and me."

In the morning, as they continued along the trail, they saw a large group loading their packs.

Maryam asked one of the women, "Are you traveling to Damascus?"

"Yes. That is our home."

"May we walk with you?"

"That would be up to Abdul."

"Will you point him out?"

She called to the leader. "Abdul!" He came to where they were standing. "This couple is going to Damascus. May they walk with us?"

Mark added, "Yesterday we had a close call with bandits."

The caravan leader looked them over and nodded. "I see no harm in it."

"Thank you. We will be no trouble." Maryam and Mark immediately embraced. They never should have started out alone. Now they would be safer.

41

They arrived in Damascus on a Friday. Maryam asked the woman in the caravan if she could point them to any Christians in the city. She led them to the home of the presbyter, and there they said goodbye.

The city had a mixed population of Syrians and Jews, with just enough Roman troops to maintain control. Nero once ordered the slaughter of ten thousand Jews in the gymnasium. The figure probably was an exaggeration, but since that day the people had been compliant.

The presbyter's name was Amir, and he insisted that the couple stay and get rested. It felt good to sleep inside, bathe, and eat a good meal. Mark even shaved. They needed to rest their legs, to say nothing of their hopelessly blistered feet.

"Stay at least for Sunday Eucharist," said Amir. "You have been too long without the Body of Christ."

"Thank you," Mark replied. "We have missed gathering with others for prayer."

"Where do you plan to go from here?" Amir asked them.

"I am from Gennesaret, in Galilee," Maryam responded.

"Gennesaret! But Vespasian is there now!"

"We expected that. After the armies move on, I want to nurse the wounded there."

"They will need a great deal of nursing," the presbyter agreed.

"What have you heard about the troops?" Mark asked.

"Vespasian brought Legions V and X to Ptolemais on the coast, where he was met by Titus with Legion XV, who had been in Alexandria. With other forces that had joined them, they totaled sixty thousand strong. Then they marched to Sepphoris, the regional capital, to take stock of the situation. Joseph ben Mattathias had been drilling local recruits in the skills of warfare, and after stirring them into a fighting fervor, he led them right toward the city."

"I am afraid to ask what happened then."

"When Joseph's men saw the Roman columns, most of them turned on their heels and ran. Only a few wanted to fight, and they retreated to Tiberius on the sea. But Vespasian pursued them, so they rushed up into the hills, to Jotapata, which had fairly strong walls."

"Did that work?"

"No! You know the Romans. They besieged the city."

"What happened to Joseph?"

"Well that is the odd part: Joseph found a place to hide just as the troops were breaking through. They caught him, though, and brought him to the feet of the generals. But then, if you can imagine, Joseph struck up a friendship with Titus, they are about the same age, and displayed an eagerness to collaborate with the Romans!"

"No!"

"Yes, and Vespasian believed him. An informant said that Joseph flattered Vespasian, saying that he would be emperor after Nero. And knowing how useful collaborating local leaders can be, Vespasian took him into his circle."

"What a traitor!"

"That is how the Jews see him now. But the Romans like him; they call him Josephus. He is their ally!"

While Mark was pondering the image of the turncoat Jewish leader, Maryam asked about the towns.

"They are crushing every fortified city that holds rebel forces—and many that do not. The armies spread out, and are destroying everything in their path: burning, looting, slaughtering. There won't be much left."

"That's why we want to go as soon as we can."

"Well, as you say, there will be a time when the armies move south. Jerusalem is their goal. But they will move with deliberation, leaving no one behind who might retaliate. I would not go any farther than Caesarea Philippi without being sure it is safe. That will put you on the border of the rebellion."

Mark cut in. "That is our plan. In a few days we will go there, and determine when we can cross into Galilee."

"Be careful. Do not rush into the holocaust."

It felt good to pray with Christians again and to receive the Body of Christ. Both of the pilgrims thanked God for their safe passage over the hills and prayed about what was to come.

After the liturgy several people took an interest in the visitors—assuming, of course, that they were a married couple, which neither corrected. These also cautioned them about going into Galilee. Mark and Maryam took in every bit of helpful information.

They were planning to leave on Monday, but it only took a small amount of coaxing from Amir to get them to stay longer. They were very tired, and their bruised and blistered feet were slow in healing.

Back in Antioch, Amos began using the gospel, and people loved it. He still was uncomfortable with the ending, where Mark had left Mary Magdalene and the other women fleeing from the tomb in terror. As his scribes began making copies, Amos added,

And all that had been commanded them they told briefly to Peter and those around him. And afterwards Jesus himself sent out through them, from east to west, the sacred and imperishable proclamation of eternal salvation.

Amos had no idea that someone else would add an even longer ending later.

Bishop Evodius was feeling weak, and a few days later he died. As he had hoped, the church selected Ignatius to succeed him.

Two weeks later Mark's mama also passed away. She did not suffer long. Her last words were, "Marcos, Marcos. I join your papa. We will all meet again."

Caesarea Philippi was an ancient city called *Paneas* or *Banias*, located at the southwestern base of Mount Hermon, adjacent to a spring and shrines dedicated to the Greek god Pan. The huge spring gushed from a cave in the limestone bedrock, tumbling down the valley and into marshes below.

King Herod the Great captured the region and erected a temple of white marble in honor of King Philip II, a descendent of Alexander. Later it became the administrative capital of Philip's tetrarchy, and he added the name Caesarea in honor of Caesar Augustus. On the death of Philip, the tetrarchy was incorporated into the province of Syria.

Vespasian's troops had been in the city, but went south again after ensuring that it did not hold any Jewish rebels. Large numbers of refugees were streaming north, getting away from the destruction.

The short trip from Damascus had been uneventful for Mark and Maryam, but they again arrived tired and hurting. They agreed to rest for a few days and listen for the latest information.

The next morning Mark said to Maryam, "This was the turning point for Jesus."

"When he headed for Jerusalem?"

"Yes—to his death in Jerusalem."

"Are you saying you want to turn back?"

"No." Mark was determined. "There is no use turning back now."

"That's the way I see it. We came here to do something. Just because refugees are streaming past us doesn't mean we have to turn back."

"So? We enter at Bethsaida and go through Capernaum to Gennesaret?" asked Mark.

"Yes, and beyond that is Magdala."

"And you feel most compelled to nurse your people at Gennesaret?"

"Yes—more than any other town."

"If we can make friends in Gennesaret, then we can use it as a hub to connect with the surrounding region."

"That will work. The towns are not far apart."

"Is there a church in Gennesaret?" he wondered.

"There was when we left; that was six years ago. Who knows what happened since. I know where we met. We'll find out when we get there."

42

They headed south, past Lake Huleh, and down along the east side of the Jordan River to within a few miles of Bethsaida. The next morning they rose early, slipped past the town, and headed for the bridge that would take them into hostile territory.

"There is my homeland," whispered Maryam, pointing across the narrow river, "the beautiful land of Galilee."

"When will we see the sea?"

"In just a little way. It's not far."

"We've got to watch out for Roman troops, and stay away from them. We look suspicious carrying these packs south."

Around the next corner they caught sight of a blue sea surrounded by a border of green, created long ago in a rift valley by the tectonic separation of the African and Arabian plates. While only thirteen miles long and eight miles wide, the Sea of Galilee has the distinction of being the largest body of fresh water on earth that lies below sea level. Its principle source is the Jordan River at the north end. The reflection of clear blue skies gives it remarkable beauty.

"Let's stop and pray here, Mark. Isn't this beautiful?"

"The sea is magnificent—lovelier than I imagined."

Maryam put her arms around Mark, and he held her close. For a moment they just stood there, taking in the awesome view. Then they prayed for safe passage, even more seriously than they had prayed on the road.

"Oh look. There is the bridge," Maryam pointed out.

Mark nodded, and they continued toward it.

On reaching the bridge, everything looked safe. But when they got to the other side, they saw a group of men in the distance, coming toward them.

"Quick! Let's hide under the bridge." Taking Maryam's hand, he led her down to the river's edge and under the shelter of the bridge.

"Do you think they saw us?"

"Listen."

Tromp, tromp, tromp, tromp. It was the characteristic sound of troops marching. Tromp, tromp, tromp, tromp. The footsteps were getting louder.

Mark pointed up to where the river bank met the bottom of the bridge. They put their packs up, out of sight, and came back closer to the water.

The soldiers reached the bridge. Tromp—tromp—tromp—tromp. The sound of heavy sandals stomping on the bridge set both of their hearts racing. Tromp—tromp—tromp—tromp. But when the footsteps got to the eastern side, they stopped!

The silence was even more frightening than the noise, as the couple speculated as to what might be happening. For what seemed like an eternity not a sound was heard. Mark was surveying their options.

Then a man's voice barked in Latin, "I don't see anything here. Do any of you want to fill your water bottles?"

Mark whispered. "We have to act fast. Do you see that shaded area with ripples? Let's lie down in the water with only our noses sticking up. Since they are on the other side, they might not see us." Maryam followed and did as he instructed. They held hands tightly while under the water, each using their free hand to smooth the air bubbles out of their clothing and keep out of sight.

They had no idea what the soldiers were doing. Presumably they were by the water on the other side of the narrow river, but they didn't dare move to look.

Finally, after what seemed like endless long minutes, they heard the sandals march back across the bridge to their side. Now, at least they knew where the soldiers were. Lifting their heads, they heard the sounds diminish back in the direction from which they came.

Maryam grabbed Mark around the waist and cried on his chest. For the longest time he just sat there in the water, holding her and caressing her hair—one ear listening to the fading footsteps and the other taking in every one of her anguishing sobs. *I must get her safely to Gennesaret*, he vowed silently as he kissed her forehead. *I must take care of this beautiful soul that our Lord has put in my care.*

After retrieving their packs and letting their clothing dry a while, the couple continued south.

"I know a house in Capernaum." Maryam had been pondering alternatives. "Let's not try to go any further today."

"That sounds fine to me."

A caravan of refugees came toward them. The couple chose to sit at the side of the road while the people passed. They looked weary and dazed, like they had been through a terrible ordeal. Most didn't even look at the wayward couple, and those who did simply shook their heads. One man shouted, "Don't go past Capernaum! They are still ravishing Gennesaret."

Maryam winced, but said not a word in return.

When the last had passed, she put her hands on Mark's face and looked straight into his eyes. "We need to talk about what we will do if they capture us."

"What is there to say? We understand the risks we are getting into."

"But I mean—if we are captured, what do we intend to do?"

Mark still didn't realize what she was getting at.

"I can't let them capture me. They will rape me and sell me into slavery. I will kill myself first."

"Don't talk like that!"

"Mark, we must be realistic—and have a realistic plan. I told you my thoughts. What are yours?"

"I don't want to make hypothetical plans. We can decide when the time comes."

"The possibility of getting captured is not hypothetical. It is all too real."

"I can't imagine killing myself."

"I can—and I will, if I need to. I know how to do it. I saw a patient once, in Antioch, who fell on a sword. But she didn't do it right. It went through her abdomen, which was very painful."

"My God, Maryam!"

"She lived for several days."

"How awful!"

"You have to point the sword up—toward your heart. If you do it right, it's all over very quickly."

"Don't speak like that!"

"You don't want me to speak like that, but you don't have a better plan."

Mark didn't say a word.

"Listen to me. I am telling you how it is done. You secure the base of the sword and put the tip under the lowest rib on the left side, pointing up at an angle toward the heart. Then you fall on it."

"All right. Now I know how to do it. But that doesn't mean that I ever will."

"You would rather that they crucify you, or make you a slave?"

"No. Of course not."

"Then say what you would do."

"I will think about it."

"Please do think about it. When the day comes, there may not be time to think."

"I will die defending you."

"Oh, Mark, I believe that you would try to defend me. I love that about you. But don't pretend that the possibilities are not possible."

"I know."

"Besides. Would you attack a soldier who was coming after me? You follow the command to love your enemies and resist not evil."

"That is correct. I don't carry a sword for that reason. I don't ever want to use it on someone, even a Roman soldier."

"Then what other option is there, but to take our own lives?"

"Don't make me talk about it today. Anyway, suicide is what pagans do—not Christians."

43

When they reached Capernaum, the sight was devastating. Half of the houses were destroyed. The city was virtually deserted, and the smell of death was everywhere.

The home of the people Maryam had known looked like it recently had burned. When the wind stirred the lifeless coals, wafts of ash and dust rose into the air. She looked at her companion in despair.

"Is there anyone else that you knew?"

"They were all in this neighborhood. No one seems to be here anymore."

For several moments they just stood there surveying the damage.

Then they heard a voice. "Who are you looking for?" Turning toward the sound, they saw an old man with tangled white hair and beard. "They are gone. Very few of us are left."

"It was several years ago. I have been away," Maryam explained.

"You should've stayed where you were. There is no reason to come here."

Mark interjected, "May we stay with you for one night? Then we will go on to Gennesaret."

"You may stay with me, certainly. But don't hurry south. It might be best to wait until we hear that the worst is over."

"My name is Mark, and this is Maryam."

"A Greek and a Jew. My name is Daniel—I am a follower of Jesus."

"So are we! We are from Antioch. Maryam grew up in Gennesaret—in a Christian family. You are brave to state your beliefs to strangers."

"Strangers are the only ones who are safe to speak to. Most of the Jews here leave us in peace, but their leaders say we are traitors because we will not fight."

"I don't fight either. I don't carry a weapon."

"So you are a serious follower of Jesus?"

"Yes. Did you know him?"

"Of course I did. We were about the same age. I am sixty-seven now."

"You are the same age! Jesus was born sixty-seven years ago."

"How do you know such things?"

It was Mark's turn to trust a stranger. "I spent eight years with Peter."

"Simon Peter!" The man couldn't believe what he was hearing. "You spent eight years with Peter. Where?"

"In Rome. I first met him when I was a boy in Antioch. But later I went with Peter to Rome."

"Come! Come to my house. We have much to talk about. Come inside where we will not be seen."

They followed Daniel to a small stone dwelling not far from the water. "I lived here with my Beth and our sons. One day when I was working, the Romans came and took them all, even the little ones."

"Do you know where they are?"

"No. I have no idea where. I dread that they sold them as slaves," lamented the old man.

Maryam gasped.

"You will see them," Mark added. "One day you will see them all."

"And I hope it is soon," the old man said. "I'm ready to go to meet them. I am ready to meet Jesus. This place is no longer home for me."

Inside the house the man asked more questions about Peter. Mark told him all that he knew, including how happy Peter was in Rome overseeing the church and teaching people about Christ. When he explained how the Christian leader was taken by the soldiers, Daniel at first showed signs of grief, but this changed to laughter when he heard how Peter demanded to be crucified upside down.

"That's Peter, always acting on impulse! Did he get his way?" the man smiled at the image.

"Yes! They placed him with his feet up and his head down. He was the first of the group to die."

"Oh my. But that meant he did not have to suffer as long."

Mark paused and then asked, "So you knew Peter, personally?"

"Yes. Oh, yes. And Andrew, and James and John—they were all from Capernaum. I got fish from them. Tomorrow I'll show you where."

"And you heard Jesus preach?"

"Yes, of course. Jesus was here many times. I'll show you the places. Why do you have so many questions? Didn't Peter tell you these things?"

Mark explained how he had made notes of what Peter taught about Jesus and how he had combined the notes into a gospel narrative. The man was astonished because he knew so few people who could read or write. "Where is the gospel now?" he asked.

"I left it with the church in Antioch. But I have a copy with me. I am in Galilee to verify what I have written and to see if there are more things to add. May I read it to you?"

"You certainly may! I would love to hear it. But first we eat!" Daniel got out some bread and olive oil. "I don't have much to offer. No wine. The soldiers took everything."

The bread was a welcome sight to the travelers, who ate heartily.

When they had their fill Daniel poured cups of water and begged, "Now. Read to me about Jesus."

"Will you interrupt me, if I say anything that doesn't sound correct?"

"Yes. Certainly. Now read."

Maryam also prepared to listen attentively; she had only heard Mark tell parts of the story.

He began reading the gospel from the beginning.

"I didn't go to see John the Baptist," the man interrupted. "I was too busy working."

Mark continued.

Now after John was arrested, Jesus came to Galilee, proclaiming the good news of God and saying, 'The time is fulfilled, and the kingdom of God has come near. Repent, and believe in the good news.'

"That's exactly what Jesus said!" Daniel was ecstatic. "We were all shocked to hear it—and delighted. We had prayed for God's day to come, but it never did."

"It did not come in one glorious day, but it is growing like a mustard seed," Mark explained.

"That's what Jesus said! But it seems so remote now."

Mark corrected him. "The faith is spreading all over the world."

Maryam added, "In Antioch both Jews and Gentiles are embracing Christ."

"Not the rich, though."

"Yes, even the rich and powerful. People are humbled by his words."

Mark added, "It looks dark here because of the revolt and the invasion. But believe me, the faith is spreading quickly."

"Well, that certainly is good to hear. Read some more."

Mark continued, reading line by line. Daniel frequently added a comment, particularly when the story was about something in Capernaum. But he offered no obvious corrections, which disappointed Mark a bit.

"If anything is inaccurate, please tell me."

"No. I can't say that anything needs to be changed—nothing that I am aware of. I can think of some things you could add, though."

"Like what?"

"It's getting late for me to think clearly. Tomorrow we'll go out. I will show you places and tell you some additional things."

"That will be wonderful."

Daniel showed his guests to a large room with a bed. "This is where my oldest slept. You can rest here."

Mark and Maryam thanked Daniel. Neither wanted their host to know that they were unmarried. They had become accustomed to sleeping near each other on the road, holding hands, and this night was no exception. They were very tired, and even though Mark was anxious for what he might learn the next day, they both fell fast asleep, sharing the comfortable bed.

The next morning Daniel was cheerful. He had a mission to pursue, and he wanted to get to it. "Why don't we walk down to the water before we eat? We might find something good there."

The two agreed. It was only a short way, and the waterfront was almost deserted. The cool breeze felt fresh on their faces. Four small boats were out on the water.

"This is where they tied their boats," Daniel said, pointing to a stone pier and steps. "Quite a few families fished. Peter and Andrew worked with the sons of Zebedee."

"It looks so pristine," commented Mark. "And so simple. I had imagined a scene more bustling with activity."

"It was busy in those days. But it doesn't take much space to tie up a few boats. Some just pulled them onto the beach."

Mark picked up a stone and skipped it across the water. All of his adult life he had wanted to stand on this shore. He hadn't known how it would feel—being in a historical place can set loose a flood of emotions. This is a sacred place, he told himself. I am so fortunate to be here, even under these circumstances. And Daniel has confirmed so much of the gospel.

"Do you have any questions?" asked Daniel.

"One thing I have wondered about: Did the apostles first meet Jesus here in Capernaum, or when he went to the Baptist?"

"I've never thought about that. They were with Jesus when he went to John, and they were with him here. I can't say which was first. Is it important?"

"Probably not. I just want to get as many facts straight as I can."

"They were with Jesus most of the time."

"Yes."

"Ah ha! Just what I was hoping to see." The old man crept over toward a good-sized crayfish and reached for it. It tried to scurry away, but was no match for the experienced crustacean hunter. Before long he caught two more, and they headed back to the house for a warm breakfast.

As they were cleaning up, Daniel announced, "I want to take you up on the hill before it gets too hot."

"We are ready. Lead on."

Near the edge of the city, the hillside shot up steeply. They were puffing when they reached the first sight.

"This is where Jesus multiplied the loaves," Daniel shared. "He had the people lie down on the grass, and he put the loaves and two fish on this rock right here." As Daniel pointed, Mark and Maryam used their imaginations to picture what it may have looked like with thousands of people gathered around. It was a big rock—several feet long and maybe three feet high. "Jesus used it like an altar. He placed the food on the rock and raised his eyes in prayer. Then he had the apostles pass it all around. It was amazing! Even after everyone had their fill, they gathered up twelve baskets of fragments. That's when I became a believer—that very day!"

Mark always delighted in stories of conversion to Christ. "Some people stayed with him, but not everyone."

"I could never understand why some fell away," continued Daniel. "They were expecting a mighty king, but Jesus didn't give that impression. He was gentle—and humble. And for some, they felt his teachings were too hard."

Mark added, "I wasn't sure if the miracle was done here, or somewhere else?"

"Jesus multiplied the loaves on at least two occasions that I know of—once here and once near Magdala."

"That confirms my suspicions, and why the accounts are not exactly the same."

"Sure. Now do you want to see where he did his teaching?" Daniel asked.

"Yes, of course. Where?"

"We are going there next. But it is quite a climb."

"We will follow," said Maryam.

It was a long climb, but worth it. As they struggled up the slope, the view of the sea became breathtaking—even more beautiful than when they saw it above Bethsaida. A few scattered clouds gave perspective to the lands beyond. The higher they went, the more deeply blue the sea became.

"Here!" Daniel stopped and let his companions catch their breaths. "This is where he preached his Great Sermon." The two noticed that they were in a natural depression in the hillside, possibly caused by an ancient slide. "Now shout and listen." They heard his words echo. "The acoustics are perfect. Jesus stood here, and people all around heard him clearly."

Maryam tried it first. "Hello!" The sound carried. "That is amazing! Try it Mark."

Mark did it too. "Hello!" He listened. "I never would have thought. So large numbers heard his teachings?"

"Yes. The day of the Great Sermon was like no other. He spoke about loving your enemies and forgiving seventy times seven times. We all were so inspired."

"I may have some of those words in my bag. I didn't know where they fit in the gospel, so I have not yet added them. Perhaps this evening we can go over them, and you can tell me when he said them."

"Yes. I can do precisely that."

Mark was in no hurry to leave the place, but the sun was getting high in the sky. It would be a hot trek down.

That evening Mark took his copy of the Sayings of Christ from his bag and asked Daniel when Jesus may have said each of them.

"Jesus probably repeated his teaching in the various villages," admitted the aging witness. "I can tell you this, the teaching about anger and retaliation and 'love your enemies' was right up where we were today. It was early on—when he first came to Capernaum."

Mark was excited to at last receive some new information. They spent the evening going over the sayings, and for each one that Daniel recognized, Mark made a symbol near it, noting when and where it was spoken. A great many of the sayings were from Capernaum.

"This was a profitable day," Mark told Maryam as they lay down for the night. "When we get back I will add much more to the gospel."

"How many more days will we stay here?"

"Oh, I don't know. Why do you ask?"

"I am just thinking about the wounded in Gennesaret. Do you think Daniel has much more to tell you?"

"Not much more, I guess. I'm willing to move on. We can always come back."

44

When morning came Daniel pleaded with his guests not to go. "I have not yet heard that it is safe there."

"Part of our mission lies in Gennesaret. We need to get there as quickly as possible."

"It's only a short way. But you don't know what you will run into."

"We will be careful," said Maryam. "I know the city."

"Go along the water. That way you can avoid the soldiers. They mostly stick to the road."

"We didn't know, but we will take your advice."

Then after exchanging goodbyes and embraces and many expressions of gratitude, they picked up their bags and left.

Going by the road would have taken only a little more than an hour. It took longer strolling along the shore, but they arrived without any encounters.

Gennesaret was just as devastated as Capernaum. Vespasian's troops had been ordered to 'teach a lesson' in each of the towns, and they did it well.

Maryam found several wounded in the section of the city in which she had lived, and immediately went about replacing their bandages and lifting their spirits. But she did not see anyone that she knew.

Late in the day, she spied one familiar face. "Sarah. Is that you?"

An elderly woman stared at her for a moment, then came up close and peered at her face. "Do I know you?" The woman seemed to have lost some of her sight, and supported her left side with a cane. Her white hair was neatly combed. The back of her head was covered with a small shawl.

"I am Maryam—daughter of . . ."

"Maryam! You *are* Maryam. It has been many years. You have matured—and you have a husband, I see."

Maryam did not correct the impression. She just gave Sarah a big hug.

"And your parents—are they well?"

"Yes. They are in Antioch, and doing well."

"What are you doing here?"

"I came to nurse the wounded. I am a skilled nurse now."

"Imagine that—a skilled nurse. We have plenty of need for that here."

Maryam smiled.

"Where are you staying?"

"We don't have any place to stay. We just got here a few hours ago."

"And you started helping people even before you found a place to stay. Well, you can stay with me, at least until you find others you recognize. Many have fled, you know."

Sarah led them to a humble little dwelling and immediately got them something to eat. "I remember that you didn't marry Samuel—and then you moved."

"It would not have worked out with Samuel; he was committed to the Jewish faith. And quite frankly, none of the other men interested me. I got tired of how they stared at me and tried to get my attention. Then papa wanted to move to Antioch, and we went."

"And that's where you met Mark?"

"Mark came along later. I met a woman who nursed, and for several years I just devoted myself to the work. I kind of liked being on my own, even though I lived with my parents."

"And later you met Mark?"

He answered. "I arrived in Antioch a few months ago. Before that I served with Peter in Rome."

"Ah! So you were with Peter. I remember when they came through here. I liked Jesus, but Peter talked too much."

"Peter matured—like we all do. He became a fine leader of the church."

"That's good. At first I thought they were fakes. It wasn't until we heard that Jesus allowed them to crucify him in Jerusalem that my Joseph and I understood that he was a man of God. We didn't listen to him while he was here."

Maryam interrupted, "I remember when you and Joseph joined our church. And the presbyter also was named Joseph."

"A number of men were named Joseph. They all grew old and died. We got a new presbyter a few years ago. His name was John."

"He *was* John? Is he not alive?"

"No! The soldiers slaughtered them—he and the rabbi—everyone in a position of leadership. And they burned his house, where we met—and the synagogue too. They are destroyers. They make their kind of peace by crushing and destroying."

"We have seen it. We passed caravans of refugees heading north."

"There is nowhere else to go. But some of us will stay here—us older ones.

We will die in our homes."

Mark asked, "Does your church still meet?"

"No. Not since they killed our presbyter."

"You could meet together, and pray together."

"Not before the rest of the soldiers go south. We have talked about it. Perhaps we will meet to pray again when there is only one squad left here. I don't know."

"When the time comes, I will help you."

"Are you a presbyter?"

"No. But I have assisted bishops in two cities and the presbyter in another. I will help you."

"That's good. We need to pray—and we need one another."

Maryam had a question. "Is there a physician in the city?"

"No, no. He left before the troops came; he knew better."

"Where will I find the wounded, so that I may nurse them?"

"There is no place for the sick anymore. They burned that too. We will just go from house to house, and when people hear about you, they will ask for you."

"But what about the soldiers?"

"The soldiers are beginning to leave us alone. They know that we help one another; they only want to eliminate any leaders who may encourage rebellion. Tomorrow I will get you started. I'm getting sleepy now."

"Yes. We will get a fresh start tomorrow."

"I don't have a bed to offer you. It was just my Joseph and I here. But you can spread those mats."

Maryam saw the pile of mats and began arranging them on the floor. "This is better than sleeping along the road. Thank you for letting us stay."

Gennesaret is located in a broad valley at the west side of the Sea of Galilee, with good water resources making it well-suited for agriculture. Once a haven for those living off the land, the changes in ownership and taxation in recent decades had left the valley economically depressed. Now, with the invasion of the Romans, everything was taken away, a plague worse than locusts.

In the morning, Sarah led Maryam and Mark to a house with two seriously burned brothers. The pungent odor of seared flesh permeated the room, and when she removed the bandages, he had to look away.

A few moments later he looked at her face, calm and purposeful, going about her task. She is an angel, he thought. But when he again caught sight of the oozing blisters, he immediately went outside.

The next house was similar. Under a makeshift bandage on the man's right side was a deep gash from a Roman sword. Mark did not want to look, but when Maryam told him to get some water, he quickly responded.

At another house they saw two children whose fingertips had been chopped off. They were too frightened at first to even let Maryam touch them. But she coaxed them and spoke with them until they became calm enough for her to inspect the wounds. "Your fingers are healing quite well. In a month you will no longer need bandages."

"But they still will be traumatized," moaned their mother. "They were only reaching for a bit of grain. Now they are afraid to hold out their hands."

"You children must be brave now. Your mama will tell you who you can trust. God wants you to grow, so you can take care of your mama and one another. Can you do that?"

The children nodded cautiously, but the mother hung her head.

It was that way in house after house after house. Mark was growing tired, but Maryam kept at her work like a bee buzzing from flower to flower. She seemed happy and totally engaged with whatever was needed.

In mid-afternoon a woman offered them some bread and oil. Mark ate hungrily, but Maryam simply took a few nibbles and talked with the woman about her pregnancy. "You will have a fine baby."

"But what kind of world will he be born into?"

"It will be the world that we make. With God's help you will make a good home for him—or her."

The woman smiled, the first time since the soldiers came.

They continued throughout the afternoon.

In the evening both were tired. Mark spoke about what he had seen in Maryam. "You are excellent with the people, so patient and kind. I love to watch you."

Maryam said nothing.

"You are like an angel."

"I need more than kind words, Mark. I need you to do more than watch."

"I want to help, but . . ."

"There are no buts when we are caring for people. We must do what we must do."

"You are so good at it. I am so—unaccustomed."

"You need to get over being unaccustomed."

"I don't know how. I want to help, but something prevents me."

"You are afraid."

"Yes. It is like I am repelled. I know that the wounds can't harm me. But I look away."

"You are afraid for yourself. You can't bear to look at wounds because you fear being wounded."

"You may be right."

"I am right. It was that way when I first started. But I got over my fear."

"How did you get over it?"

"I just kept facing situation after situation—doing what was needed. You need to focus on the person, not yourself."

"I'll try to learn that."

"It won't change in one day—or one week. But in time, you will grow accustomed to it."

Mark changed the subject. "You are the best thing that has come into my life."

"You flatter me, Mark. What about Jesus coming into your life? And Peter? And the gospel?"

"Well, those were vitally important. But with you, Maryam, I feel myself becoming mature. If I had died from the Fever, I never would have grown fully into a man. With you I am finding out what adult life is about."

Maryam blushed. "Don't give me too much credit. I've seen you grow, though. You were a babbling brat while you were recovering, in many ways a thirty-two year old boy. But on the road you have become more sensible."

"I have to be sensible. I have to take care of you."

She blushed again. "I've perceived that in you. And I have more confidence here because you are with me. We are good for each other."

Mark pulled her close, and she rested her head on his chest. He caressed her hair and kissed her forehead. Maryam didn't say a word, but pondered the feelings in her heart.

A few days later most of the soldiers marched south. People were talking about how only eleven were left to control the city. That was a sufficient presence to ensure order. Everyone knew that any uprising would lead to hundreds streaming back, along with their swords and torches.

In one house a woman greeted Maryam and Mark, and showed them her husband and son who had been wounded the previous day in Magdala. "They were fighting to save what was left of the synagogue."

Several children sat in the corner, staring at them.

MARK'S PASSION

The man was unconscious. She could tell there was little hope for him.

The boy was about fourteen years old, with a nasty cut in his side. Maryam cleaned and bandaged it.

"How did you get your father back here?" she asked.

"I floated him in the water."

"You are a good son."

"It took a long time, wading through the water, but I got him here. Dragging him up to the house was easier."

Mark put his arms around the boy. "You will be the man of this house now."

"I know."

"To take care of your mama and family, you must stay away from the fighting."

"I can fight like a man!"

"And you can die like a man. Then who will be left?"

The boy looked at his father and began to sob. Mark held him closer and let him cry.

"What is your name?"

"Ezekiel."

"Well, Ezekiel. A great man once said, 'Blessed are the peacemakers.'"

"He was not a real Jew."

"Oh, he was a real Jew, all right. When he was your age he studied with the rabbis. And I pray that one day you will know him and love him, like you love your father."

The man let out a slow moan. Maryam reached for his hand. There was only one more moan; then he was silent. When the mother began to cry, Maryam went to her and held her in her arms.

When the woman spoke, they were surprised by her words. "You people are so different. You stay out of the fighting, and you survive. Yet after we fight, you help us."

"Jesus did all that he could for your parents, and we do what we can for you," said Mark.

"Will you speak when we bury him?" the woman pleaded. "We have no one else."

"I don't know . . ."

Maryam interjected. "Yes. Mark will do it. When will you bury him?"

"Tomorrow, I suppose."

Maryam washed the man's body and helped his wife dress him in a clean tunic. They laid him on a mat in the center of the room. "We will come tomorrow morning. Tell your friends." Then, after smoothing the wrinkles in the dead man's tunic, she bent over and kissed him on the cheek.

A crowd of about thirty gathered the next day, relatives and friends of the deceased. They brought the body outside where there was room for everyone to stand.

Mark explained that he was unfamiliar with the Jewish prayers for the dead and suggested that anyone who wished to add anything should feel free to do so. Then he invited Ezekiel to recite a passage from the Book of Wisdom. The boy knew it by heart.

The souls of the just are in the hands of God,
  and no torment will ever touch them.
In the eyes of the foolish they seemed to have died,
  and their departure was thought to be a disaster,
  and their going forth from us to be their destruction;
  but they are at peace.
For though in the sight of others they were punished,
  their hope is full of immortality.
Having been disciplined a little, they will receive great good,
  because God tested them and found them worthy of himself;
like gold in the furnace he tried them,
  and like a sacrificial burnt-offering he accepted them.
In the time of their visitation they will shine forth,
  and will run like sparks through the stubble.
They will govern nations and rule over peoples,
  and the Lord will reign over them forever.
Those who trust in him will understand truth,
  and the faithful will abide with him in love,
  because grace and mercy are upon his holy ones,
  and he watches over his elect.

Mark was not sure what he would say, but he began, "Sometimes there are tensions between Jews and Christians. But on days like today, we gather to show our respect for our neighbor and our friend, a fellow child of God, who God has lifted to his own heart with tender love.

"Ezekiel, your father is at peace. The Lord loves your father and is at this very moment caring for him.

"These past few weeks your papa fought with all his might to protect his homeland, and his city, and his family. He even went to Magdala, to help his friends there. We wish that he had not gone—perhaps he wishes this too. But he was a man who did what he did out of love. There was love for all of you in his heart, even in his last moments. And now he is at peace. Like it said in the scripture, *'grace and mercy are upon God's holy ones, and he watches over his elect.'* We must trust God in all things—even in death.

"The scripture tells us, *'Those who trust in him will understand truth.'* We can never understand the truth, unless we first trust in God. That is true Wisdom. And at this point in the history of Galilee we must trust and understand. We must trust that there is a reason for us, who are living, to go on. Can we understand this?

"And if there is a reason for us to survive, then we must remove all malice from our hearts. We cannot hate one another and survive. We cannot hate the Romans and survive. We must pray to God that all hatred will be removed from our hearts and be replaced with love—with divine love—that flows from him, through us, to all those around us, who will see how perfectly we trust. I cannot say that it will be easy—I can only witness to each of you that it is possible.

"Trusting in God means trusting in the future. Ezekiel, you and all of us here need to trust that there is a future. A time will come when the attention of the Romans will be drawn elsewhere. A time will come when their power will wane. We may not see it in our lifetimes, but if we trust in the God of life, our descendants one day will see it. And it will be a wonderful day—a beautiful day for all who choose life and choose love. It will be a glorious day for all the earth.

"We grieve now. We grieve the loss of a good man—your husband, your father, your friend. We can't change what happened. We can't make the grief go away. But let us grieve in hope. Let us feel our loss with hope—hope for all of us—hope for the future—hope that God's ways will prevail. And let us show our trust in God by putting away our swords. Let us show our trust by putting away all malice. Let us show our trust by loving one another as our God loves each of us.

"Better days are ahead for all who trust with understanding."

Then after leading some prayers, Mark bent over and kissed the dead man on the cheek.

Everyone thanked Mark for his helpful words. Then some said, "Don't come with us to the tombs. The guards will notice you."

"But we want to come."

"No. Stay here. It is best. We need you to stay alive for us. We want you in our city."

45

The next several weeks were a blur. Each day they nursed the sick and the wounded. Mark brought the Christians together for prayer. He continued to do funerals for both Christians and Jews. More and more began gathering for prayer. The city was becoming a community again. But the people kept Mark and Maryam out of sight; they didn't want the guards to see them as leaders.

Whenever Mark met someone he could trust, he asked about Mary Magdalene. No one knew where she was or even if she still was alive. The older ones remembered Mary as a good woman, who was very devoted to Jesus. They said that if Mark could find her, she would have much to add to the gospel—she was an honest woman and a faithful witness. But that is all they could tell him.

Several families offered Mark and Maryam lodging. Eventually they moved in with another widow whose sizable home gave them some space of their own. People gave them food and shared their medical supplies; no one had any money.

One night, as they were preparing to sleep, he asked her, "How long do you want to stay in Galilee?"

"I haven't thought about it. Why do you ask? Don't tell me that you want to go south for more research. It will be terrible there."

"No. I don't have in mind going to Jerusalem—at least not before the war ends. I thought at some point we might want to go back to Antioch."

"I do miss my family. And I would like them to know I am all right."

Mark whispered, "If we went back, we could get married."

Maryam drew back and looked at him, almost in disbelief. She knew that she had heard him right, but it was not what she was expecting.

"I mean . . . I would like for us to be married. Do you?"

"Oh yes, Mark." She threw her arms around him and kissed him. "Of course I want to marry you. It's just that we haven't talked about it."

"Well, let's talk about it now. Shall we go back to Antioch and be married?"

"Yes! Yes! Yes!" She kissed him again and again. "For many years I thought that I would never marry. But since we have been together, all that has changed. Nothing would make me happier than to have you as my husband. I love you and love you." Her kisses became more generous, from the depth of her soul.

"I love you, Maryam. I have felt this way for weeks, only I couldn't get the courage to say it before now. It is a deeper love than I have ever felt. In fact, there is no comparison. You are the special soul that God has brought to me. I am sure of that."

"Oh, Mark. I do love you. I felt so alive with you on the road. But here in Gennesaret I, too, have become certain. What we have shared together these past weeks is but a taste of what we will share for years and years."

"It is what we will share for all eternity."

"All eternity—my goodness—can you stand me for that long?"

He kissed her so long it took her breath away. "I can stand you forever. Even after we are old and gone you will be my wife."

"I want that. I want you to be my husband forever."

Their kisses became passionate. But both knew that they were not yet joined before God.

"Shall we consider ourselves betrothed?" Mark asked.

"Betrothed. My goodness yes!"

"I would like Amos to marry us. What do you think?"

"Yes. Amos is fine, as long as we are joined in the church."

"We'll speak with him as soon as we get back."

"Oh, Mark. You have made me so happy."

He cradled her in his arms, and it was a long time before either fell asleep.

Vespasian was satisfied that Galilee was pacified, and he began bludgeoning south through Samaria and the coastline west of Judea. He would use overwhelming force until all of Judea was under control and his troops had surrounded Jerusalem in preparation for the final battle.

With few wounded remaining in Gennesaret, the couple made it known that they were planning to return to Antioch. The people understood. They were grateful that God had brought them to their city during the most crucial weeks. Maryam felt satisfied that she had done what she could for her people. Mark was happy to see the Christian community coming together again and felt that the information he had gathered would enable him to fold many lines from the Sayings of Christ into the gospel. He suggested going back to Antioch by the main route, so they could stop in Nazareth on the way. They were ready to leave.

Then Sarah died. She had not been sick long, and Maryam did everything she could to make her comfortable. Both Maryam and Mark were with her at the end.

Sarah was well-liked. About sixty people gathered the next day for the funeral in the courtyard of the house in which the two were staying. Some had to stand out in the street.

Because Sarah had been so kind to them, Mark put on the toga with the red border. It added to the solemnity of the occasion.

The funeral began, and Mark asked the only other man who could read to proclaim the gospel.

Jesus said to the crowds, 'Is a lamp brought in to be put under the bushel basket, or under the bed, and not on the lampstand? For there is nothing hidden, except to be disclosed; nor is anything secret, except to come to light. Let anyone with ears to hear, listen!' And he said to them, 'Pay attention to what you hear; the measure you give will be the measure you get, and still more will be given to you. For those who have, more will be given; and from those who have nothing, even what they have will be taken away.'

Then Mark spoke about the woman they had known.

"When Jesus said these words, he was thinking of people like Sarah.

"She let her goodness shine all through her life. To anyone who needed anything, she gave it. Yes, she gave in good measure. And it is our faith that Christ has welcomed her and is rewarding her now in equal measure—and much, much more.

"This is the first time I have worn this formal toga in Gennesaret. I put it on to honor the first person who befriended us in this city. I put it on to demonstrate in a small way how Christ will honor his saints in a big way—just as we heard in the reading.

"Be good to one another. Be good to one another just as Sarah was good to you. Be good to one another and let your light shine. Be good to one another and spread the good news of Jesus Christ.

"Every time that you let your light shine, remember this day. Remember the hope that you felt in your hearts. Remember the gratitude that you felt for the abundant ways in which God has blessed you.

"Do not count your losses. Do not count your losses because that puts a basket over your lamp.

"Count your joys. Count your joys and your blessings—let your light shine.

"You have thanked Maryam and me for being with you these past weeks. Well, we thank you, also. We thank you for giving us the opportunity to live with you and learn from you. We both have grown because you let your faith shine on us. As you know, this is our last day with you—our bags are packed, and we will be leaving tomorrow.

"None of us are ready when our time on earth is done. Even Sarah felt that she had more to do. But if Sarah did not die, she never would see her Joseph and never see her relatives and friends—and she never would see Christ.

"It is that way for all of us. Jesus never promised that we would not die—he only promised that we will have new life with him and with our loved ones. And it will be a happy life, with no more tears and no more sorrows. And anyway, when we no longer are here to do the things we consider so important, someone else will do them.

"Help one another to keep the faith. And help each other to spread the gospel. That is what Sarah wants—and it is what Christ wants of us. It is the way we express our faith—and show our gratitude.

"Keep the faith alive. Keep the faith alive, here in Galilee."

Even before Mark could collect his thoughts and lead the people in prayer, a shout was heard from the street. "Soldiers! Soldiers!"

The squad burst through the gate and pushed through the crowd. Their eyes were on the leader in the toga with the red border. "Kill him! Kill him now!" shouted the commander. Two soldiers grabbed Mark by the arms while a third raised his sword and cut a big gash across his throat. Blood gushed forth in bright red spurts as they let him slump to the ground.

Maryam did not say a word. She picked up a small stone water jar and hurled it at the guard, striking his head. He wavered momentarily and dropped his sword. Maryam picked up the sword and ran to Mark's side.

"Seize her! Seize the wench!" cried the commander. But the crowd rushed toward the guards and blocked their way.

Maryam quickly went to Mark's side and smoothed his toga. Then she bent down and kissed his cheek.

The crowd shrieked as she placed the hasp of the sword securely against his body. Then she positioned the tip beneath the ribs on her left side and got ready to let her weight drop upon it. No one uttered a sound.

Then she heard a voice. "Suicide is what pagans do—not Christians." She heard Mark say it twice. "Suicide is what pagans do—not Christians."

She couldn't tell if she heard him through her ears, of if it was a memory of their conversation after the close call with the soldiers at the Jordan Bridge.

Maryam stood up, and the sword fell to the pavement with a loud clank.

Then moving her arm in a broad arc, she pointed her finger directly at the officer. "You cowards! You pretend you are strong with your swords and your torches. But you are little boys—all of you—drawing what strength you possess from a system that takes and steals.

"This is a real man." She used her free hand to point to Mark. "This Man that you killed—gives and reveals. He shares the vision of a kingdom that surpasses any you could ever imagine—a kingdom of justice and love.

"We are followers of Christ! We follow the one you crucified, and God raised from the dead—the holy Son of God. He unites us more strongly than any Caesar ever will. And with his Holy Spirit within us, you have no power over us—no power at all. With every new invasion your power is weakened. One day your empire will crumble into dust.

"You can't see him. You cannot see the Savior because that is only granted to those who have faith. And everyone who has faith, receives Christ's divine life into their very soul. We are saved. We are forgiven. We have eternal life with Him! But you are doomed to die in your sins." She continued pointing her finger at the officer.

Everyone held their breath. For a moment there was absolute silence.

Then moving his arm in a broad arc, the officer brought his hand down and pointed his thumb at the ground.

The two closest guards pushed through the crowd and thrust their swords through her abdomen. She felt pain beyond any that her patients had ever described and she knew that it might be a long time before it took her life.

"How wonderful," she thought. How wonderful that I will join my husband and not be made a slave. How wonderful that I could give witness to these people and die as a Christian martyr. How wonderful that I will see Christ face-to-face." She fell to the ground, unconscious.

"Damn the woman," cursed the officer. "Damn her. Toss them into the house and burn this place down."

With the precision they had trained for, the guards made a pile of everything combustible within the house, heaped the two bodies upon it, and set it ablaze. The crowd ran away as fast as they could. In a few moments, only the soldiers remained to watch the flames. They made sure that everything was incinerated—particularly the bodies. Mark's pack—with all of his books—burned completely, page after page after page.

Before the guards returned to their quarters, all trace of the two travelers having ever been in Galilee was destroyed.

46

Mark floated up and looked down upon the scene. Then he saw his love—his betrothed—floating toward him. He took her hand and they floated higher and higher.

They saw the Mediterranean coastline, and in the east a beautiful blue lake surrounded by green.

Descending lower again, they saw massive armies, mowing through the region, punishing—abusing—looting. It had become fall, and then winter. And when it was spring again, the armies continued south, conquering Perea, Idumea, and virtually every city of Judea, except for the capital—killing—taking—burning. Refugees streamed into the Holy City, but by summer the vise had tightened around them.

Then the movement of the armies stopped—or at least paused. Word came that Nero was dead. The Emperor, who did everything in excess, had ordered too many executions of noble leaders, and both the Senate and the military were deserting him. Nero considered poisoning the entire Senate at a banquet, but did not pull it off. Working in close cooperation with the Praetorian guards, the Senate declared him a public enemy and sentenced him to be flogged with rods until he was dead. When he heard hoof beats of cavalry coming to capture him, he stabbed himself in the throat, but only after declaring, "What a loss I shall be to the arts."

In Rome, there were three new emperors—Galba, Otho, and Vitellius—each with short reigns ending in assassination. Vespasian waited to see how the intrigues turned out.

During the lull, many of the Jerusalem Christians escaped and went to Pella, to the north and on the east side of the Jordan River, a position of relative safety. The community flourished there for many years.

The following winter the Senate called upon Vespasian, the most able leader and friend of the guards and legions, to take control of the Empire. In the spring of the seventieth year after Christ was born, he sailed for Rome, leaving the armies in the command of his eldest son. Titus had about sixty-five thousand men at his disposal. It was time to bring the Jewish revolt to its inevitable conclusion.

Inside the walls there were at least three antagonistic factions—the Zealots, the displaced Galileans, and some freedom fighters from Idumea, south of the Holy City. Each sought to impose its own brand of revolution on the fight for independence. They all held the conviction that with God on their side, Jerusalem would be protected. Titus' repeated calls for surrender fell on deaf ears.

So in May the siege began. The general built platforms for his artillery, and his rams were put into action. The outer wall was breached on May seventh, and the second fell four days later. Then Titus concentrated on the Antonia fortress and the temple district.

As the shortage of food became critical, Titus had his men feast in full view of the rebels, but this led to few defections. Instead, vigilantes searched their neighbor's homes for hidden stores of food, and when they found any, they beat the hoarders. Bodies piled up in the streets, but the rebels shouted, "Death—not slavery!"

In July the Romans wrapped the city with a wall of their own, to protect their forces and cut off all chance of escape. Titus captured the Antonia fortress. Then as the Jews retreated into the temple, he decided that this must be his next target. When the rams could not penetrate the thick gates, he ordered them set afire. Soldiers tossed torches into the temple until the blaze became a conflagration. Thousands burned to death in the holocaust. After taking out all that they could carry, the troops watched what remained of the magnificent structure crumble in sections to the ground.

The siege lasted for one hundred and thirty-one days. Several hundred thousand Jews perished. The most able-bodied survivors were sent off as slaves, while the weaker ones were executed on crosses or ravaged by beasts as entertainment for the troops. Titus ordered the total destruction of Jerusalem; all that remained was a section of wall on the western side. Just as Jesus had predicted, not one stone was left upon a stone.

But Masada remained, holding about one thousand Jewish rebels. They had plenty of food and water within the impregnable mountain fortress, but neither of these would stop Titus. As he sailed for Rome—and a victorious hero's welcome—he left Flavius Silva with the task of destroying the stronghold and its inhabitants.

It may seem like a massive undertaking just to punish a handful of holdouts, but that was the Roman way. After an ingenious and lengthy siege of Masada, the forces broke through and set fire to the gates. Realizing that they had only one night in which to deliberate, the rebel leader Eleazar suggested that they all die an honorable death at their own hands, rather than allow the Romans the pleasure of killing them or selling them into slavery. When Silva's forces entered the fortress the next morning, they met only still silence. Each man slew his own family members, then one another, and the last fell on his own sword.

But then—and both of their hearts leapt when they saw it—most of the soldiers were gone from the Holy City and caravans of Christians were streaming back. They were those who had fled to Pella, earlier. The families were joyful as they returned to their homes, set on rebuilding their lives. Maryam and Mark gazed at one another in delight.

Floating higher, Mark saw many of those he knew. Habib's and Palut's children were working in the family business. Alexios and Irana had hired a cook from Odessus on the Black Sea, and she and Ariston were growing close. Zosima and Basil both had new spouses, and Anyte had learned more poetry. Sosthenes had become bishop of Corinth, and he made one of the central area deacons the head of the eastside church. Agathe was hurt when she was not chosen, but she continued to labor where she was and in time developed a fine working relationship with the new presbyter. Timon had become quite an evangelist in Thessalonica—bringing one by one, all of his friends to Christ.

Then rising even higher, Mark simultaneously saw into two homes in different cities. In each, men were hunched over tables with open booklets—the Sayings of Christ on the left and the Good News of Jesus Christ, the Son of God on the right, and they were writing into a third codex. Matthew was copying some inspiring words of Jesus, *'Blessed are the poor in spirit, for theirs is the kingdom of Heaven.'* Luke was penning a story about a prodigal son. They were adding the kind of detail that Mark had so diligently sought to include in the gospel. And in a third house, which suddenly came into view, an elderly John was dictating to a younger man a story about Jesus washing his disciples' feet.

Now higher—and off to the east—he saw a vast crowd of all ages, dressed in white robes. "Who are they?" he wondered. He recognized Antonius and Niko, and their child Stephanos with his little sister. "Are they the martyrs?"

Then a voice answered, "Yes, they are." It came from the leader of the apostles, with whom he had spent eight years. The former fisherman was clad in a white toga with a red border, like the one Mark had on. "Come. We have been waiting for you." His eyes flashed as he smiled through his curly beard. "The Teacher is pleased with what you both have accomplished. Come—he is near. He has prepared a place for you. He wants to show his gratitude for your dedication."

Everything was bright, as they walked toward the light. The one whom they sought was seated on a golden throne. He had been reading a book, but when he saw them he lifted his eyes. "I like what you wrote," he indicated to Mark. "You got it right. And I am very pleased with how you joined one another and helped give life to the people in Gennesaret." Then closing the book and extending his arms toward the diligent author and his bride, he walked to them and took them into his arms.

After a few moments of unimaginable bliss Jesus asked them, "Do I hear that you wish to be married?"

"Yes . . Yes," they exclaimed together.

"Would you like to be married now?"

"Yes. Yes we would!" They couldn't believe what was happening.

"Peter, come here. Antonius and Niko, bring your children. I will find Mark's relatives. Would you like to invite Sarah and the others from Gennesaret?"

"Of course."

"Niko. Can you get Maryam something nice to wear?"

"Right away."

Jesus went one direction, and Niko the other.

"Can you believe this?" Maryam said to Mark.

"I am speechless."

"Oh Mark. I'm so happy. I never thought in a thousand years that I'd get married in heaven."

"With you, my bride, I feel so fulfilled." He held her close.

"I am your bride, my husband." They kissed long and passionately, oblivious of the hundreds of saints and angels who were watching.

"Oh my! Kissing you in heaven is better than on earth."

"A year ago I thought I never would marry. Now I'm having a wedding in heaven." Maryam began shedding tears of joy.

"From the moment I first saw you in Antioch, I hoped for your love."

"It took me longer. But I became totally committed to you."

"You were heaven-sent."

"I was created to care for people, and I will love you and care for you for all eternity."

As they kissed again, their hearts became closer than anyone on earth could possibly imagine.

Niko reappeared with a parcel in her arms. "Can you two tear yourselves apart for a while, so we can get Maryam ready?"

Mark laughed and let go. Maryam gave him a loving little wave as she followed Niko. Mark just stared in amazement as he watched her. "She is so beautiful," he uttered through his breath.

Peter came to Mark with a clean toga. "You will look nicer in this." It was white with a red border.

"Do people get married in heaven often?" Mark asked.

"There are lots of surprises here." Peter answered. "In heaven we fulfill our intentions. And if our intensions on earth are loving and faith-filled, then here they become reality. You get what you hope for."

"I always hoped to see Christ in heaven. My last hope, as I remember, was to marry Maryam."

"See. It's like I told you."

Mark put on the clean toga. It fit perfectly.

Then a group of angels brought flowers. A choir began to sing as the heavenly scent filled the air.

Jesus returned, accompanied by Mark's family and friends. His mama rushed to him. "Oh Marcos. I've been praying for you."

"Mama, mama. I didn't know you were here."

"It hurt my heart to see you leave. I came here to meet you."

"Oh mama. I love you so."

"And here is your papa."

"Papa! It has been so long."

His father took him in his arms. "You have been an excellent son. I am so proud of you."

Their eyes were filled with tears of joy.

Jesus gave them a few minutes together, then said, "Well Mark. If you are ready, we can begin."

"Certainly."

While papa escorted mama to her seat, another choir of angels joined the first. Then Jesus walked to the front and smiled.

"Will you be my best man?" Mark asked Peter.

"Of course. I'll be honored." Peter led Mark down the aisle. Jesus was beaming.

When they turned, twelve bridesmaids came toward them—all ancestors of Maryam, dressed in the colors of the rainbow. Mark's heart raced.

The music changed, and he held his breath as angels opened two great golden doors with silver images of Adam and Eve, Mary and Joseph, and all the great couples of history. He looked at Maryam and gasped. No woman on earth ever looked so beautiful. She was aglow in a flowing white gown with a garland of white baby roses in her hair. The first sight of her took his breath away.

Bishop Evodius led Maryam down the aisle and presented her to Mark. Taking her arm, they turned toward Jesus. Then the music stopped.

"We are gathered here today to join Maryam and Mark in holy matrimony."

Holy matrimony, Mark savored the image. At last, I have my true love. Holy God I praise thy name.

"Have you come here freely, to give yourselves to one another in marriage?"

"We have."

"Mark, do you take Maryam for your wife? Do you promise to love her and honor her for all eternity?"

"I do."

"Maryam, do you take Mark for your husband. Do you promise to love him and honor him for all eternity?"

"I do."

Everything else was a blur. They were as united as two people can be, and yet in love with all who ever lived or ever will. Christ smiled upon them, and as they exchanged their rings, he gave their union his divine blessing.

ABOUT THE AUTHOR

Dedicated religious educator and deacon Gene Vanderzanden writes for those who like to search for and discover gems of insight that deepen their understanding of scripture and connect their faith with their life experience. He holds Master of Pastoral Ministry and Master of Divinity degrees from Seattle University, and has served in parish ministry for nearly three decades.

Gene's other books include *Christ Speaks about Peace: His message for today* and *How to Preach Peace: ten tips for pastors*, available from Amazon.com.

For a free download of illustrations, maps and facts about the 1st Century, or to learn what New Testament scholars are saying about the gospels today, go to the author's website at www.markspassion.com.

PLEASE SUBMIT A REVIEW

Did you enjoy this book? Did you learn what it is like to pursue a spiritual calling and what life was like for Christians in the 1st Century?

I will greatly appreciate your submitting an honest review on Amazon.com. Reviews help us authors to reach more readers, and that helps to get the word out about Mark and the gospel. It will take you only a few minutes.

To submit your review of *Mark's Passion*, go to the Amazon page where you bought the book. Then scroll down until you see Customer Reviews and click where it says Write a Customer Review. Hit the number of stars that you want to give the book and write a few sentences that tell how you feel about it.

The most helpful reviews are simple, honest and to the point. Simply say why you liked the story, what you learned and what people can get out of it.

Thank you for expressing your opinion about *Mark's Passion*.

KEY HISTORICAL EVENTS

39 BC	Herod the Great is made King of Judea
19	Herod completes the temple in Jerusalem
4	Rebellion and slaughter in Sepphoris
0 AD	The birth of Jesus
6	Herod Antipas becomes Tetrarch of Galilee
20s	Herod Antipas rebuilds Sepphoris
30	The baptism of Jesus at the Jordan River
30-33	Jesus teaches and heals in Galilee and Judea
33	The crucifixion of Jesus in Jerusalem
36	The conversion of Paul
42	Peter moves to Rome
48-60	Paul's missionary journeys
64	The Great Fire of Rome
64-65	Martyrdom of Peter and Paul
66-70	Jewish Rebellion against Rome and civil strife in Jerusalem
66-69	Probable date of Mark's Gospel
67-68	Vespasian leads the Roman invasion of Palesine
68	The death of Nero
70	Vespasian becomes Emperor
70	The destruction of Jerusalem by Titus
80s	Probable date of Matthew's and Luke's gospels
90s	Probable date of John's gospel

Made in the USA
San Bernardino, CA
02 February 2016